The Iranian Deception

To Sean,

Happy reading!

Matt Scott

Books by Matt Scott

SURVIVING THE LION'S DEN SERIES
Surviving the Lion's Den
The Iranian Deception

COMING SOON!
The Ayatollah Takedown

The Iranian Deception

Matt Scott

SPEAKING VOLUMES, LLC
NAPLES, FLORIDA
2022

The Iranian Deception

Cover design by Hannah Linder

ISBN 978-1-64540-732-4

For my brother

Characters

Americans

Ben Thrasher, a.k.a. Jay Jacoby (code name *Jaybird*)...........CIA Counterterrorism operative

Jackson Whang, a.k.a. "Dub" (code name *Sandpiper*)............CIA Counterterrorism operative

Beth Jenkins, a.k.a. Katherine Jennings (code name *Raven*)....CIA Head of Iranian Affairs desk

Tom Delang...Retired CIA Agent

Kirk Kurruthers...............................American of Iranian Heritage

Tequila Griffin............................CIA Counterterrorism Operative

Vik Wheaton.......................................Hollywood Filmmaker

Chad Ward...Hollywood "Fixer"

Vivian Walsh...............................Former United States Senator

Roger Cannon ....President of the United States

Iranians

Farhad Khorsandi.......................smuggler, People's Mujahadeen of Iran (PMOI)

Donya Karimi..People's Mujahadeen of Iran (PMOI)

Vahid Avesta...President of Iran

Marzban Shir-Del......................................Supreme Leader of Iran

Dr. Shahid Aslam..................Personal Doctor to the Supreme Leader

Ramin Lajani...........................Major General, Iranian Revolutionary Guard Corps (IRGC)

Captain Mahmoud Yazdani...........................Iranian Revolutionary Guard Corps (IRGC)

Sgt. Najib Bameri.....................................Iranian Revolutionary Guard Corps (IRGC)

Indians and Pakistanis

Kedar Dhoni, a.k.a. Ketan Jadhav...............India Intelligence Bureau (IIB) operative

Akshay Sharma..President of India

Ameer Raja.......................................President of Pakistan

Lt. Hasan Wasim...Pakistani Marines

Wahab Malik..Pakistani Terrorist

Prologue

ISLAMABAD, PAKISTAN
4:44 AM

Beth Jenkins was jolted from a deep, much needed sleep by the loud ring of her phone. As she spun around the clock on her nightstand, she winced at the intense glow of the lime-colored numbers. She once believed in the concept of numerology. In this case, the repetition of numbers would indicate good luck about to manifest into one's life. Considering that it was the middle of the night and that she was the new head of the Iranian Affairs desk for the CIA in Pakistan, Jenkins doubted that this interruption would generate any good fortune. She grabbed her phone, flopped back on the bed and braced herself for whatever was waiting. The voice on the other end didn't even wait for her to speak.

"He's dead."

Recognizing the voice, her eyes popped open, and she sat up. She had met Farhad Khorsandi a year ago when he was an unknown Iranian who helped rescue Tom Delang, a fellow agent and her colleague, from Iranian custody. After Delang's escape, she had debriefed Farhad and was struck by the twenty-six-year-old's display of courage during the unorthodox events that enabled Delang's escape. She also appreciated Farhad's enthusiasm for helping the American cause in Iran. He was everything a CIA agent would want in a source—loyal, motivated, and plugged into the country's inner workings. Farhad had agreed to go back into Iran and stay in touch. In a country where such sources are in short supply for the CIA, the kid was a godsend.

Except Farhad had recently thrown a bit of a tantrum. As someone used to sneaking in and out of the country to smuggle illegal goods, he naively thought he could do the same and operate his business freely, as long as stayed below the radar. But Farhad was already a marked man by the Iranian Revolutionary Guard Corps (IRGC).

Before his execution style death outside the embassy where Delang had been rescued, IRGC captain Azam Aslani had made sure that Farhad's name was fed into the group's database as a traitor to be apprehended on site. This meant that "The Pirate of Iran," as Farhad had come to be known, was forced to keep a lower profile than usual. Given Farhad's naturally extroverted personality, this expectation was unacceptable. He had spent the last two months brooding over his new situation and had cut off all contact with Jenkins.

"When did he die?" Jenkins asked.

"Three hours ago."

"Okay, I'll contact the Deputy Director's office and let him know. Who do you think his successor will be?"

"That's why I called. They've named his replacement."

"Wait. He died *three hours* ago, and his successor has already been voted in?"

"Yes. The Assembly of Experts knew who they wanted."

Jenkins thought about making a wiseass comment about wishing the U.S. Congress worked as fast as the leaders in Iran but held her tongue.

"Who is it?"

"You're not going to like it."

As Farhad revealed who had been anointed as the new Supreme Leader of Iran, Beth Jenkins felt the pressure tightening in her temples. It was time to get moving. Today was going to be the first of many long days ahead.

Chapter One

TEHRAN, IRAN

Newly appointed Major General of the Iranian Revolutionary Guard, Ramin Lajani, stood on the balcony of the Edifice of the Sun at Golestan Palace and gazed out in astonishment at the people below. When the Supreme Leader had gotten sick, he and his fellow members of government had foreseen this moment and had done their best to prepare for it legally, logistically, and emotionally, but he had not expected *this*.

It is one thing to say in an offhanded comment that a million people may show up but to see those numbers materialize in person was a surreal experience. It wouldn't have surprised him if the actual numbers were even larger. He had never seen such an ocean of people collected together. The cheering produced by so many people was nearly deafening.

The Supreme Leader's selected successor, Marzban Shir-Del, had been considered a shoo-in to be the new Ayatollah, long before his predecessor succumbed to the heart disease that killed him. What wasn't widely known was that additional stress had been placed on the man's heart when he was given news that Israeli hackers had penetrated the servers of Iran's military computer system.

The two men had not grown up together, but their friendship slowly developed into a formidable force, one not to be challenged. Shir-Del had become the 'go-to' man when back door deals or matters of discretion were required. In effect, anyone speaking to Shir-Del in those moments was speaking to the Supreme Leader.

Shir-Del and his predecessor had distinctively different styles, though. While the deceased spoke boldly about destroying America and wiping Israel off the map, he tended to work more covertly on projects and stay below the radar when it came to foreign affairs. He was by no means a weak man, as his willingness to hang those who either betrayed or failed him was well documented. But the economic sanctions imposed on Iran increased in each of the thirty-three years he had held the title of Supreme Leader and he became more preoccupied with keeping his house in order.

When Ayatollah Khomeini died, he had big shoes to fill and the weight of preserving the legendary man's vision for the Iranian way of life weighed heavy on him. With each new addendum to the sanctions, his country's economy became weaker, and the natives became more restless. After a slow, twenty-six-year burn of oppression by the Shah, the revolution burst onto the scenes in 1979 with relative ease. The former Supreme Leader knew quite well that the government he inherited from Khomeini could just as easily suffer the same fate as that of the Shah. He would be damned if he would let that happen on his watch. Khomeini's legacy for Iran would be preserved at all costs.

His show of force on the international stage was limited to the sporadic car or suicide bomb in foreign lands, as well as some naval tensions with America off Iran's coast. While these incidents continued to demonstrate Iran's willingness to inflict damage anywhere it deemed necessary and reminded both the Americans and Israelis of Iran's presence on the world stage, in terms of long-term strategy, they ultimately amounted to little more than the occasional summer thunderstorm.

On the other hand, Shir-Del was much more calculating and had a grander vision for Iran than his predecessor. He would rarely make a big decision that he hadn't examined from every possible angle and seldom acted on emotion alone. He did this by doing what all true leaders do: he studied the material and listened to the subject matter experts around him. When he spoke, those around him listened, and once he made a decision it was final. Those who disagreed or tried to get him to revisit the issue were dealt with appropriately. Replacements amongst Shir-Del's inner circle were a rarity.

Personality-wise, he was usually serene, but was known for random, violent outbursts and mood swings, which kept the people in his presence distinctly on their toes. Before meeting with Shir-Del in person, it wasn't uncommon for the invited guest to inquire with Shir-Del's aides as to what type of mood he was in that day.

But making the legal decisions imperative in maintaining Iran's constitution as part of the Guardian Council were a far cry from military decisions or those related to foreign policies that shaped the country's role in the world. For those inside Shir-Del's circle of trust, he was well-known for being ruthless when he had to be and fair when he needed to be. For the Ayatollah loyalists in-country, the question was whether their new man would step up and do what both his predecessors had consistently talked about but neither did: finally confront the Israeli pigs and their American puppet. For the rest of the world on the outside looking in, the question was, is this a man with whom they could negotiate or was he their newest nightmare?

Lajani didn't know the answer to either question. He'd only been promoted to commander of the IRGC six months ago and had only spoken to the new Supreme Leader a handful of times, at the annual special event at the old U.S. Embassy, commemorating the day their countrymen stormed the gates. The lack of contact was not intentional. The occasion simply never arose for them to formally meet.

He'd heard rumors about his then future leader, though. The last person that failed Shir-Del was his predecessor at the IRGC, Rahim Shirazi. Lajani hadn't been brought into the loop regarding the general's most recent plan, which upset him, but apparently the man made one of Shir-

Del's close friends a sacrificial lamb as part of a larger plot to reclaim Bahrain as part of the Persian Empire. The plan fell apart when the general was unable to make a simple exchange of a captured American agent for a missile program built by the Russians.

Lajani didn't make any inquiries into the matter, not because Shirazi was executed for his behavior, which was understandable, but because of the way he was executed. When he heard that his friend had perished as part of the general's scheme, Shir-Del secretly had a hot box constructed especially for the man. When the general failed, which Shir-Del feared, he was taken to a relatively uninhabited area outside Isfahan, where he was chained, unharmed, into a steel container equipped with a hundred UV lights, each outfitted with a 1500-watt bulb, and all out of his reach. The gossip around Tehran was that Shir-Del flipped the switch himself. Over the course of one evening, the lamps' brightness increased, along with the temperature inside the box. Shirazi suffered an excruciating death from being slowly cooked to death.

When they opened the box the next morning, the soldiers saw a disgusting and putrid scene that could only make the most eminent of serial killers proud. What was left of his skin was littered with boils and blisters. The rest of it, along with what were once his eyes and cartilage, melted onto the steel floor into a liquid ooze that created an unimaginable, acrid stench as it spilled out of the container.

The poor souls selected for this horrid assignment puked and dry heaved for hours as they attempted to clean out the box. On their way back to Tehran, they stopped to throw the General's bones into the Maranjab Desert, but his skull was supposedly brought back to Shir-Del for safe keeping. It would undoubtedly serve as a trophy to the man who would become the new Supreme Leader.

From that moment, Shir-Del laid the foundation for his future rule as Grand Ayatollah. For those inside the Iranian government, in and out of his inner circle, the message regarding the price of failure was clearly delivered. In short, Shir-Del scared the living hell out of everyone.

As sweat trickled down his spine, Lajani snapped out of his daze when Ayatollah Shir-Del grasped his hand. Looking down the row to his right, he noticed that Shir-Del's other hand was connected to the newly elected Iranian president, Vahid Avesta.

"Ready?"

Shir-Del turned to each man. Lajani and Avesta nodded. The crowd erupted as their arms were raised in unison. Lajani could feel the cheers from the crowd reverberate from beneath his feet, as if the Earth itself was moving. In that moment, Lajani learned two things about his new Supreme Leader. One, he was a showman who knew how to play to a crowd. Two, this display of the three men joined together was a clear signal that his talents and the president's would not go unutilized. When the roar of the crowd died down, Shir-Del gestured his head inside the palace.

The rooms within Golestan Palace never ceased to amaze Lajani. In this particular room off the second-floor balcony, the powder blue walls were adorned with individually cut mirrors that made the room sparkle like diamonds in the morning sun. Their steps echoed across the polished white marble floor and the larger mirrors that lined the ceiling loomed over them. While the designs were exquisite, Lajani felt that the room's use of mirrors was a symbolic attempt by Shir-Del to let him know that every move he made from this moment forward, both inside the room and out, would be carefully monitored.

"Well? Do you have good news for me?" said the Supreme Leader, barely speaking above a whisper.

Avesta sighed.

"Sir, our friends in Pakistan won't do it," he said.

Hoping for a different answer, Shir-Del turned and looked to Lajani.

"He's right, Supreme Leader," said Lajani. "I've tried myself, repeatedly. No matter what I've offered them in return, Pakistan won't sell us the nuclear war heads."

"Is Captain Yazdani continuing with his experiments?"

"Yes, Supreme Leader, but progress has been tough to come by," Lajani said.

Disappointed, Shir-Del chewed his lip and slowly nodded.

"I think it's time that we take matters into our own hands. Have you thought about my plan?"

Lajani looked to Avesta, who gave a slight nod.

"It would take a few weeks to set up, but our current relations with India are such that it may not be needed."

"You shouldn't be so confident in our Indian friends. They are slowly becoming puppets of the Americans."

"I think we can do it, if needed."

"You think?"

Lajani swallowed nervously. He didn't want to display a lack of confidence, but he didn't want to disappoint his new leader on the day of his coronation either.

"Sir, there are no guarantees in such an operation, but in speaking with President Avesta at length, I believe that it's a formidable plan. Complex with many moving parts, for sure, but if executed correctly, Iran will make a major dent on the international stage."

Shir-Del turned to Avesta.

"Will it be executed correctly?"

"Yes, Supreme Leader," said Avesta.

Shir-Del paused as he listened to the crowd chanting "Death to Israel" and "Death to America." Their passion fueled him with motivation. Although he wasn't willing to admit it out loud, Lajani was right. It was a bold play. If it was botched, he will have failed in his first major act as

Supreme Leader. He couldn't afford those optics. To those inside his country, he would appear to be a bumbling fool. To those in the international community and the rest of the world, he would appear weak.

The crowd's chants became louder. Shir-Del stepped outside to the balcony to wave to them. Once again, their roars erupted across the land. Listening to the masses, he watched the sun continue to rise over the panoramic view of Tehran. His reign was the start of a new dawn for his country. The bad times were not there to stay. They had come to pass. It was his time to shine. It was Iran's time to shine.

Lajani and Avesta stood at attention as the Ayatollah returned from the balcony.

"This is an historic moment for our country, wouldn't you agree?"

"Yes, Supreme Leader," said both men.

"We carry a heavy responsibility for our people, don't we?"

"Yes, Supreme Leader."

"Iran has suffered at the hands of the Zionists for far too long, hasn't it?"

"Yes, Supreme Leader."

"And I have your full support on all endeavors, don't I?"

"Yes, Supreme Leader."

"Very well. You have my permission. Start making the necessary preparations to execute my plan."

Both men nodded.

"Now, go. Leave me with my people."

"Yes, Supreme Leader."

Lajani and Avesta walked away as Shir-Del returned to the balcony.

"One last thing," he added.

"Yes, Supreme Leader?"

"Heed my words about *executing* the plan."

Shir-Del stared them down with his small but terrifying eyes.

7

Lajani and Avesta glanced at one another. They could read between the lines.

Execute the plan successfully or I will execute you.

Message delivered. Message heard.

Chapter Two

It had been one hell of a day for President Roger Cannon. Upon being elected, all new chief executives quickly come to terms with the pressures of the twenty-hour job. Rarely does a day go by that they are not presented with some type of bad news, accompanied by world-wide criticism and a continuous news cycle, not to mention social media. Having a bad attitude and whining about any of it is a luxury that no one who sits behind the Resolute Desk can afford.

Today's news, though, was more distressing than most, especially when it came to the two-front war America was fighting. The president's lunch had been interrupted with news that the Supreme Leader of Iran had died. While Cannon wasn't the type of person to do cartwheels at the news of someone dying, he wasn't exactly going to shed any tears over this man no longer being amongst the living. He would, of course, publicly offer his condolences and reach out to the new Iranian leadership in an effort to rebuild the strained rapport between the two countries. While the idea of a new, peaceful chapter in the United States-Iran relationship was hopeful, Cannon knew that it amounted to little more than wishful thinking.

In theory, the Grand Ayatollah's death should have made Cannon's job easier because it meant that new negotiations with Iran was possible. But the briefing he received an hour later from the Director of the CIA immediately extinguished any small flame of hope. Unfortunately, this was a feeling he was getting used to. Again, one of the pitfalls that came with the job. Apparently, the new Supreme Leader ticked every single box on the undesirable list: calm, exacting, decisive, ambitious, patient, and a true believer in the Khomeini-style government.

Cannon managed to lower the prickly stress levels of the Joint Chiefs of Staff and his Secretary of Defense, who pleaded with him to increase the DEFCON, but Cannon refused, claiming that it would send the wrong signal and that the country had to at least attempt to show that they were giving peace a chance with the new leadership.

In the spirit of the old Ronald Reagan moniker of "trust but verify," Cannon took every precaution without officially increasing the DEFCON. He ordered all military bases and embassies to double their security as well as instructing the battleships in the Arabian Sea to keep their eyes peeled just in case the Iranians tried to make a statement on the new Supreme Leader's first day.

Israel, though, was a different story. Minutes ago, the prime minister had placed their military on maximum readiness. The West Bank had been closed and was starting to look like the front lines of a war. Although he didn't specifically say so, Cannon was certain that they had a plan ready to attack Iran if the Persian country so much as twitched in their direction. Although Iran hadn't yet made any moves that signaled aggression, the tense situation felt eerily similar to that of the Cuban Missile Crisis.

But, as the savvy, ex-CEO of multiple Fortune 500 companies, Cannon was able to talk the Israelis down from the edge by offering them a different strategy in U.S.-Iran relations. For decades, the economic sanctions against Iran had steadily put more pressure on the throat of the Iranian government. Little by little, the bad boy of the Middle East had been reeling from the effects. Had one of Cannon's predecessors not unfrozen $150 billion in Iranian funds, the U.S. might have been able to bring the regime to its knees.

Alas, it was not to be. Cannon had an idea, though, that would allow the U.S. to play more covert offense while strengthening its own economy and bettering foreign relations with other Middle East leaders who were opposed to the Iranian regime.

"Good evening, Mr. President. I'm sorry to bother you so late," Cannon said, as he began his video conference call in the Situation Room.

He was well-aware of the nine and a half hour time difference between Washington, D.C. and New Delhi, but it was a deliberate strategy on his part. One of Cannon's secrets to success in the corporate world was getting people to make decisions so that they could get off the phone and go to bed.

"Roger, please. We've been over this before. Please call me Akshay."

Cannon and Indian president Akshay Sharma had never dealt with each other prior to their respective presidencies, but they knew each other by reputation and had come to work well with one another in their national roles.

After being discharged from the Air Force following the first Gulf War, Cannon spent much of his corporate career jumping from company to company as their 'Mr. Fix-It' CEO. He never stayed at any company longer than two years before hopping to the next. Each time he skipped to a new company his payday grew. His success was largely attributed to his trained eye for looking at companies with an obsolete technical infrastructure. He would spend the necessary funds on revamping it and then secure compensation for the additional spending by offshoring a healthy chunk of the local IT and finance positions in the U.S. to India. Doing so was never a popular decision for the employees within the companies he headed, which would eventually be a point of contention for his opponent during the election, but the results were always the same: better systems, reduced head count in the U.S., lower spending, and higher profits.

While Cannon couldn't claim the title of being the person to start offshoring jobs from the U.S. to India or Philippines, he unabashedly waving the scepter and embraced the trend. It was even his idea to have India's customer service colleagues trained to speak more like an American so that the customers on the other end of the line would be more at ease if they felt that they were speaking to a fellow citizen. Cannon's team had to train them to pronounce words such as "can," which was naturally pronounced like "Khan" in India, to instead pronounce the latter part of the word like "Ann."

When he became CEO of his first company, only five percent of Fortune 500 companies offshored U.S. jobs to overseas locations. By the time he resigned from his final role, that figure was up to forty and small businesses were starting to do the same for their miniscule financial tasks. His business dealings laid the foundation for tremendous relationships in India. So much so that Cannon would later be called on to be the U.S. ambassador to his friends in New Delhi, an opportunity he dared not turn down.

Sharma, on the other hand, grew up relatively poor but managed to work his way up through the Indian Congress before becoming the country's Finance Minister during the Kargil War, where he oversaw increases in the military budget. The war was also where he lost his first cousin to an ambush by Pakistani forces, which would forever plant the seed of hatred for Pakistan in his soul. He would later learn that the man in charge of the ground forces that day was Ameer Raja, who would go on to become the President of Pakistan. His strategy of fighting fire with fire with Pakistan was not a popular one within those inside the Indian government, but voters loved him for being known as a man who would stand his ground. The fact that the Pakistani leaders thought of him as a wild card, he concluded, was a good thing.

Both men were experienced in war, had a strong sense of business, and a reputation for being blunt. They respected each other from the start but they were not friends.

"You're right, Akshay. I do apologize for the late hour, though. I assume that you've heard the news coming out of Iran?"

"And the quick election of the new Supreme Leader."

"Indeed. I think this may present an opportunity for both of us," Cannon said.

"How so?"

"Well, personally, I'm sick and tired of playing defense with the Iranians. I want to go on offense and put a stop to this bullshit once and for all."

"Given the history of U.S.-Iran relations, I can certainly understand how you feel, Roger. But Iran has shown no such aggression towards India. In fact, we receive fifteen percent of our oil supply from the Iranians. I'm not sure that I can help you."

Sharma leaned back in his brown leather chair, knowing that Cannon would entice him with an offer.

"Actually, I think we can help each other. Today, I've been on the phone with the CEOs of seven Fortune 500 companies that want to relocate additional positions to the global service centers in Mumbai and Pune."

Sharma raised one of his thick, caterpillar-like eyebrows.

"How many?"

"Eight thousand."

Sharma rubbed his forefinger across his lips. The offer would help get the nagging members of Congress off his back.

"What's the catch?"

"I want to shut the door and cut off your country's oil imports from Iran completely."

The expression on Sharma's face immediately changed from one of intrigue to one of provoked irritation.

"Roger, that is absolutely out of the question. As much as India needs those jobs, it is not even close to being a comparable trade. Eight thousand jobs, especially at wages your companies pay our people, can't begin to compare to the tremendous effects the lack of oil would have on our economy."

Cannon would give Sharma a point for the crack about American companies paying its Indian colleagues dirt wages, but he wasn't done yet.

"You didn't really think that I wouldn't have a plan for you to get the missing oil, did you?"

"By all means, tell me more."

Sharma had the feeling that he was about to be set up.

"I can convince the Saudis and the Iraqis to step up their oil production by forty percent each. You would get the last twenty from us, at a discounted rate."

"Do I want to know how you plan on doing that?"

"Oh, come now, Akshay. I can bring you to a magic show and show you the tricks, but I can't show you how they're performed."

Sharma smiled. Cannon was a slick customer.

"I don't know. I'm not sure that I want my country to join yours on Iran's hit list."

Cannon did his best to contain his grin. The trap was set, and it was time to drop the net.

"Akshay, that list only exists as long as the Ayatollah regime is in power. Now, if you don't like this idea, I can easily call not only those CEO's back, but *all* CEO's with service centers in India and tell them that you and I have hit a snag in our negotiations and their tax credits for offshoring those jobs are going to be a thing of the past."

Sharma could now feel himself backed in a corner.

"Really? Is that the card you want to play?"

"It's just business, Akshay. I'm sure the Philippines would love to have those jobs."

Sharma knew that he had little choice in the matter but he needed to get something out of this mouse trap.

"Fine, agreed. But you owe me one."

"I can live with that."

"I'll call President Avesta in the morning and give him the news."

"Thank you, Akshay. Have a nice evening."

Sharma gruffly ended the call, but Cannon couldn't have cared less. He smacked his hands together in celebration and each of the staff members in the Situation Room who had been observing the call gave him a thumbs up. He had thrown a hard-right hook to the Iranian regime's jaw. This undeclared war between the U.S. and Iran was going to end and he was going to make damn sure it ended under his watch.

Chapter Three

HIGHLANDS, NORTH CAROLINA

Ben Thrasher was sitting in a rocking chair on the porch of a cabin owned by a friend of the agency, drinking a highball of Hooten Young American Whiskey. Despite the fact that he was momentarily enjoying the sunset over a breathtaking view of the Blue Ridge Mountains, the Special Activities Center operative was in the CIA's doghouse. He crunched the ice from his glass with disdain. It was one of the few therapeutic methods he knew of to express how pissed off he still was over his suspension.

Thrasher originally hit the CIA's radar in South Dakota, where he'd been on a solo vacation in the Black Hills to see Mount Rushmore. One of the travel tips to the monument is that a parking permit entitles visitors unlimited access to the national park for one year from the date of purchase. In an effort to ensure that he got pictures of the monument in the best light possible, Thrasher took advantage of the government's generosity during the week he was there. On one of his daily visits, he noticed two Islamic men who seemed out of place. It wasn't the fact that they were making the same consecutive daily visits as him. It was the way they were walking around the observation platform and the staircases around the presidential trail. Their movements felt like inspections.

On his last day in the area, he spotted them at Desperados Cowboy Restaurant, where he was having lunch. Thrasher noticed that the two men ordered bourbon that they weren't drinking and were collectively looking at one phone. Most Americans would be checking their social media pages on their individual phones. After paying his tab, Thrasher's curiosity got the best of him, and he discreetly followed them out of the restaurant.

His instincts proved correct as he watched the van carrying the two terrorists pull over to the side of the road on Route 244. Upon seeing the rocket-propelled grenade launcher from the sliding door that was being aimed directly at the mountain side sculpture of the former American presidents, Thrasher hit the gas on his pickup truck and slammed into the rear of the van. Fortunately, this caused the grenade to fly wildly off course without hitting the monument.

Wasting no time, Thrasher pulled his boot knife and approached the van. The terrorist who had previously been holding the RPG had fallen to the ground and was in the midst of pushing himself back up when Thrasher grabbed him by the hair and slit his throat. The driver exited the vehicle, pulled his gun, and aimed to shoot Thrasher. Outgunned, he flung his knife at the man's chest. The shock of the blade sliding between the man's ribs caused his gun to go off erratically in Thrasher's direction, but the bullet whizzed past him. Thrasher charged the man and repeatedly slammed his head into the hood of the van until he was sure he was unconscious.

The rangers from the National Park Service swiftly responded by following the RPG's smoke trail. Thrasher was arrested on site and spent two days in custody, explaining his patriotic story. He was released on the third day but not before coming to the attention of the FBI's Special Agent in Charge of the incident, John Bennett, who happened to work in the Counterterrorism Division. The terrorists who Thrasher subdued had been on their watchlist but had snuck into the country without their knowledge. Bennett had enough field experience to know that a man with Thrasher's instincts needed to be on Uncle Sam's side.

Only weeks after Thrasher arrived for training at Quantico, the instructors quickly advised Bennett that Thrasher's personality and persistent rule breaking had no place in the FBI and that he should cut Thrasher loose. But Thrasher's patriotism impressed Bennett and he alerted a friend over at CIA of Thrasher's potential. Bennett had worked with Tom Delang on more than a few occasions on terrorism cases that had crossed U.S. borders and he knew that Delang was reliable. After meeting Thrasher, Delang came to the same conclusion as Bennett and got Thrasher enrolled in the CIA's training program.

Thrasher wasn't much easier on the CIA's instructors at the Farm, but they were a little more used to handling recruits with a reckless disregard for authority. His personality aside, Thrasher stood head and shoulders over the competition in his class. His high functioning brain could see a scenario play out well in advance, his adaptive instincts were off the charts, and his creative solutions were fascinating. But the agency psychologists warned the instructors that Thrasher wasn't well-suited for a team environment. When confronted with such feedback, Thrasher was adamant about proving them wrong. For one, he needed to show himself. Second, despite his quirks, Thrasher was smart enough to know that one man couldn't do everything himself. In a team environment, success was best achieved where each member fed off of the others' energy, especially in the field of anti-terrorism.

However, when given the chance, Thrasher failed at his first team assignment when it was determined that he missed a hidden cell phone in a Beirut home, which he was supposed to have cloned. This error resulted in his team only hearing one side of a conversation between two Hezbollah terrorists. Had they been able to hear the other side of the conversation, they may have known what was being planned. Instead, the team walked into an ambush and all its members except Thrasher were killed by a suicide bomber.

It was later determined that the burden of the mission's failure ultimately fell to its lead agent, Jacob Webb, whose poor judgment led him to make contact with the suicide bomber without properly assessing the scene. Thrasher's error may have been a contributing factor to the team's death but not the root cause.

Thrasher took the incident personally. Devastated that his miscue was responsible for the deaths of a team that had put their trust in him, he used the burn marks from the blast on his hands and neck, as well as his survivor's guilt, as motivation to never fall prey to an incident like that again and to never let any team member down.

Dr. Dorothy McCoy, the lead psychologist at the CIA, ardently objected and even took her conclusions straight to the director's office, citing that Thrasher's fragile psyche would inevitably result in his death, the deaths of innocents, or both. It was a valid concern, but the director had made his career in espionage by evaluating people. His glimpse into Thrasher's inspired eyes was all he needed to know. Thrasher was a man he needed on the front lines.

The director's intuition would prove correct. In the two years since the Beirut incident, Thrasher's investigative skills had successfully solved six suicide bombings and one drone strike, which was proven to be a setup by the Iranian Revolutionary Guard.

Thrasher's success was not devoid of problems, though. He often exhibited a confrontational attitude and his moodiness made him difficult to be around, even under the best of circumstances. He tended to unknowingly snap when it came to responding to questions, and he disobeyed orders when he felt his moral code was being insulted or broken. It was the latter that landed him on the front page of the CIA's personnel shit list. He understood the reason he was being punished, but that didn't mean he had to like it.

Despite his situation, Thrasher had come to enjoy the quiet afternoons in the mountains, rocking back in forth in his chair. His sleeveless t-shirt exposed a colorful array of gargoyles and evil clowns running the lengths of both arms as he watched the sunset through his brown rimmed Arnette sunglasses that he was never without. For an agent who spent most of his time in the Middle East's desert heat, he should have felt cold. The temperature was only forty-five degrees, but he was indifferent to it. His anger kept him warm.

Tipping back his glass to down the last ounce of whiskey, he was about to refill his glass when the screen door opened.

"You have a phone call. She's been calling for the last ten minutes."

Tom Delang handed the young agent his phone, which was still ringing.

Recognizing the number, Thrasher grunted as he contemplated answering, but knew that the caller wouldn't stop trying to reach him until he answered. After refilling his drink, he finally put the phone to his ear.

"Enjoying your vacation?"

"This ain't no fucking vacation, Beth."

Jenkins sighed in frustration. She had hoped this conversation would go in a different direction but should've known better.

"Can you blame me for what I did?" Thrasher asked.

"No. But you had orders. That guy you killed in Karachi was India's best source inside Pakistani ISI. Did you really think that there would be no repercussions?"

"You know what I saw him doing. There was no way in hell I was gonna let that pass."

"And when you snapped his neck, there was a large piece of me that said 'bravo,' but you're lucky the Indian Intelligence Bureau didn't come after you right away."

"Feel free to give those bastards my address and tell them I'll be waiting!"

"If you keep up the attitude, I just might. But have you forgotten who talked them out of doing it in the first place? Matter of fact, I don't think I ever received a proper thank you!"

Thrasher's lips made a smacking sound as his tongue slid down the front of his teeth. Not only was Jenkins right, but she was one tough cookie.

"I'm waiting, Ben," Jenkins insisted.

Following a long pause, Thrasher responded in a milder tone.

"I'm not sorry that I killed that sorry sack of dog shit, but I *am* sorry that I made things hard for you, and that you had to clean up my mess. Is that sufficient?"

"I guess it'll have to do. Look, had it been me, I would have found another way to deal with the situation, but I understand why you did what you felt you had to do. But you need to understand that the Deputy Director and I both stuck our necks out for you. Any other agent would have been served up to IIB on a platter."

Admitting he was wrong was hard enough for Thrasher. But knowing that he had people in his corner who he put in a bad situation was what twisted the knife in his orphaned soul. It was this thought that made him take another large swig from his glass.

"I get it," Thrasher said.

"Good. Now, are you ready to get back in the game?"

"Damn right, I am."

"I know that Tom doesn't watch a lot of TV in that cabin of his, but have you seen the news on your phone?"

"The new Supreme Leader?"

"Exactly. How much of that bottle do you have left?"

Thrasher pulled the phone from his ear and stared at it.

"If you and Delang planted cameras in here to watch me, you're gonna see a side of me that you don't want to see, and real fast."

"Relax, tough guy. I know you. Finish the bottle and then pack up. First thing in the morning, you catch an agency plane to the station here in Islamabad."

"Fuck tomorrow. Tell them to get the plane ready now. I'll be there in three hours."

"The plane's not even in Atlanta yet, Ben. Just be there first thing in the morning."

"Fine, I'll see you soon."

"Good. And Ben?"

"Yeah?"

"When you get here, try and behave. Put Tom back on the phone."

Thrasher rose from his chair and went back into the cabin where he found Delang appearing to read the latest Jack Carr novel. No doubt, he had been eavesdropping on the conversation.

"Here. She wants to talk to you."

Thrasher tossed the phone back to Tom before walking back onto the porch.

"Hey, girlie," Delang said in his customary greeting to Jenkins. "What's up?"

"How's he doing?"

"Hang on. Let me go upstairs."

Delang walked up the staircase and into his private, soundproofed office.

One of the conditions of Thrasher's suspension was that he had to spend some time with Delang. It was a cool move by Jenkins. She needed Thrasher to keep an eye on Delang to make sure that he didn't become a recluse and reintegrated himself into society after his time in Iranian captivity. At the same time, she needed Delang's skills as a veteran agent to help sand down the sharp edges on Thrasher's elbows, to help mold the up-and-comer into what would hopefully be a long career. While she would never call what they were doing babysitting, in essence, that's exactly what it was. She knew it was best for both of them.

"It sounds like you hammered him pretty good," Delang said.

"He needed to hear it. Plus, I wasn't letting him off the phone until I heard an apology."

"I'm not disagreeing with you. He and I have spent the last few weeks swapping stories. I finally got him to open up about that ambush in Beirut."

"Really? What'd he say?"

"It's not what he said. It's what he didn't say. Beth, I think that incident cut him *way* deeper than you realize. He feels like he let everyone down, especially you. I'm not saying that you don't need to ride him hard when its warranted, but I am saying that you've got one hell of a loyal agent. He'll do anything to keep something like that from happening again. You may want to keep that in mind, okay?"

"Okay, okay," Jenkins said.

She sighed.

"What about you? How are you doing these days?"

"The nightmares are still there, but I'm taking fewer Xanax in the morning. You'll have to ask Abby about the panic attacks. They're less frequent, but pretty strong when they happen. Talking to Thrasher has helped a bit, though."

"Good to hear. What's the latest on the movie?"

The day after Delang testified before Congress about his time in captivity, Hollywood producers were lining up at the CIA's doorstep for rights to the story.

Delang huffed out a laugh.

"Between the Iranians and the Hollywood producers, I'd rather deal with the Iranians."

Jenkins busted out laughing. At least Delang's sense of humor was still intact.

"Seriously, some days it seems like things are running on all cylinders and other days it seems like things are at a dead stop. I honestly don't know what to tell you other than the fact that a producer is making a trip out here in a few days."

"He's making a special trip to see *you*? It's usually the other way around, isn't it?"

"I'm not complaining. It saves me the hassle."

"Alright, fair enough. Let's get back on the clock. You think Thrasher's good to go? I know that he's got the chops to make it in the field, but I can't have him flying off the handle."

"He likes being pushed. It drives him. But only you can know where the line is before he's pushed too hard and blows a gasket."

"Point taken. Thankfully, I don't think that will be a problem."

"What's that mean?"

"If I'm right, this new Supreme Leader is going to push all of us."

Chapter Four

TEHRAN, IRAN

Vahid Avesta sat at his desk in the Presidential Administration building, anxiously awaiting a video call from the president of India. The clock on his computer read 9:01 a.m. While Avesta was known for his punctuality, President Sharma was not. It was a reality that Avesta detested but had come to accept.

Today, though, Avesta was feeling more lenient. His aides had informed him that India was going to be rejoining the gas pipeline deal between Iran and Pakistan. It was an agreement that Avesta had personally worked on for several months. Given their feelings toward one another, it had been annoying serving as the nanny between India and Pakistan, but now, it was about to be worth it. Thanks to the United States, the economic sanctions against Iran had decimated his country's economy. This deal with India would increase the crude oil exports from fifteen to upwards of twenty percent, which equated to seventy billion in additional annual revenue that would flow into Iran's economy. It was the exact type of good news that Avesta was chomping at the bit to bring to the Supreme Leader.

Avesta came out of his daze as a noisy alert of the incoming video call came to life on his screen. He adjusted his burgundy tie and could see the condensation from his sweaty palm on his black mouse as he hit the *Join Now* button.

"Akshay. It's great to see you, my friend," Avesta said.

"You as well, Vahid," said Sharma.

Avesta noticed something 'off' about Sharma's tone of voice.

"We've worked many months on this pipeline deal, and I know it hasn't always been a smooth road to travel. Every good deal leaves all parties involved wishing they had gotten more out of it for themselves, but I think we've come to a result that will satisfy everyone involved. Wouldn't you agree?"

"Actually, Vahid . . ."

Uh oh.

Avesta's palms became sweaty again.

"I think we are going to have to put our agreement on the back burner for a while."

"Excuse me? Akshay, we've worked on this for months. What's the problem now?"

"A new offer has come in within the last twenty-four hours and we've received a better deal. One that I cannot turn down and also prohibits me from moving forward on this with Iran."

Avesta was stunned.

This can't be happening.

Panic started to set in, but one word from Sharma's statement caused his ears to perk up.

"In the last twenty-four hours, you said? As the new Supreme Leader assumed his role?"

"I'm not sure that has anything to do with it, but yes," said Sharma.

He lied and hoped Avesta did not recognize it.

"Of course, it does. Don't treat me like a child, Akshay."

"Vahid, let's not make this personal."

Avesta ignored the statement.

"This new deal that you've accepted *prohibits* you from moving forward with our deal? Is that the word you used?"

Sharma bit his tongue. He should have known that it was a poor choice of words.

"That's right, Vahid. We . . ."

"What did those pig Americans offer you?" Avesta said.

"Vahid, please. You know I can't go into those details."

"So, it *was* the Americans. How much?!"

Sharma let out a heavy breath.

"Put it this way. My country will no longer be able to import oil from Iran for the indefinite future. But let's not forget that our two countries can still trade a variety of goods together that will benefit everyone. In fact, . . ."

"Those maggots! You've been in bed with them for far too long. Now, what? You agree to be their full-time mistress?"

"Vahid, let's keep this in perspective. This is a business deal. I have to do what's best for my country. It's as simple as that. Between you and I, our countries can find a way to continue to trade without damaging our relationship."

"Save it. You can be courted by the Americans all you want. They can wine you and dine you, and promise you the stars, but don't come crying back to me when you get fucked!"

With that, Aventa signed off from the call and threw a massive punch at his monitor that sent it flying off his desk. He tried to calm himself by pacing his six-foot frame around his spacious office with his hands on his head, clenching his thick, greying hair in both fists. He stopped at the full-length window that overlooked downtown Tehran, hoping that the scenic view would comfort him, but it was no use. Nothing was going to cushion the blow of Sharma's statement. If he didn't figure something out, and fast, he was going to be the next victim of the Supreme Leader's wrath.

Avesta closed his eyes and took a nervous breath as he pinched the bridge of his nose under his thick, black-rimmed glasses.

How am I going to break this news to the new Supreme Leader?

Not only had the deal to guarantee additional crude oil fallen through, but the other fifteen percent of all crude oil exports to India that were a staple of his country's current economy would soon be gone. Forget the seventy billion of additional revenue lost. The loss of their other oil exports to India would cost Iran billions per year. There was no way to spin this.

Those fucking Americans!

Then a thought popped into Avesta's head. The Americans. They may be the bane of Iran's existence, but they might also enable him to not only worm his way out of his current predicament but make a bold move on the chess board in front of the new Supreme Leader.

He called out to his assistant from the doorway.

"Saeed, see if you can track down General Lajani. I need to speak with him right away."

"But, sir, the general is already here, waiting for you."

"What? He's here?"

"Well, yes, sir."

The young assistant pointed to him. Avesta was shocked. He had been so focused on his idea of speaking to the general that he hadn't even noticed that the man was literally ten feet in front of him.

"General, please come in. What brings you by?"

Avesta closed the door behind them.

"The Supreme Leader asked me to give this to you."

Lajani removed an item from under his arm and handed it to Avesta.

Inside the polished, cherry frame was the photo of the Supreme Leader, Avesta, and Lajani, standing unified at Golestan Palace a few days earlier. On the white mat surrounding the 12x16 photo was a handwritten note from the new Supreme Leader that touched Avesta.

Vahid,

Let us do great things together. For the glory of Iran and in the name of Allah.

—Marzban

"It's beautiful. But you could have gotten one of your aides to bring it by."

"He wanted me to deliver it to you personally. What did you want to see me about?"

"What?"

Avesta was still stunned by the personal gesture of the Ayatollah.

"When you stepped outside your office, you asked your assistant to track me down. What did you want?"

Avesta snapped back to attention.

"Yes, I did. Remember the plan the Supreme Leader mentioned to us moments after this photo was taken?"

"I don't forget any military plan," Lajani said. "My staff is already making arrangements."

"Are they ready? Based on the conversation I just had with the president of India, we need to proceed."

Lajani paused. It was a valiant plan, but he would have never thought that Avesta had the balls to take such a political gamble.

"If it doesn't work, you'll be the one standing without a chair when the music stops. Even I won't be able to save you."

"Fortune favors the bold, my friend."

"You'd better hope so."

Chapter Five

ISLAMABAD, PAKISTAN

Izad Hyat's day started early, but it was already stressful. After reviewing his morning reports, the veteran Pakistani ISI officer had his required annual physical at headquarters before lunch, a chore he found annoying. He knew that he was in perfect working order, but rules were rules. Most of all, he despised being poked with needles, even for routine blood work. As someone who routinely utilized needles when injecting suspects with sodium pentothal, which he used as a truth serum, he was around needles enough that he should be used to them, yet there was something about being injected himself that increased his anxiety.

No one likes being treated like a lab rat but for Hyat it was more than that. He never truly trusted the person on the other end of the syringe. As far as he was concerned, the intelligence world was a dark pit filled with nightmarish monsters. The idea that his DNA was being thrown into this pit never sat comfortably with him. By nature, the spy world was corrupt, and ISI had more than its fair share of questionable characters.

Later that afternoon, he took a brisk five-mile drive to a local park to meet Jackson Whang, a friend of his at the CIA. Hyat and Whang first crossed paths in 2019 when Pakistan needed U.S. assistance in crushing the Baluchistan Liberation Army (BLA) in the southwest part of Pakistan. They had been setting up a series of ambushes against Pakistani Armed Forces. During their collaboration, Hyat found Whang to be likable but learned quickly not to be fooled by his politeness. There was a darkness looming below the surface that he admired. Hyat liked him right away.

While the BLA wasn't totally quashed, CIA's high-tech surveillance equipment and drone usage helped the Pakistani government regain the upper hand in the area. Unfortunately, Whang was injured on the mission when he took some shrapnel to the back. Hyat got him to safety, and the two decided to keep in touch. When Hyat called his friend two days ago, requesting a meeting as soon as possible on an important issue for him personally, Whang told him that he was already in-country.

The personal issue that required Hyat to meet with his CIA counterpart concerned his nephew on his wife's side, Hasan Wasim, who was a Lieutenant in the Pak Marines. Normally, Hyat wouldn't have thought twice about the fact that his twenty-nine-year-old nephew had not been heard from for a few days. After all, he was young and in the military. He could've been on assignment with orders of no outside contact or on leave, doing whatever it is that young people of his country do in their spare time. But Hyat's wife, Aisha, and her nephew, had a close relationship. Privately, Aisha proclaimed to her husband that Hasan was her favorite of all of the nieces and nephews, due to their love of football and the national team. So, when Hasan missed his aunt's birthday without a text or phone call, his wife was perturbed and Hyat became curious.

When he called the Marine base in Qasim and spoke to his superior, he was told that Lieutenant Wasim had not yet returned from an assignment in the Baluchistan region near the Iranian border. Hyat knew instantly that this was not a good sign. When he dug a little further, he learned that Wasim had a regular job transporting nuclear rods to and from the state-run facility in Karachi. From there, his investigation came up empty. He realized that he had no other choice than to reach out to his contacts in the intelligence world for assistance, hoping that they would be willing to momentarily put aside their daily tasks to help him. It was a slight breach of etiquette in the spy world, but Hyat decided to roll the dice and see if he could cash in on some of his credibility for this type of personal use.

Because of scheduling conflicts on Whang's end, Hyat wasn't able to meet with his CIA friend until four in the afternoon. Whang expressed the sincere concern that Hyat had been hoping for and told him that he would look into it, but he also told him that he should go speak to his boss. Since he was already acquainted with her, Hyat figured that the extra meeting couldn't hurt. Before parting ways, Whang noticed that the collar to his friend's shirt was partially flipped upward so he adjusted the collar.

"I'll get back to you," Whang said.

"That's all I ask. It's most appreciated."

As he made the short half-mile walk through crowded sidewalks, where people kept bumping into him, Hyat replayed the conversation in his head. His instincts told him that the meeting had gone well. He trusted that Whang would do what he said he would, even though he had no obligation to do so.

When he reached the gates of the U.S. Embassy, a square jawed Marine frisked him.

"Who are you here to see, sir?"

"Katherine Jennings," Hyat said.

***

It wasn't as if Jenkins had a ton of spare time, but whenever she needed a break, one of two things happened. She either went to her bookshelf to continue her studies on Hitler's Nazi regime or she pulled out her copy of the Tom Delang file and pored over the list of his old sources. Today, it was the latter. They had all been vetted and notified upon Delang's return to the United States. His debriefing had been exhausting on both ends. For one, there was a reason Delang had been the most trusted agent in the region. Over the years, he'd made a ton of contacts in the field and every one of them had to be researched for any potential links to his capture.

Second, there was no way to tell what Delang had given up during his interrogations at the hands of the Iranians. He did his best to recall what he could, but the Iranians had slipped him more than a few drugs to loosen his tongue. Though he resisted them with the full force of his will power and maintained that he stayed tight lipped, he admitted that he couldn't be one hundred percent sure. Given the information that Delang gained over his years of experience, these weren't odds that the CIA was willing to risk.

There were also the torture sessions. Jenkins was absolutely sure that Delang remembered, and the details were gruesome. As professionals, the CIA agents who interviewed him should've been used to hearing the finer points of how a vegetable scraper can be used to peel back layers of one's skin or using a chisel to knock out a person's teeth, but in the end, they were human like everyone else. The team performing the interviews had to excuse themselves more than once to give their stomachs the opportunity to unknot.

While the details Delang disclosed about his torture were precise, things became fuzzy when it came to how the Iranians caught on to the sleep deprivation technique. There was a reason why the CIA employed such tactics on Al-Qaeda terrorists after 9/11: even Navy Seals find themselves compromised after seventy-two hours. But the Iranians took the next step with this enhanced interrogation tactic. Delang called it "catnapping." The Iranians would utilize the sleep deprivation tactic for three days and then allow Delang to sleep for short periods of time, which he suspected were no longer than thirty minutes. When asked how he knew it was only thirty minutes, he said that one of the IRGC guards would habitually roll up his sleeves and expose his watch. The catnapping allowed the brain to reboot and process thoughts more clearly after the sleep deprivation had taken place, but the ability to maintain its lucidity faded quickly. Over the course of time, the back-and-forth tennis match of deprivation and catnapping took a toll on Delang's brain. When coupled with drugs, his brain's ability to efficiently reboot itself was reduced each time, to the point that he was almost literally a zombie.

Considering what he had to endure, it was amazing that Delang didn't go insane. In Jenkins's estimation, no one could have withstood his aggressors better. Still, everyone eventually breaks and Delang was no exception. Every piece of information that Delang knew was considered a national security risk. His file was an intelligence and diplomatic horror show.

No one wanted to deal with it, but Jenkins knew that she had to. She would never be able to let go of the fact that she had begged her boss to send Delang to Saudi Arabia to meet with the U.S. ambassador. She knew the two men had a close friendship and she took advantage of it in order to get some quick answers regarding the Shiite uprising in Bahrain. Her insistence was what led to him being captured and nothing was going to change her mind. His file was her responsibility and she planned to kick over every stone inside it to recover any lost information.

She was so deep in thought that she almost didn't notice junior agent Tequila Griffin standing at her door.

"Oh, hey. What's up?"

"Sorry to bother you, but ISI is here to see you," Griffin said.

Jenkins's eyes narrowed and stared at her curiously. She knew that she didn't have a meeting scheduled with ISI today.

"They asked for me, personally? Or did they ask to speak with a security officer?"

The difference between the two was distinct. By asking for her by name, it meant that whoever it was knew Jenkins personally. If they asked to speak with a security officer, anyone from the CIA could speak with them under the guise of working for the State Department.

"He asked to speak with a Katherine Jennings."

Question asked and answered. Katherine Jennings was Jenkins's legend as an employee of the State Department, but anyone from ISI that was using that name either knew her only by her cover name or was being polite enough to not say her real name out loud. She would have to see for herself which one was the case.

"Okay. Put him in interrogation room 112. I'll be there in a minute."

"Will do."

Once again, Jenkins closed the Delang file, put her iPad in the wall safe, and made her way through the maze of hallways leading to the interrogation rooms on the other side of the building. They were generally reserved for walk-ins, claiming to have either vital information that may be of use to United States national interests or to report potential threats.

As she arrived at the interrogation room door, Jenkins straightened her charcoal blazer that matched her sky-colored, satin blouse and flipped the switch on the button outside the door, which let everyone know that the room was in use. This switch also blocked all electronic and GPS signals to and from the room. She took a deep breath, scanned her badge, and walked in to see Izad Hyat sitting at the table, waiting for her.

In 2012, Tom Delang had introduced Jenkins to Hyat under his real name, but he had used her legend name. Together, they had tracked down a terrorist with links to ISIS who was hiding in Karachi. They had spoken on various issues since then and she considered him to be a consummate professional, a rarity for ISI in her experience, but they were more acquaintances than friends. Given the recent occurrences in Delang's life, she was far more guarded when sitting in front of Delang's trusted sources for fear that she might suffer a similar fate.

"Katherine, how are you?"

"I'm well, Izad. What can I do for you?"

She sat across from him at the metal table but didn't exchange any pleasantries.

Hyat hesitated. The American wasn't her usual chipper self.

"I, uh, need your help."

Hyat proceeded to fill Jenkins in on the same information about his nephew that he had shared with Whang earlier. He didn't specifically know that Jenkins handled the Iranian Affairs desk for the CIA in Pakistan, but he knew her to be a smart agent who was well dialed-in to the region close to the Iranian border.

"I'm sorry to hear that. But, why come to me?"

"Two years ago, you came to me, asking for the same type of help regarding Tom. While I wasn't able to deliver on any information as you had hoped, I want you to know that I did my best to find him. I'm hoping that you will extend me the same courtesy regarding my neph-ew."

Jenkins looked for any facial tics or mannerisms that would indicate that Hyat was lying. She saw only kind eyes that appeared to be pleading for her help.

"Please, Katherine. I wouldn't be here asking if I didn't need your help."

Jenkins deliberately tried not to let her emotions govern her decisions, but she could tell the man was sincere. Plus, he was right. She had asked the same of him when Delang went missing. Fairness wasn't a quality that normally factored into the spy world, but in this case, she thought that she should return the favor.

"Certainly. I'll do some digging and keep my ear to the ground. If I hear anything, I'll call you."

"Thank you, Katherine."

"You're welcome."

With that, Jenkins waved at the two-way security mirror. For the safety of an agent under cover or any embassy workers, it was standard protocol for any questioning to be observed by someone outside the room. Her hand wave signaled that the agent in the observation room, Griffin, could escort the walk-in back to the front of the embassy.

As he left, Jenkins remained seated and tapped her fingers on the table, thinking about Hyat's request. If his nephew was working around the Iranian border, there was a good chance that he could have been captured.

What would the Iranians need with a Pakistani soldier?

She would have to ask Farhad if he knew anything about it.

As she stood to exit the room, Jenkins was knocked off her feet, and hit her head on the table when an explosion rocked the side of the building.

Chapter Six

CHAKLALA AIRPORT
ISLAMABAD, PAKISTAN

Thrasher saw a familiar face leaning against the side of an Agency issued Dodge Durango, waiting for him on the airport tarmac. Jackson Whang was a naturalized Korean American, who had grown up bouncing around between army bases, like the children of most military families. His parents had met when his father was stationed at Fort Benning, Georgia, where his mother lived. Most military brats hated being relocated every year or two, but Whang embraced the sense of adventure. Along the way, his father had instilled his patriotism and deep love of America in his son while trying to be true to his family's Korean roots.

"Always look at North Korea, see it for what it is, and know that you could be living there. Then look at America, see it for what it is, and you'll realize how lucky you are."

His father's statement, often repeated, stayed with Jackson.

The combination of his Korean heritage, a sense of adventure, and his genuine patriotism sprinkled on top made him the ideal candidate for the CIA. While Whang was a relatively polished candidate, it was at the CIA's training facility outside Williamsburg, Virginia that he met a brash, up-and-comer named Ben Thrasher. Early on, the two clashed like oil and water, but thanks to some tough love from the training instructors, the two trainees found the chemistry that the agency had hoped they would, and they soon discovered that their combative personalities actually made each other stronger. Thrasher admired Whang's skill set as a master safe cracker and Whang was in awe of Thrasher's ability to assess a crime scene and offer creative solutions. By the time they graduated, they came to respect one another.

Their friendship, though, was a work in progress. Given the initials of his first and last name, JW, it was not uncommon for his friends or those he worked closely with to call him "J-Dub." Thrasher hated urban lingo. For the first few years of their careers, he refused to call him by anything other than his last name. But as they worked cases together across the Middle East, it came as a shock to Whang when Thrasher called him "Dub" out of the blue. At that moment, both Jenkins and Whang knew that Thrasher had accepted him into his personal inner circle.

After sustaining an injury during an op in Pakistan, the CIA had tried to medically retire Dub. Fortunately, his father had some deep connections to friends in Congress, and used his leverage to allow the CIA to keep him on board.

He was currently the senior assistant to the Iranian Affairs desk in Islamabad. Given his good relationship with ISI, he'd thought that he was going to be promoted to the top job, but it went to Jenkins. He wasn't happy about it, but the promotion would have to wait.

The two men hopped into the car as soon as they spotted each other.

"I didn't know you would be here," Thrasher said.

"Good to see you, too."

Dub handed his colleague a holstered Sig Sauer P226 and his embassy ID.

Thrasher grimaced as he tucked the holster into his belt and lassoed the ID card around his neck. He'd been on the ground for two minutes and his anti-social tendencies were already rubbing his colleagues the wrong way.

"Sorry. How are you?"

In an attempt to make up for his rudeness, Thrasher held up a fist looking for a bump.

"Stylin'."

Dub returned the bump and drove off.

"Your folks okay?"

Dub smirked as he noted how Thrasher was trying to be social, even though he knew the man's natural tendencies were quite the opposite.

"They're hanging in there. Thanks for asking."

"Seriously, though, I didn't know you would be here. How long have you been in the country?"

"About two months, but I think the boss lady had plans for us to work together even before your suspension. Welcome back, by the way."

"How is she?"

"Nervous. I think this new Supreme Leader thing has her spooked. A true 'unknown unknown.' Know what I mean?"

The "unknown unknown" phrase was still not one that was received well in the U.S. intelligence community, even twenty years after the Secretary of Defense had used it to describe the pre-invasion regime of Saddam Hussein in Iraq. Unfortunately, the term was as true today as it was then.

The rest of the forty-five-minute trip to the embassy unfolded in silence. Both men were not inclined to make chit-chat, but the bigger reason was that they were CIA officers driving the streets of a country where at least ten percent of its population wanted them dead. Constantly checking the mirrors and being fully aware of the surroundings was crucial for assets in any region of the world but especially in the Middle East.

When they stopped at the light outside the American embassy, Thrasher caught a glimpse of a boy and his father across the street, fishing in the Jinnah Stream. Since Thrasher never knew his father, he grinned at the idea of the boy and his dad making a memory of their first catch together.

As the car started moving again, Thrasher noticed a strange formation of rocks downstream from the father and son. The grouping of rocks was the same size as the others on the bank but lighter in color. When the car was two hundred yards away from the front of the embassy, the angle of the road gave him a better look at the arrangement. It was located on the bank that situated it above the embassy fence, positioned perfectly between the diplomatic structures, which gave it a clear line of sight to the rear of the building.

"Back up! Get outta here, now! Move! Move!"

Dub had no idea what his partner had spotted, but he trusted Thrasher's instincts implicitly. He immediately shifted the car into reverse and slammed on the accelerator. The tires squealing against the pavement barely muffled the sound of an RPG streaking above the ground toward the embassy. It was a sound that Thrasher was all too familiar with from his run-in with the terrorists in South Dakota.

The rear corner building exploded, and debris sailed everywhere. Pieces of brick fell from the sky and landed on the Durango, denting the hood and roof with a pronounced thud. Thrasher threw his hands up in defense to protect himself from the falling pieces that cracked the windshield but thankfully didn't penetrate it. Once they were clear of the embassy complex and back on the main road, Dub stopped the car so that they could get a clear view of the destruction.

But before they could make heads or tails of what happened, another RPG came screeching over the ground and hit the building again in nearly the same spot. Thrasher traced the streak of smoke from the weapon and knew immediately that it came from the bank across the stream.

"Look, there!"

Dub pointed. Emerging from the façade of rocks was the terrorist who had fired on the embassy. Spotting Dub and Thrasher across the road staring at him, he discarded the grenade launcher strapped to his shoulder and made a run for the forest, like a squirrel hustling away from oncoming traffic.

Without hesitating, Thrasher and Dub jumped back in the car, engaged the four-wheel drive, and hauled ass toward the stream.

"Don't you let that little bastard slip away," Thrasher said.

"Let me do the driving. Keep your eyes on him!"

Dub cut such a hard left that Thrasher felt the wheels come off the ground even when he leaned heavily against the passenger side of the car. Once back on all four wheels, they drove parallel along the stream as they watched the terrorist run toward the forest. Dub jerked the wheel right to cross the stream, but as they made their way to the other side, the large vehicle came to a grinding halt. Dub kept slamming his foot on the accelerator. The tires were spinning but nothing was happening.

"We're stuck!"

Thrasher wasted no time and leapt from his seat, gun in hand, and hit the ground running in relentless pursuit of his suspect. Dub got out to see that the front axle of the car was propped up by one of the stream's natural rocks.

As Thrasher made his way up the embankment toward the forest, he could see dust kicking up from the terrorist's feet.

Damn, the little shit is fast.

Thrasher recognized that he had to be faster and smarter. The distance between him and the suspect narrowed as he felt his adrenaline kick into turbo and his muscles burn, trying to exceed their capacity.

As he entered the forest, the terrorist couldn't have been more than one hundred yards in front of him, but Thrasher had no choice but to slow down. There was no telling what kind of booby traps could be waiting for him or if the enemy was lurking, ready to surprise him with a shot of their own. Thrasher had to be careful, but he had to keep moving and following the footsteps in the powdered clay dirt.

He followed them for a quarter of a mile before they unexpectedly disappeared. With sweat dripping from his brow, Thrasher's eyes darted in every direction. The suspect couldn't disappear like Houdini. He made a conscious effort to control his breathing and think his way through the situation. There was no road up ahead and running back down to the stream was useless. It was too shallow so there couldn't have been a boat waiting for him.

Continuing his search, his mind replayed the images of the pursuit in his head. It dawned on him that the skinny coward was wearing a brown t-shirt and pants, which camouflaged him in the brush. Thrasher knew that he was there, lying in wait.

Thrasher crouched down, which gave him cover and allowed him to concentrate on his hearing rather than his eyes. As he lowered himself, he noticed that the sun was directly behind him, projecting his shadow front and center. His large frame had given his opponent some cover. The squatting motion, though, had taken the man by surprise, and when Thrasher saw his shadow, now towering in front of him, he realized that the terrorist prick had doubled back and gotten behind him.

He saw a shadow of the man with a nine-inch Damascus machete reaching above his head to plunge the blade into him. Thrasher pivoted, pushed away from the ground, and shot the man three times. Wide-eyed and caught by surprise, the man tipped over and fell face first into the ground.

Thrasher wiped the sweat from his brow and sighed in relief. Hearing other footsteps rushing up, he intuitively raised his weapon, but lowered it when he saw that it was Dub.

"You okay?"

Thrasher nodded as Dub kicked the body over, face up.

"Recognize him?"

Thrasher shook his head.

"No, but I'm gonna carry this sack of shit back to the embassy and find out."

Chapter Seven

The scene at the embassy was pure chaos. Sirens blared and emergency lights lit up the area. EMT's did their best to tend to those who managed to stumble away from the wreckage. Some Marines tried to secure the scene and prevent any other attacks, while others aided unharmed embassy workers, trying to pull their injured colleagues to safety. Fortunately, both RPGs had hit the same corner of the building, leaving much of it relatively undamaged.

Dub found an American EMT he recognized, and Thrasher dumped the body of the dead terrorist with her.

"I'll go with the body to the morgue to see if we can get an ID," Dub shouted to Thrasher over the commotion.

"Roger that."

When the ambulance pulled away, Thrasher rushed into the tumultuous scene. He was immediately met by an amped up Marine, Arkevis Truesdale, who could have been no more than twenty-five years old and didn't hesitate to shove the barrel of his M27 Infantry Automatic Rifle in Thrasher's face when he saw the Sig Sauer P226 in the agent's hand.

"Hold it right there! Drop the fucking gun!"

"Whoa! Easy, kid, easy! I'm one of the good guys."

"Where's your ID?"

Thrasher reached for the ID card that should have been hanging from his neck, but it wasn't there. In all of the commotion while chasing the terrorist and getting back to the embassy, he must have either lost it or the weight of the dead body had yanked it off its chain.

"It's okay, Arkevis," a graveled, hacking voice shouted behind the Marine.

Truesdale spun around to see who was speaking to him. Thrasher immediately recognized Tequila Griffin. Her dark black face and long flowing cornrow braids were covered in soot and her rose-colored blouse had been torn. She placed her hand on Truesdale's shoulder.

"He's with us."

Once he heard her confirmation, Truesdale lowered his weapon and nodded at Thrasher. He caught a wobbling Griffin from falling to the ground, and escorted her back to the nearest EMT, who gave her an oxygen mask.

"What happened?" she asked.

"Two RPG's fired from the stream embankment behind the building just as Dub and I were pulling up. Where's Beth?"

"I don't know. She was meeting with a guy from ISI who had come in unexpectedly. I was escorting him back to the front when the explosion hit."

"What ISI guy? Who was he?"

"Beth said his name was Izad Hyat. I'd never seen him before, but she seemed to know him."

The name sounded familiar, but Thrasher couldn't remember why.

"Look! I think that's him," she said.

Thrasher turned to see a line of embassy workers and Marines carrying what appeared to be a lifeless body from the rubble on an orange, plastic rescue stretcher. He flipped the oxygen mask off Griffin's head without even so much as a head's up, grabbed her hand, and pulled her toward the body, which was moving their way.

Thrasher helped carry Hyat's body back to the same spot Griffin had been sitting and laid him as gently as he could onto an empty stretcher. His arms dangled from the sides as Thrasher put two fingers to his neck and checked his pulse.

"He's alive, but I think he's in bad shape. You're sure that this is the guy?"

"Yes," Griffin said, still hacking for air.

"Okay, you stay with him and get to the hospital," said Thrasher, pointing his finger at her. "Call me with any updates. If he dies, you go with the body, no matter what."

Griffin would have normally smacked Thrasher's finger away from her face, but in her weakening condition, all she could do was nod.

"Good. What room were they in?"

"One-twelve. At the end of the hall."

Without so much as a goodbye, Thrasher ran toward what was left of the building. Shuffling through the maze of debris, he tried not to fall or cut himself on any exposed metal beams or glass. Fortunately, the interrogation rooms at all U.S. embassies are built with reinforced steel to assist with noise cancellation. It appeared to Thrasher that this engineering tactic had helped sustain the overall boxy structure of the rooms, but two direct hits from an RPG had dramatic effects.

As he reached the area that was once a hallway, Thrasher began tossing away pieces of brick and loose debris with reckless disregard for anyone around him. Creating a pathway as best as he could, he finally came across the warped door, labeled 112. Thinking that he could use it to escort any injured persons he might find back to safety, Thrasher picked it up and set it aside.

After several minutes, Thrasher began to notice that this particular mountain of debris was stacked higher than the others he had dug through. Halfway through it, one piece of metal he had been pulling at with all his might wouldn't budge. This piece wasn't junk. It was a table in the interrogation room. He felt a surge of adrenaline as he tore away the rubbish below his waist.

When he created enough of a sustainable hole, Thrasher pulled a penlight from his tactical cargo pants and clicked it on. Inside, he saw a curled-up body with thick, pitch-black locks of hair.

"Beth!"

Jenkins moaned a response.

"Hang on, I'm gonna get you outta there."

Thrasher continued to kick and pluck away at the debris surrounding the table until he could lift it away, but then he remembered that interrogation tables are deliberately bolted to the floor, which prevented one of the persons sitting at the table from using it as a weapon by pushing it toward anyone else in the room. Each table was also outfitted with wiring that embassy personnel could use to control the recording system in the observation room.

Thrasher hunched under the table and tried pulling Jenkins out by hooking his hands under her armpits but she wailed in pain.

That's not good.

He then gently placed her arms around his neck and scooped her legs up with his other arm. Because of the table above him, he was unable to lift with his legs and nearly pulled his back out trying to emerge from under the table. Her head rested against his shoulder. She was mumbling something, but Thrasher couldn't make it out as he carefully walked his way back to the door he had set down on the ground.

"I need some help over here!"

Thrasher motioned to some paramedics.

"Hang on, boss lady. You'll be outta here in a jiff."

Perhaps it was the sound of a familiar voice or the fact that he called her "boss lady" but Jenkins's brown eyes cracked open. Thrasher looked down when she unexpectedly lifted his hand and placed her cell phone in it. Her lips moved but the words forming in her brain wouldn't come out. Thrasher turned his head to her ear to try and hear what she was saying over the sounds of the calamity around them.

"Far...Farhad. Find Farhad."

As she passed out, another EMT arrived to help Thrasher carry Jenkins's body to safety. Before he loaded her into the ambulance, Thrasher held Jenkins's phone to her face. He lifted her eyelid, allowing it to scan her eye and grant him access. Then, he went into her settings to turn off the security feature. When the ambulance drove away, he immediately called Dub.

"What's up?"

"I found her. She's headed your way, so be sure to meet her. She doesn't look good."

"Roger that."

Chapter Eight

HIGHLANDS, NORTH CAROLINA

Tom Delang felt like life was looking up. For the first time in weeks, he'd slept through the night. His flashbacks of being tortured were still there and probably always would be, but they were dissipating. He tended to become a little more shut off from the world at night, when the rule in his house was that the television stayed off and it was his quiet time to read. But he thought he was turning the corner on that as well when he and his wife, Abby, decided to watch some *Married...with Children* reruns on Hulu.

Being the career CIA man that he was, old habits died hard. Delang was sitting on the outdoor patio of his favorite eatery, Lakeside Restaurant, facing the door and basking in the afternoon sun emerging from behind puffy clouds, when a familiar, pony-tailed figure emerged from around the corner with a leather messenger bag around his shoulder.

"Hey, I know you, don't I?"

The man was smiling.

"It's been a while, so I wasn't sure you would recognize me," Delang said.

He stood to shake the man's hand.

"Looks like you've gained some of your weight back. That is, you look healthier than you did when I saw you on TV."

"Thanks, I'm feeling better."

Delang had known Vik Wheaton from way back in their high school days. They had once been good friends but had a small falling out over a girlfriend. Then, life took them in different directions. For Delang, it was to a sales position with a tech company out west and eventually the CIA as the agency's most trusted spy in the Near East division. Wheaton headed to Hollywood where he was a struggling screenwriter for years until he made a splash with a series of horror films. Noticing his friend's success, Delang reached out and offered his sincerest congratulations and the two kept in touch from time to time.

Wheaton's screenwriting success led to gigs as an executive producer. It wasn't long before he was directing his own projects, where, over a period of four straight years he made several critically acclaimed slasher flicks that made him the latest golden boy in Hollywood. The characters he created would be used in silly sequels for years to come.

Since he wrote the scripts for the original films, it meant that he owned the rights to the characters. This had the added benefit of having a check arrive in the mail each time a new movie was made, whether he was involved in production or not. He partied with the biggest stars, sailed on luxurious yachts to the most exotic locations, cruised at fast speeds in his custom-made Lamborghini on the Pacific Coast Highway, and dated even faster women.

But as success goes, the highest highs are usually followed by the lowest of lows. Four years ago, one of the big three studios put a hundred million dollars into an epic Civil War fantasy-drama, *The Ungodly*. Think *Ghost* meets *The Godfather* in the Confederate South. Wheaton served as the sole writer, producer, and director. It was his largest and most expensive production to date as well as his first drama film, but Wheaton was confident that he could make it work. During principal photography, though, one of the sets caught fire, due to a safety error, which resulted in the deaths of two crew members and an up-and-coming actress with a supporting role. Production was shut down for a month. A week after it resumed, in a stroke of sheer bad luck, the Los Angeles area was hit with a 5.4 earthquake that damaged the set. When it was all said and done, the film was thirty million dollars over budget and payouts to the families of the deceased actors and crew had not yet been negotiated. To help keep the studio off the ledge, Wheaton offered his ten thousand square foot, seven-bedroom Malibu mansion and $10 million of his own money as collateral.

Wheaton knew the history of Hollywood well-enough to keep the studio from cancelling the picture altogether. He used *Apocalypse Now*, a film with legendary stories of issues during production, as his example of how films can recover and go on to live in infamy. By leaking fictional stories from production to social media, he was convinced that the series of controversies would create enough curiosity on the part of the public to get to the theaters. Since the stories on social media were retweeted and shared on Facebook more than fourteen million times, this convinced the studio to throw in an additional twenty million in marketing beyond what had already been planned.

The results were disastrous. On opening weekend, the film grossed only nineteen million dollars. Overseas releases were even worse. By the time the film was released digitally ten weeks later, it had recouped less than half of its budget. There was little doubt among the Hollywood elite that the film would be ranked as one of the most colossal flops of all time.

The disaster put Wheaton on a Hollywood blacklist that no independent or mainstream studio would touch. Even the horror genre that he essentially redefined wanted nothing to do with him. All planned spin-off films based on the characters he created were shelved.

He was relegated to the rafters of doing podcasts in the basement of a one-story house he rented in West Hollywood. This put him back into the arena of the horror genre, which best suited him. He discussed the in's-and-out's of his earlier, successful films with eager fans, which allowed him to relive the memories of his glory days. The podcasts were a success, but barely kept him afloat financially. Night after night,

Wheaton sat on the stoop of his backdoor, smoking cigarette after cigarette. He missed his old life and knew that the only way to get it back was to find another hit.

With his successes and failure in Hollywood consuming him, he lost touch with many of his old friends, including Tom Delang. It had been three years since he had heard from Tom, and it wasn't until he saw the breaking news coverage of him testifying before Congress that Wheaton had even seen him, let alone knew that he was in the CIA.

When Delang detailed his torturous time in captivity at the hands of the Iranians, it sparked an idea in Wheaton's head. His one-time close friend had a true story to tell that would specify the severe torment he had suffered before he emerged safely on the other side. That would play well into his horror genre wheelhouse. Wheaton knew in his gut that this tale was one that had to be told on the big screen and would taste like warm, gooey, southern apple pie to the masses.

While other Hollywood producers were relentlessly knocking on the CIA's door the day after Delang's testimony on Capitol Hill, Wheaton knew Delang well enough to know that he needed and wanted his privacy. For six months, he meticulously planned how he would approach Delang to make the pitch for the rights to his story.

Not all of his intentions were insincere. His friendship with Delang had once been treasured and he was genuinely glad to know he was alive. At the same time, Delang's story could be Wheaton's golden ticket back to the big time. When he thought the time was right, he touched base with a common acquaintance in the Department of Defense, who got word to Delang that his old high school buddy was reaching out. The two men traded phone calls for a week. After Wheaton sent over some ideas he had sketched out, Delang agreed to meet.

"Was your flight and drive up okay?"

"Oh yeah. Nothing but smooth sailing."

"Good to hear. So, what's the latest?"

"Well, I'll make it short and sweet."

Wheaton knew that Delang never liked to beat around the bush.

"The ball is in your court, but I've got Robert Rodriguez lined up to direct and I should be getting the green light from the studio in the next day or so."

This statement was less than true. It had taken Wheaton three weeks to even get Rodriguez's people to take his calls, and he was far from being onboard with the project. All they would say was that the director had shown interest in the project. Columbia Pictures had also expressed curiosity, but had kept Wheaton at arm's length, due to his most recent flop.

Delang remained skeptical. Given that he had been recently betrayed by a longtime source that led to his capture, his willingness to trust old friends was on a short leash.

"Is that right? Let me guess. You're going to tell me that you have a director and a studio lined up, and all you need now is for me to sign away the rights to my story? Then you'll go to the studios and tell them that you have me and Rodriguez, and need their greenlight. Finally, you'll go to Rodriguez and tell him that you have me, and the studio and need him to sign on as director. Sounds like the classic Hollywood three-way. Sound about right, Vik?"

Wheaton sat back in his chair and sipped a glass of water, trying to rid himself of the massive lump that had instantly formed in his throat. So much for his strategizing. Delang's mind was still as sharp as ever and he had him dead to rights.

"For old time sake, I'm willing to give you a shot at this, Vik, but not if you're going to treat me like I'm another Hollywood scumbag," Delang continued.

The two men sat in silence for a moment before a young waiter took their drink order. Delang ordered a craft beer that would go well with his Philly cheese steak sandwich. Wheaton asked for a Bloody Mary. When the waiter left, Wheaton dipped his toe back into the icy waters.

"Okay, you got me."

Wheaton turned his palms upward.

"But your story *is* generating a lot of buzz in Hollywood circles. Plus, who knows? If the movie is a hit, it could lead to other films about your career."

"I can't speak to that, Vik. That would require the government to declassify some of my other adventures."

Wheaton sighed. With no choice on his next move, he leaned forward, folded his hands together, and looked at Delang.

"Look, I flew all the way out here to meet you. And I won't lie to you; I really need this deal. I know that we haven't been in contact for a long time, but I'm really hoping you can help me out—for old times' sake. Please."

Delang studied his old friend's smoky blue eyes for a moment.

"Do you really think that you're the guy to get this done? I'm willing to help out an old friend, but I don't want this movie caught in purgatory for years on end. If it's going to be made, its gotta happen fast. I'm too impatient to deal with a bunch of Hollywood bullshit."

"I get it, man. Unfortunately, it's a business that is built on bullshit, but I know that I can navigate the waters."

Wheaton's phone pinged with a text message. Within seconds, a smile stretched from ear to ear across his face.

"How's this for an offer of good faith?"

He showed Delang his phone screen.

$50 million if you can get the rights.

Delang looked at the sender's name and knew that she was in charge of one of Hollywood's major studios.

"I'm impressed. Think you're up for the challenge? This isn't a standard horror film."

"I know I am, Tom. I swear to you that I won't let you down."

"Okay, then. Pull out the paperwork."

Wheaton radiated with joy as he slapped his hand on the table. He pulled out his iPad and swiped through it, looking for the particulars he needed with Delang. For the next hour, the two men discussed the next steps in the filmmaking process and merrily enjoyed discussing the crazy pranks they pulled in high school, still wondering how they ever got away with them.

When they were through, Delang and Wheaton gave each other a firm handshake-hug and went their separate ways. As he strolled to his car, Delang tossed his keys up and snatched them from the air, knowing he had made the right deal with the right person. Once he reached his car, Wheaton leaned against the door and breathed an immense sigh of relief, knowing that better days were ahead.

Unbeknownst to them both, down the street from where a local policeman was writing out a parking ticket, a man had been sitting in his Ford F350, meticulously observing the two friends' interaction. Once their meal was over, he marked Delang's patriot-blue, Jeep Gladiator and followed him down the road.

Chapter Nine

Delang's eyes were twinkling. He felt exhilarated as he navigated down the twists and turns of Route 1603, heading back to his cabin. A movie about his life was being made. He could practically hear the chorus of 1975's hit song *Celebrate* in his head. Thwacking the steering wheel in celebration, he couldn't help but let out his inner child. He had been through hell in Iran and quickly remembered the quote from Milton's *Paradise Lost* that was made famous by another film, *Se7en*: "Long is the way and hard, that out of Hell leads up to light."

"Damn right!"

His moment of jubilation was suddenly interrupted by a ping on his iPhone in the cupholder. Knowing better than to look while driving on a spiraling mountain road, Delang pulled off into an observation station for travelers to enjoy the hazy mountain view. As he glanced at the breaking news, his moment of ultimate joy was stolen away like the Grinch on Christmas Eve.

U.S. EMBASSY IN ISLAMABAD
ATTACKED BY MULTIPLE RPGs

That's where Beth is stationed.

His knee began to nervously bounce up and down and his eyes darted back and forth as he shuffled through the files of potential scenarios in his head.

Had there been reports of potential attacks? What prompted this?

He was out of the game, but he made a habit of keeping up with world news and was unaware of any friction between the Pakistani and U.S. governments.

Had an extremist group gone rogue? Or was it something worse and Iran had made a move by way of another group?

Before his mind could spring to the next thought, his body lurched forward, and his forehead hit the steering wheel as a car slammed into him from behind. He instinctively grabbed the back of his neck as the whiplash tore through his muscles. Delang looked in his rearview mirror to see who had hit him, but was immediately met with another impact. The truck behind him continued to push. Whoever it was, they were trying to push him over the railing and down the mountain.

Delang put his Jeep in reverse and slammed on the accelerator, pushing back against the truck behind him. The tires from both vehicles squealed against the asphalt and smoke rose up, along with the distinct smell of burning rubber. The truck behind had a ram guard mounted to the front and it was crumpling his Jeep's rear end like an aluminum soda can. It also had far more horsepower. He could hear the guard rail scratching against his passenger side door like fingernails on a chalkboard. He needed to do something fast. Otherwise, he would be rolling down the side of the mountain.

Unfortunately, Delang had left his gun at home. He had convinced himself that he didn't need it for a short drive up the mountain to meet with a Hollywood executive. Lesson learned. Even in retirement, an agent of his stature should *never* be without armed protection.

Pulling his 1200 Lumens flashlight from the console, Delang clicked it on and pointed it back toward the driver's face. He watched as the man instinctively threw up his hand to block the blinding light. This momentary break gave Delang the time he needed to steer away from the guardrail and haul ass down the road. He could feel the rear end squashed underneath. The friction from the aluminum was scraping against the rear tires and inhibited his speed.

Delang steered down the mountain as fast as he could, but he dared not push the car faster than it needed to go. If he did, the twisty roads could easily turn the Jeep on two wheels and he would lose control, sending him down the side of the mountain just as easily as if his enemy had done it himself. The roads were still slick from the rain the night before. Delang turned right, hit the accelerator, and then eased on the brake, which enabled him to make the turn to the next left. The rocks from the mountain made it impossible to see if there was another car coming from the opposite direction. As he leaned left on the steering wheel, his Jeep veered into the other lane. Luckily, he made it past the first turn without running into any oncoming traffic.

Thank God.

But the truck was back. It raced toward him and gave him another jolt from behind, propelling him forward. The Jeep swerved left and right but managed to stay on the road, but the last impact from the truck had been substantial. It hit the exhaust pipe, which restricted the flow of fumes out of the car. They started flowing through the air vents and into Delang's face. He coughed and hacked, using one hand to wave away the toxic haze coming at him while trying to drive down the mountain. He had at least another five miles to go before he could turn onto his neighborhood road.

As he eased his foot off the gas heading into the next turn, a white Kia Sorento was waiting for him around the bend. He was forced to keep control of the Jeep and stay in his own lane. The driver pounded his horn and Delang saw that she had locked her elbows and forced herself against the seat as she braced for impact. Thankfully, he only shaved the side of the Kia down his driver side door. With the car now behind him, Delang looked in the rearview mirror and watched the truck bulldoze through the Kia's front end like it was nothing but tinfoil. The truck looked as if it was getting ready to make another run at him when it oddly eased off and allowed the distance between them to increase.

What the hell?

He knew what was next, another right turn that was sharper than the others. Delang slammed on the brakes and tried putting the Jeep into park, but it was no use. His speed was too high. He steered the car right in order to successfully make the turn and to keep the car from tipping over.

The result was mixed. Delang felt the left side of the car lift up from underneath him, though it didn't fully tip over. He could hear the under-side of the front and rear axles scraping against the reinforced guardrail as the force of the spinning tires rode the railing down the curve. His chest heaved up and down as he felt the sweat drip down his forehead. Because of the angle of the Jeep, he couldn't see the pursuing truck, but he could hear the driver revving up the engine for a big charge. All Delang could do was lean to his right, brace himself against the steering wheel, and pray that he survived.

The large diesel truck came at him like a freight train. The monstrous collision of metal echoed against the mountains, and shoved Delang's Jeep over the guardrail. It stalled for a moment as the underside of the passenger side tires caught the railing, but it was too weak against the weight of the vehicle, and Delang's car tumbled down the side of the mountain.

Once it went over the side, the driver of the truck exited his vehicle and leaned over the side to get a look at the carnage he had caused. Delang's car rested upside down in the middle of an oak tree more than two hundred feet down from the road.

The driver smiled.

Seat belt or not, no one could have survived that.

Satisfied with his work, the driver spit over the edge and pulled out his phone to send a text to his employer.

IT'S DONE

With no other traffic around, he got back in the truck and drove down the mountain road as if nothing had happened.

Chapter Ten

ISLAMABAD MEDICAL AND SURGICAL HOSPITAL

Thrasher tapped his foot impatiently as he sat in the waiting room, hoping for any good news he could get. When Jenkins arrived, the paramedics had been quick to point out the purple bruise on the side of her head, and what they believed was a hematoma on her right side. Thankfully, the doctors had gotten her into the ER right away but there was no word yet of her prognosis. There wasn't much Thrasher could do except sit and pray for a positive result.

Positive thinking wasn't exactly Thrasher's strongest characteristic. Instead, his mind wandered to places it shouldn't. He thought about what would happen if Jenkins didn't make it.

How would the leadership on the seventh floor of the CIA react?

More important, how would the president react?

Would this be another case of talking hard at Pakistan and then treating them with kid gloves?

His thoughts of concern swiftly shifted to rage. If he had to do it all over again, he wouldn't have shot that little cow turd in the forest. He would've beat him to a pulp, made him talk, and then shot him. Hopefully, he would get a second chance if he found the person responsible for this attack.

Thrasher's blood pressure increased with every thought of revenge. He could feel the tips of his ears burning. In an effort to calm himself, he tried to think of more practical things. Two hours ago, not long after Jenkins had been admitted, the doctors released Griffin. How she survived with only minor scratches and bruises was nothing short of a miracle. When she saw Thrasher pacing in the waiting room, she had walked right up to him to offer her assistance. He gave her the phone from the terrorist, and told her to get to the nearest operations center with a secure connection to see what she could uncover with the analysts in Langley.

His phone buzzed. It was Griffin.

That was fast.

As Thrasher read the text message, he felt his adrenaline surge. He barely had time to process what he'd read when a door squeaked open. Thrasher hopped to attention, but it wasn't a doctor who walked through. It was Dub.

"Hey."

"Any word on the ID of our guy in the forest?"

"Just got it. That's why I came to find you. Remember the attack on the Taj Mahal hotel back in 2008?"

"In Mumbai? What's that got to do with this?"

"Our guy didn't pop in any of our databases, but the snake brand coiled around his arm did. His name was Wahab Malik, and he belonged to the terrorist group, Lashkar-e-Taiba."

"The same group responsible for the Mumbai attacks."

"Right. So, I called your best friend at the Intelligence Bureau in India. He recognized him instantly. They've been looking for him ever since those attacks."

Dub could see Thrasher's brain running through the maze of intel.

"What are you thinking?"

"That it doesn't make sense for someone connected to those attacks to want to attack us. Our boy was for hire."

"What about his phone? Come across anything?"

"That's what I was looking at when you came through the door. I gave it to Tequila so she could go over it with Langley. She sent me this."

He handed Dub the phone.

The phone was a burner. No pics or text messages. The call history showed that the same number called him twice in the last two days. No record of the number in the databases, but the country code didn't come up from Pakistan. It came from TEHRAN!

Dub was shocked.

"What the hell?"

"Yeah, that was my reaction, too."

"Now what?"

"Tell me about this source of Beth's, named Farhad. That was the last thing she said to me before she passed out."

"Oh, him. I thought you would know more about him than I did. After all, you've seen him in person."

"Huh? When?"

"Last year when you guys rescued Tom Delang. Remember that? Delang had three people with him when they walked through the embassy gates. One was another American. The second was an Iranian girl, the guy's girlfriend. And the other was this dude Farhad, who helped them escape. Farhad Khorsandi. Beth thought he looked like a USC grad student, but it turned out that the guy had a lot of connections in Iran since he primarily smuggled goods into the country, booze mostly. He and Beth decided to stay in touch, but I remember her saying that he went dark."

Thrasher replayed the events from the previous year outside the U.S. Embassy in Ashgabat. He remembered he and Jenkins escorting Delang through the gates with a couple of companions, but he was busy trying to get medical attention for Delang. Plus, one of the three had been shot. He didn't get any names and caught an agency flight to out of the country a few hours later. When he spoke to Delang separately about the drone strike in Basra, they did so by phone. With his personality being the way that it was, he hadn't bothered to ask Delang about his escape or even how he was doing. Once again, his lack of compassion continued to haunt him.

But Thrasher remembered the guy with Delang, the one who got shot, being older, in his thirties. The other guy was much younger, late twenties with a tight haircut. They both looked like hell from their trip over the mountains, but the second guy had to be Farhad.

"This guy Farhad. He's Iranian, right?"

"Yeah, some type of freedom fighter. Why?"

"The pieces don't fit. Beth had no way of knowing who the bomber was. Yet, the last call he received was from Iran."

"Maybe she knows something we don't."

Thrasher pulled Jenkins's phone from his cargo pants, punched in Farhad's contact info into his phone and then tossed her phone back to Dub before walking away.

"Whoa, where are you going?"

"Stay here and keep an eye on her. Set up shop outside her room and kill anyone besides a doctor who tries to get past you. Keep me posted. I'm gonna track this Farhad guy down if I have to kick over every fucking rock in Iran."

Dub gave a sarcastic salute as Thrasher burst through the waiting room door.

Chapter Eleven

BANDAR ABBAS, IRAN

Farhad stood in the dank, dimly lit basement of a house owned by one of his colleagues, taking inventory of their remaining beer and liquor. Their stock was getting low and he needed to make another run fairly soon. Not that he minded. Living in Iran and not being able to legally enjoy the fruits of life was a major pain in the ass, but he had come to revel in his self-employment as a smuggler. As an avid *Star Wars* fan, it made him feel like an old school Han Solo.

But the stakes were higher for him now. A year ago, he was just another smuggler in a country of many. If he were caught, he would have to endure his punishment, such as a lashing, but he would ultimately be released and return to his old ways after his wounds healed or the heat on him died down, whichever came first. Now, his picture had been specifically added to the IRGC database as an American conspirator. If caught, the punishment for that was not lashing. It was death.

His previous smuggling jobs had been pulled off in conjunction with a friend he had met in Tehran when he was nineteen, Simin Dehghani. For the first few years, he and Simin were friendly competitors until they both realized they were doing each other more harm than good. Rather than continue competing, they decided to join forces. They shared contacts, but her list was more extensive, and he knew the secret routes better than anyone. He and Simin had a handshake deal of fifty-fifty, minus expenses, and their arrangement worked well for six years.

Six months ago, however, that changed when an American named Kirk Kurruthers came to Iran, hell-bent on revenging his grandfather murder at the hands of the former commander of the IRGC. Since

Farhad also had a side business of escorting tourists around Iran, Kurruthers had contacted him, looking for help. As fate would have it, the person that Kirk wanted to assassinate was also Simin's biological father, who had raped her mother. Hating the IRGC as much as Kirk did, they agreed to help.

What Farhad did not expect was for Simin and Kirk to fall in love. The assistance they provided, though, quickly snowballed into full blown chaos. While Kirk managed to get his revenge, he did not know that the IRGC had been watching him. While he was incarcerated at a secret prison, formerly called "The Lounge," and after an all-out brawl with IRCG soldiers, the two not only managed to get away but helped facilitate the escape of CIA agent Tom Delang, who was also being held there. With Simin's help, the three men had made a daring run over the mountains of bordering Ashgabat. Once they were secure, Simin left the country to live with Kirk in America. While Farhad knew that he had done the right thing by helping Kirk and the CIA agent escape, the adventure had its punishments. He was now on the IRGC's radar full-time, and he'd lost his friend and business partner.

After hearing about his exploits, he was contacted by a member of the People's Mujahedeen of Iran (PMOI), a revolutionary group inside Iran dedicated to fighting the Ayatollah regime. Through a mutual smuggling friend, they accepted him into their group. With few places to turn and being the socialite he was, Farhad embraced the invitation. The members of the PMOI liked him right away and decided that he would be an asset to the organization.

But his association with the PMOI, along with being known as an American conspirator, meant that he had to fly even lower under the radar than normal. Guards at the border stations now demanded much higher payouts to look the other way, and he often had to use elaborate disguises to get the job done. At one point, he had to lose ten pounds and minimize his iron intake in order to pass for a sickly patient seeking medical attention in Turkey. In short, life sucked. The Ayatollah regime had put him on a short leash at birth, and now he was more confined than ever.

"How's it looking?"

He heard a female voice as she descended down the steps.

"Huh? Oh, hey, Donya. Not good. By the looks of things, we'll be out of beer and wine in three weeks. We may be able to make the vodka last a little longer if we watch ourselves."

Donya Karimi was a talented hacker and the third highest ranking person in the PMOI. She was the one who had approached Farhad about joining. She also had more than a few contacts in the state-run television station, which came in handy when needed.

"What are your contacts saying?"

"A friend of mine in Karachi said he may be able to get us a few more cases of red wine, but it will take about two weeks. I'll try and figure out the logistics of that later."

"Is he trustable?"

"He's been reliable so far, but . . ."

Before he could finish his sentence, Farhad felt one of his cell phones vibrate. Pulling it from his back pocket, he saw that it was not the standard phone he normally used but the encrypted one given to him by the CIA. He didn't recognize the number but only one person ever called that phone.

"Donya, would you mind giving me a minute? I have to take this."

"I'll be upstairs. We can talk later."

"Sure thing."

He waited for her to reach the top of the stairs and then closed the door. He flipped the switch on the side of the phone to put it in scrambling mode so that the call could not be traced.

"Hello, *Raven*. What can I do for you?"

He was referring to Jenkins's code name.

"This isn't Raven," a male voice answered. "This is *Jaybird*. We haven't met, but we saw each other briefly outside the Ashgabat embassy with an agent we both know. I have sleeves of tattoos on both arms. Do you remember me?"

Farhad had to think for a minute. The final moments of getting into the Ashgabat embassy had been chaotic. He did recall a large man with tattoos shooting his former IRGC nemesis in the knee before escorting him and his friends into the embassy, but he needed to verify that this wasn't a ploy by the IRGC to draw him out.

"If that's true, what color striped hair did the girl who was with us have?"

Farhad was referencing Simin's streak of highlights.

"Blue," said Thrasher.

"What's Raven's favorite food for lunch?"

"Grilled chicken tacos."

Satisfied, Farhad proceeded.

"Okay. Why are you calling me?"

"Have you seen the news? I'm sure even the state-run media in that shithole country of yours is covering this."

Offended, Farhad glanced down at his phone with a furrowed brow.

"No, asshole, I haven't. Hang on."

Going to the other side of the room, he grabbed the remote and turned on the twelve-inch TV that dated back to the early 2000's. When the small screen came to life, he saw the news broadcast about the embassy attack in Islamabad.

"Oh, no. Is she okay?"

"She's in surgery right now. I killed the guy who launched the attack, but his phone said someone from Iran had been contacting him.

Before she passed out, she told me to contact you. I don't know how the puzzle pieces fit, but I'm relying on her instincts that Iran is involved this. Our database doesn't recognize the number that called the terrorist. Is there anyone there in your group who can run these against any of the numbers for people in the Iranian government?"

"What company made the phone?"

"Tracfone."

"Send them over. I'll see what I can do."

"Dammit, kid, do you have someone there who can do it or not?!"

Thrashers voice was so loud that Farhad had to jerk the phone away from his ear.

"Take it easy, man! Yeah, there's a hacker here. I can't make any guarantees, but she's pretty good."

"Okay, call me back as soon as you get something."

"Fine, but Jaybird, if we're gonna be working together, then our next call better be a lot more civil. You got me?"

Thrasher breathed hard into the phone. He knew his emotions were running high.

"Kid, if you get this right, I'll find a way to get you a case of the best whiskey in Ireland. Deal?"

"I'll get back to you."

Chapter Twelve

HIGHLANDS, NORTH CAROLINA

Delang blinked as he tried to concentrate and get his bearings. He wasn't sure what was happening. Blood was dripping from his nose, which was almost certainly broken, and he had a massive headache. As he wiped blood from his face, his neurological system kicked back into gear and the pounding on the sides of his head began to rival the thunderous drums on college gameday. He could see more clearly but remained confused, so he relied on his old training and performed a situation assessment.

He wiggled his toes to make sure he wasn't paralyzed and was relieved to know that he could feel the bottoms of his boots through his cotton socks. His arms and legs were mobile, but he could feel pain in his extremities. He couldn't tell if that was due to cuts or if something had pierced his skin. His seatbelt was still in place, so his waist wasn't moving, but he could feel that his rear was not on the seat. If he hadn't cracked a rib on his left side, it had to be badly bruised. The rest of his torso was lying lengthwise across the console, but he was dangling off the passenger seat. He was trapped underneath leaves and branches that had impaled the windshield. That's when he realized he was hanging upside down.

He recalled the meeting with Vik, and the chase afterward. The last thing he remembered was going over the edge of the mountain road and clinging to the passenger seat while he braced for impact on the way down. It appeared that his memory was intact. He was even more thankful that he had chosen to have a reinforced steel roll bar installed on the car the previous week.

The Man above is looking out for me.

He was alive, relatively uninjured, and the oak tree he had fallen into was stable enough to support the weight of the car—at least for the moment. Delang knew that he had to get help from wherever the hell he was in the mountains.

After unlocking his seatbelt, Delang did a freefall into the branches that were inside the car. He heard several of them snap since they could not bear his weight, and he banged his head when he thumped into the ceiling. Panic set in when he felt the car shift inside the tree, and he heard more branches splinter. It was time to get moving before he fell any further.

The rear window of the cab was removeable and wide enough for him to jam his body through, but with the Jeep hanging upside down, he dared not go through it because then he would have to get past the truck bed. Since he was hanging upside down, he didn't want to end up trapped under the truck if it collapsed on top of him.

The only way out was through the side windows. Delang kicked the rear passenger side window with the heel of his boot. There was a good chance that this would cause the car to shift in the tree, but it was a chance he had to take. It took only two kicks before it finally shattered, but he could feel the truck shifting as the tree began to collapse.

He had to move fast. He repositioned his body so that he could get through headfirst. But with every movement of his arms and legs, he felt the truck dropping through more branches. It rotated toward the passenger window, nailing Delang's Achilles tendon as he squeezed through and held on. He yelped and saw an assortment of green and yellow stars as he jammed his eyes shut. When he opened them a few seconds later, he watched the Jeep tumble down the rest of the tree before crashing on its side.

Clutching the rear of his right leg, he heaved a sigh of relief that the car hadn't taken him with it. He rested only a moment before an all-too-familiar aroma snaked its way up his nose.

Gas.

Injured or not, he needed to get the hell out of the tree and as far away from it as he could before a fireball mushroomed up and burned him to death.

As his right foot made his way through the maze of branches, he felt sharp pain shot with each movement. He couldn't afford to let that slow him down, even though he had to favor one leg. Every move seemed rigorous, but the real pain came when his hand slipped on wet moss and he had to catch himself using his armpit on his already bruised left side. Tears of pain leaked from his eyes.

He looked down and saw that he would have to jump the last ten to fifteen feet and land perfectly. With his Achilles damaged on one leg, he couldn't afford to roll his ankle on his good leg. Hoping he could cushion the blow, he decided to hang from his hands and drop.

Please don't let this hurt too much.

As Delang let go, he watched the ground get closer fast. He bent his knees so they wouldn't jam. The force of the final contact sent searing pain racing up his legs. He managed to land on his butt, but only after stumbling backward, and adding a bruised tailbone to his list of injuries.

He could hear gas trickling from the tank. He pulled himself to his feet and hobbled as fast as he could and managed to get fifty feet away before the Jeep ignited and sent flames roaring through the air. Delang collapsed on the debris of brush, broken branches, and dirt.

Making his way back slowly to the burning junkpile of what was once his prized possession, Delang stood back to avoid the intense heat. The rising black smoke made it difficult to see what was going on above, but he thought he could see a blue police light swirling. He thought about yelling to them, but he knew that he couldn't be heard from so far down the mountain. His phone was gone and probably burning away with the rest of what could be used to help him survive in the woods.

His best estimate was that he was at least four or five miles away from his house. He was in for a long and strenuous journey to get help. If he could make it through the peaks of Iran, he could certainly make it through the Blue Ridge Mountains. Maybe this was life's way of telling him he shouldn't live in the mountains anymore.

Next time, they'll have to come for me at the beach.

Chapter Thirteen

KARACHI, PAKISTAN

Lieutenant Hasan Wasim felt anxious as he drove his government issued FAW group truck up to the gates of Base Masroor and waited behind three trucks ahead of him. He closed his eyes and tried to slow his breathing. It was not terribly hot, but he could feel the sweat in his armpits, powering through his thickly laid deodorant and sliding down the side of his body. Thankfully, the beret he was wearing absorbed the perspiration on his brow. He repeatedly slid his hands down the thighs of his pants in order to wipe off the condensation. It was imperative that he appeared confident when he reached the gate.

When it was finally his turn, he noticed that the soldier working security was not one he recognized from previous trips, so he tried a different strategy. Feeling less than confident, he decided to seem exhausted instead, which was not much of a stretch considering the emotional duress he was under. He yawned when the officer asked for his ID badge and wiped his fingers across his eyes in fake boredom, as he waited to get back his badge.

"Here you go, sir," the young soldier said.

"Thanks," said Wasim.

"The computer says you are here to pick up five hundred pounds of explosives. Is that correct, sir?"

"Uh huh."

"Sir, when I scanned your badge, the system said that your license to drive explosives on public roads expires in two days. Protocol requires me that I ask you to finish your delivery before then and get it renewed as quickly as possible."

Unbelievable.

Of all the things that could come up, he had forgotten to renew his hazardous certification and he had a soldier, stiff as a board, now flagging it.

"I'll take care of it, soldier. Now, open the gate."

"Yes, sir."

The soldier nodded to his partner at the booth to hit the button to raise the gate.

Step one complete. Two more to go.

The knots in Wasim's gut were tightening as he made his way around the base to the explosives warehouse. Driving in Pakistan was an art unto itself, organized chaos really, but the last thing he needed was to get into an accident on the base, either by driving too fast or accidently crashing into an idiot who was. He scanned each of his three mirrors so he could keep an eye out on anyone headed his way.

As he reached the southeastern part of the base, he pushed an earpiece into his ear canal and hit 'send' on the phone. The recipient answered on the first ring.

"What is it?" the man answered.

"I made it through the gate. I'm on my way to get the C-4 now."

"That's why you're calling me? You fool. Getting into the base was never going to be a problem."

"Look, I'm just telling you that I'm here, and I'm on my way. Is paperwork in place at the warehouse? They won't let me in without it."

"Stop worrying like a little girl. Our intelligence analysts worked it up and hacked the system yesterday. Get the stuff, get out of there, and call me when you get close to Gharo. Oh, and don't try anything after you leave the base. Our drones are watching you."

"I want to speak to my family first."

"No. And if you don't man up and do what you're told, I can assure you that you will never see your wife, son, and daughter again, and I will repeatedly violate your wife before I put a bullet in her head. Now, get it done and don't forget to smile for the security cameras!"

Wasim dropped the phone and felt his heart pounding inside his chest. He knew it was unlikely that he would make it through this entire ordeal alive, but maybe he could get his family through it. There was something odd about the voice on the phone. The accent wasn't heavy enough to fluently speak the local Urdu language.

When he pulled the truck into the warehouse, he tried to calm himself by slapping himself in the face a few times. Getting the explosives may have been his mission, but he needed to make it seem like it was an average pickup on another boring day at the base. Thankfully, he ran into a familiar face.

"Hasan, I wasn't expecting you today," the man said.

Captain Samir Ali was a familiar acquaintance of Wasim's. Ali had been a year ahead of him at boot camp. They first served together on a UN peacekeeping mission in Somalia that hadn't amounted to much in terms of action in the field but the two men had bonded. Wasim and Ali stayed in touch and called each other for favors when needed.

"Yeah, well, what can I say? It's a last-minute pick up and I didn't mind making the drive."

"Don't you usually work at the nuclear facility? I was expecting Lieutenant Zaman instead."

Wasim balked.

"In the hospital with a hernia," he said.

It was the only lie he could manage.

"It must suck to be him."

"I surely wouldn't want to be."

Wasim glanced up at the security cameras. He noticed how they looked different than the previous ones.

"When did you guys get the camera upgrade?"

"Three days ago. It was a real pain. The techs were strange guys, too."

"How so?"

"I don't know. They were overly quiet. Gave me the creeps. Their paperwork was in order, but it was a weird experience. Anyway, you're here for the C-4, right?"

"Yup. General's orders."

"Do I want to know what it's for?"

Even I don't want to know what it's for.

"I guess I'll find out when I drop it off," he said.

"Sign here."

Ali handed him an iPad with a smart pen. Wasim signed and Ali hit 'submit' to log it into the database. Afterward, he started whistling and barking orders for the others in the warehouse to get the forklift and load the explosives into the truck. After they finished loading the first of two pallets, Wasim jumped in the back of the truck to examine his cargo. He observed that the C-4 has its standard green packaging with all the necessary markers so it could be identified if found or used, but Wasim had his doubts.

Could it be something else wrapped in C-4 packaging?

A high-pitched whistle from behind knocked him out of his puzzling thoughts. The next pallet was ready to be loaded in and the crew needed Wasim out of the way. Once loaded, the crew secured the pallets in place with straps and gave him a thumbs up.

"Stay safe out there with this stuff, Hasan. I'll see you next time."

"I hope so."

He held the captain's handshake for an extra second. Ali gave him a short sideways look as he drove away. Wasim looked at his watch as he made his way back to the gate. He had been in the warehouse a total of fifty minutes.

Step two complete. One more to go.

He sailed back through the gate, only stopping to have his badge scanned into the computer, which noted when he had arrived and exited the base, and made sure that his credentials matched his truck ID that Captain Ali had written down on the transfer work order.

As instructed, he drove an hour east from Karachi to the city of Gharo. But he didn't have to make the call, as instructed. Three non-standard tactical vehicles, all loaded with machine guns in the bed of each truck, honked their horns, trying to get him to pull off the road. He recognized the trucks as those used by local warlords, but this scheme was far too organized for them. Someone else was pulling the strings.

The lead car finally passed him and parked sideways on the road, giving him no choice but to stop. They *had* been watching him. Wasim raised his hands from the steering wheel. Even though he was carrying his standard issue sidearm, he wanted to get through this alive.

The passenger in the lead truck quickly exited the vehicle and hopped into his truck while keeping his gun pointed at Wasim. He was dressed in the same Pakistani army uniform as Wasim. He could see the man's muscles bulging but his skin was far too light for him to be Pakistani. His beard was neatly trimmed, even combed. If it weren't for the near unibrow he was sporting, Wasim would have said he was too polished for any Pakistani soldier he knew.

"Okay, now what?" Wasim asked.

The muscular man made a swift move and nailed him in the side of the head with the butt of his Glock 17.

"Drive toward Shakoor Lake, and step on it. I want to make it there by midnight."

Finally hearing the man speak in person, Wasim immediately recognized that the man was Iranian, although he thought it odd that he had a small swastika tattoo above the collar of his shirt.

"You're the guy on the phone?"

The Iranian returned a slight nod.

"What do I call you? I know the name on your uniform must be fake."

The Iranian thought about it for a second. He could lie and give the Pakistani a fake name, as he had been ordered, but he was a prideful man. Besides, after the mission was completed, he had plans for this soldier that would involve him forgetting his name altogether.

"Mahmoud. Captain Mahmoud Yazdani."

He momentarily took his eyes off his target to look back at the trucks and rolled his finger in the hair as if to say, "let's move."

Wasim knew that there was no need to try anything heroic along the way to their destination. Three tactical trucks were escorting them the whole way.

As they started to move, Yazdani kept his gun on Wasim and dialed a familiar number.

"Yes?"

"I've got him."

"Good. You have your orders. Get it done."

"And afterward?"

"Continue with your experimental studies. The soldier should remember nothing. Is that understood?"

"Yes, Supreme Leader."

Chapter Fourteen

BAHRIA TOWN, PAKISTAN

Thrasher had gone back to the embassy bombing site to see if he could learn anything new. When he came up with zip, he decided to head to the nearest CIA safehouse in Bahria Town, an hour south of Islamabad. In most cases, agency safehouses were situated in remote areas of whatever country they were in. This, of course, was by design. The agency wanted as little attention as possible; areas deep in the forest or on the outskirts of small towns created the privacy desired and eliminated any potential repercussions in terms of civilian interference, in case an incident occurred.

But this was less of a safehouse and more of an operations center. Bahria Town was different. It was owned by a private real estate development company, Bahria Town Private Limited, which owned, managed, and developed properties all-across Pakistan. Developing malls, supermarkets, mosques, and hotels, based on contracts with household names like Hyatt and an Adventureland theme park in Karachi that mimicked Disney World in Orlando, the real estate company had its hands full. What made Bahria Town attractive to the CIA management was the fact that it looked like a westernized, gated community, specifically constructed to cater to rich clients, which meant privacy. As a bonus, some of its properties were on the Soan River, which allowed operatives more than a few options for escape, if warranted.

The trick for the agency was infiltrating the company's management. This was made easier when ISIS thugs threatened its Chairman of the Board, Malik Alvi, for developing westernized properties which they felt dishonored Islam.

When they kidnapped his sickly, seventeen-year-old daughter, Alvi didn't think twice about walking into the U.S. Embassy in Islamabad, requesting to speak with an agency operative. Since Alvi was already on the CIA's wish list, the embassy agent on duty wasted no time passing along the information to Langley.

Tom Delang was then dispatched to rescue the real estate mogul's daughter and forge a long-term relationship with the man. The veteran agent was able to rescue the girl, but the jaundice she had developed had worsened, due to a lack of care. When Delang was able to negotiate a quick liver transplant with one of his medical contacts in Karachi, Alvi felt forever indebted to Delang, and agreed to be an agency source for life.

From the outside, the house was everything the CIA wanted, unassuming, so it blended in easily with the other beige houses around it. It was a two-story brick complex with a terrace and minimal windows, all of which were bulletproof.

Alvi was able to fudge the company's books so that an agency construction crew was able to come in and make their own upgrades without alerting the locals. The gate was solid steel with bars going six feet into the ground to prevent vehicles from ramming into it. The eight-foot-high perimeter wall was made with blast-resistant concrete. It also had a basement with a lab, thanks to agency colleagues in the Science and Technology department, and state of the art computer technology for the analysts who were always on-call.

When Thrasher walked in, Griffin was on the phone with India's Intelligence Bureau, trying to find out more about Wahab Malik, and what connections he had with the Iranians. Unfortunately, her Indian contact was more interested in getting the terrorist's body flown back to India so that their government could formally announce to the public that all parties involved in the Mumbai bombings were dead, so that they could finally put the incident to bed. As patient a person as Griffin was, the way she was shaking her head and rolling her eyes made it clear to Thrasher that she was frustrated.

There was an art to speaking with members of other intelligence agencies that Thrasher hadn't yet mastered. By nature, anyone working at any intelligence agency in the world always wanted to obtain more information than they wanted to give, so navigating the waters of those conversations was more of an art than a science. It also required patience, a trait which Thrasher severely lacked. He found the idea of dancing his way through a conversation to be nauseating and emotionally exhausting. That's why his success in the field was based on trading information rather than asking for help.

It should have been an easy exchange, the body for the intel on the terrorist's connections to Iran, but the Indians appeared to be purposely holding back. The tension between Griffin and her contact on the other end was growing thicker by the second, and Thrasher was in no mood for games. Based on his conversation with Jenkins only a few days ago, he knew that he needed to be on his best behavior, but circumstances had changed. Griffin's frustration fed into his own, and he decided that he had had enough. He ripped the headset away from Griffin and put it on his own head. Insulted, she smacked him on the shoulder, but he paid her no mind.

"Who the fuck is this?"

There was a pause on the other end.

"Agent Dhoni of IIB. Who the hell are you?"

Great. Him again. This guy is like a bad rash that won't go away.

"You should know by the sound of my voice who this is, jackass. I'm the guy that's gonna come over there to that shithole country of yours, wait outside your agency's doors and put my size eleven shoe so far up your ass that it'll tickle your tonsils if you don't give my associate

83

the information she's been nice enough to ask you for, repeatedly. So, in the spirit of cooperation, unless you want me to chop up the body of that terrorist and feed it to the sharks in the Indian Ocean, I suggest you help us out or you're gonna find out what it means when I really lose my temper!"

Thrasher said nothing further before tossing the headset back to Griffin. Then, his own phone rang.

"What?!"

"Whoa, take it easy. Is this not a good time?" the caller asked.

It took Thrasher a moment to recognize the voice.

"It's fine, Farhad."

Thrasher closed his eyes and tried to calm himself.

"Were you able to find anything?"

"Maybe. The phone number that was used to call the terrorist may have been a burner, but it's been used before. As it turns out, it matched an old number that used to call me."

"Wait, wait. That number called *you* before?"

"Yes. Remember the guy you shot outside the embassy in Ashgabat? His name was Azam Aslani. He was a constant nuisance to me. My prayers were finally answered when he was shot by one of his own men outside the embassy right after we went through its doors."

"Dead men can't make phone calls, Farhad."

"No, but if the phones aren't shut off, other people use them. My friend Donya's first cousin is an established reporter at the state-run TV station. Fortunately for us, he keeps really good records of the phone numbers used to call him. It helps him keep track of his sources. Anyway, he says that this number called him three months ago, and the caller on the other end was Mahmoud Yazdani of the Revolutionary Guard. Mahmoud used to report to Azam and took his place as captain in the IRGC ranks."

Thrasher scrolled back through the pictures in his head from that day outside the embassy. He remembered seeing more than one Iranian in an IRGC uniform.

"The guy with the big, hook nose or the one with the unibrow?"

"Unibrow. He's one of those types that always likes to ask people if he can borrow things and then never gives them back. I'm betting he inherited Aslani's set of burner phones after he killed him, so to speak."

"So, that links the Revolutionary Guard to the embassy bombing."

"I can't say for sure, but it seems that way. It's always possible that the number was reassigned to someone else. If it was, what I can tell you is that before the number was shut off, it was used as recently as three months ago by a member of the Revolutionary Guard."

"Okay, let's say it wasn't someone from the Revolutionary Guard. All that proves is that this Mahmoud guy was once issued that phone number. Big deal."

"Wait, hang on. There's more."

Thrasher paused. He was becoming impressed with Farhad's skills.

"Assuming that it is Mahmoud, and I think so, Donya was able to convince her cousin to give her Mahmoud's most recent phone number. It's different than the one that called your terrorist. Since I use Tracfone a lot on my bootlegging runs, I called one of my friends at the phone company. In exchange for a bottle of gin, he told me that it pinged on a tower outside Karachi two hours ago."

"He's here in Pakistan?"

"Well, it seems that he was."

"What do you mean *was*? Where is he now?"

"India. The last movement showed him outside the town of Bhuj. The phone went dead after that, but we have the last number he called."

"Give it to me."

Thrasher snatched a pen from a nearby desk. Farhad gave him the number and Thrasher wrote it on his palm.

"That's a Pakistan country code."

"Right. Do you think that it's a coincidence that a known Revolutionary Guard captain just happens to be in Pakistan the same day that a U.S. embassy in Pakistan gets bombed?"

"It's a pretty thin connection. The bombing was in Islamabad, and you said he was near Karachi. Something doesn't seem right."

"I don't know what that means, but I'm hoping it points you in the right direction."

"Kid, if Raven trusts you than so will I. Just don't make me regret it," Thrasher said.

"I'll try and take that as a compliment. You're welcome. Good luck."

Thrasher jumped on one of the open computers to see if there was an airport near the city of Bhuj, and there was. Tapping his lips with his finger, Thrasher decided to take a chance on Farhad's hunch. He pushed back from his chair with such force that it rolled into the person behind him, but he didn't even notice. He walked over to Griffin, who was still on the phone.

"Is that still India?" he whispered.

She nodded, still pissed at him for jerking the headset away from her.

"Ask him to run this phone number through his system."

He showed her the palm of his hand.

Although she was frustrated as hell at him, Griffin did as she was told. She knew Thrasher well enough to know that he was like a bloodhound when he caught a scent, and no one holding the leash should dare ignore it. After wiggling the information out of her Indian counterpart, she shook her head.

Thrasher cursed under his breath.

"Tell him that I'll meet him in Bhuj with the body tomorrow morning."

Griffin covered the microphone.

"Are you sure?"

"I'll charter the plane. Tell him to meet me there by nine."

Griffin gave Thrasher a confused look.

"Are you going to tell me what this is about?"

"I will as soon as I figure it out myself, but right now I'm following the breadcrumbs and I want to see where they lead."

Chapter Fifteen

ATLANTA, GEORGIA

Chad Ward did not fit the classic image of a Hollywood fixer. His husky body and Caribbean style beard didn't make him look the part, but he wasn't the least bit timid about being ruthless to get his job done. Actors and producers in the area were well-aware of his storied adventures, doing dirty deeds for studio executives who needed to keep their films free of any social wildfires. They cringed when they saw him walking their way.

Recently, he'd been hired to straighten out an executive producer, named Penny Barham, who had a reputation for getting A-list actors to star in her movies at a fraction of their standard fee. She managed that by hiring female escorts to slip Rohypnol into their drinks when she invited them to her house for a party. A female escort would lure the gentleman upstairs to take provocative pictures of the actor with her and her friends, and they would pose in sexual positions to make it look like he was a willing participant. Once the pictures were in hand, Barham would threaten to release the photos to the actor's wife.

In the wake of the Harvey Weinstein scandal, one studio president could no longer turn a blind eye to such activity. He hired Ward to ensure that Barham's antics were stopped. It was supposed to be a straight hospital job. A broken leg or collar bone would have been fine, but the details of what happened next are murky at best. It was rumored that Barham had dirt on Ward that he was stealing from his clients. This wasn't true, but the rumor was enough of an assault on Ward's reputation to ruin his career.

After a film premiere at Grauman's Chinese Theater, Barham's limo picked her up, but she never made it home. The case was still listed as unsolved. Though the Hollywood elite were suspicious of Ward, no one said anything to the police about his potential involvement. For actors in Hollywood who Barham had blackmailed, Ward was considered their instrument of revenge. Months later, an actor who had been arrested by the police on drug charges tried to use his knowledge of Ward to get his charges reduced. When Ward received word of this, he arranged for the actor to have a fatal car accident. For Ward, it was business. For those in the Hollywood circle, no one wanted to end up in a hole next to Barham.

As he recollected some of these events, Ward sat in a chair outside his departure gate at Atlanta's airport, keeping a watchful eye on Wheaton sitting at the bar of Bobby's Burger Place. Their flight wasn't scheduled to leave for ninety minutes. He was about to get something to eat himself when he felt his phone vibrate. It was the client.

"Hello, Lisa. I hope this call means that you are excited about the deal with Delang."

Lisa Chang was the president of Columbia Pictures. Having texted Wheaton during the meeting with Delang, she had shown the most interest in the picture and was working with an investor on securing the required funds. Most important, she had only been in her new role nine months and was willing to take some risks in order to make a splashy impression within the Hollywood community.

"I am. Based on what I'm looking at on TV, I'm going to fast track the film as soon as Wheaton gets back here and sign some papers."

"I was wondering how long it would take for the news to break."

"Has Vik seen it yet?"

"Not sure, but I don't think so. He's too busy stuffing his face with cheese fries and scribbling on a notepad."

"Make sure he sees it."

"Hang on."

Since Wheaton's back was to him, Ward waved his arm at the girl working the bar and pointed to the TV. She made sure to turn up the volume. Wheaton stopped chewing when he saw the headline.

HERO CIA AGENT TOM DELANG
KILLED IN ACCIDENT

"Does he seem happy?"

"I'd say that you definitely got his attention."

"You should see the numbers I'm looking at. Twitter, Facebook, Instagram. They're off the charts with the buzz of his death."

Ward snickered. He loved seeing social media ablaze. With the movie being released shortly after Delang's death, its success was nearly guaranteed, especially considering how he knew the studio planned to hype it. All Wheaton had to do was not screw up production. If Chang was lucky, the news would chalk Delang's death up to the Iranians coming back to finish off the job. She and Wheaton would have a killer ending.

"What about the script?"

"It's gonna be a little harder now because we can only base the script on the testimony Delang gave in front of Congress, his other interviews, and whatever info he gave Wheaton a few hours ago. He'll probably have to take some creative liberties to fill in the gaps, but I'll call one of my consultants who used to be a spy. He should be able to help out."

"Whatever, just send me the rest of my money."

"It's on the way."

Chapter Sixteen

COLUMBIA STUDIOS HEADQUARTERS
CULVER CITY, CALIFORNIA

On the other end of the line, Chang sat in her oversized black leather chair. She placed her forehead on the back of her hand while clutching the phone.

That was a lousy thing to do.

"You did the right thing."

A female voice came from a couch across the room. Chang tossed her phone on her oak desk, wiped the tears from her face, and gave her guest a condescending glare that could've cut through ice. Her guest was unphased as she continued puffing on her cigarette.

"No, I didn't. And you know it."

"Relax. You owed me a favor, and you did what was necessary. It's not like you won't get anything out of this. I'll make sure that you get the funding that you need, and your movie will be a smash. Win-Win."

"Don't you mean win-win-win, Senator? You're taking five percent of the box office gross."

"Well, I am entitled to a little compensation," said Vivian Walsh, "given what happened to me. Don't you think?"

Vivian Walsh had once been the Senator from Pennsylvania and one of the most powerful figures in Washington. She had been re-elected twice, chaired the Senate Armed Service Committee, was willing to make any deal she could as long as it benefitted her, and had enough dirt on her fellow members of Congress to ensure that she always got her way.

However, her reign as "Queen of the Senate" came to an abrupt end when she was forced into a deal with the Iranians, and attempted to get NSA Bahrain, the naval base that was home to the Fifth Fleet, closed. Unfortunately for her, the Secretary of Defense and Delang proved Iran's involvement in a drone strike in Iraq, which precipitated her charge to have the base closed. When video evidence of her colluding with the Iranians was exposed, it slammed the door shut on her career in Washington.

Though the Secretary of Defense was currently outside her reach for revenge, Tom Delang was not. When she heard that Hollywood producers were clambering over each other for the rights to Delang's episode in Iran, she sprang into action. She had once done a favor for Chang on a movie that her studio was producing in Pittsburgh. At the time, Chang was a low-level executive at the studio, ambitious about moving up. When her film ran into local union issues, Chang asked around and was told that Walsh was the person to see. True to her word, Walsh negotiated an off-the-books deal with the union. They would receive extra pay in exchange for keeping the production running smoothly. Chang knew she was in Walsh's debt but had no idea about the depth of what that bargain meant. It was time for Walsh to cash in and force Chang to accept the project.

"I think you're scum. I wish I'd never reached out to you."

"What's done is done. Move on. You've got work to do and so do I."

She gave Chang an evil wink as she stubbed out her cigarette and proudly made her way to the door.

"Senator, one last thing. You should've just retired quietly and worked as a board member on that phone company. Karma got you once. It'll get you again," Chang said.

Walsh turned back to look at Chang from the door.

"This time," she said. "I am Karma."

Chapter Seventeen

MUMBAI, INDIA

By western standards, Mumbai was not the cleanest of cities. The congested sidewalks were packed elbow to elbow with people and homeless dogs. There was no escape from the constant racket of car horns on the streets and thick smog polluting the air. Though the aromas coming from the food vendors smelled superb, the steam from their fryers could sting the eyes.

But Aman Bhandari didn't pay any attention. He was used to it, and having just been promoted at his company, he was in a jovial mood. It was his first day as a manager, and he was feeling thankful for attaining the next step in his career.

When he arrived at his place of business for his morning shift, he stood in awe of the concrete structure, as he wanted to savor every moment of the experience. He checked his hands to make sure they were clean and then flattened out his powder blue, button-down Oxford shirt and khaki slacks. He was thirty minutes early so he sat on a concrete bench and decided to document this moment of his life with a selfie video to post later on his social media pages. He made sure that his face and the company logo on the side of the building were in the center of his shot, but he paused as he began to speak.

He remembered performing the same ritual five years earlier when he began working for JP Morgan as an entry level call center operator. A friend of his had told him about the job and he was fortunate enough to win over the hiring manager with his confidence and tales of good work ethic, despite never having worked in a call center. In the years that followed, Aman dedicated himself to his job, working whatever hours were needed, including weekends, and performing any task handed to him. Finally, his hard work and ambitious nature paid off.

Having finished his monologue and sharing the excitement of his first day as a boss, Aman kept the camera on as he walked up the stairs, through the glass double doors, and to the security desk, where Officer Stanley was waiting for him with his new badge. He had to wait a few minutes for the janitorial staff to check in and deliver new house plants to spruce up the office, but he kept recording.

"I've been waiting for you, Aman," said Stanley. "I see you've decided to capture this moment on video."

"Absolutely. These are the moments in life that matter."

"That's right. Well, here it is."

The security guard handed him his new badge with a green leash while Aman set his old one on the marble counter. He beamed with joy as he focused his phone on his new ID with his new job listed underneath his familiar photograph.

AMAN BHANDARI
MANAGER, NORTH AMERICA CALL CENTER- EAST

Stanley grinned. Aman's eyes welled up with happy tears. Stanley and Aman took their time catching up on the happenings of each other's families and talking about how the company had changed since Aman had joined it five years ago. Their conversation ended as Aman's shift officially began.

"So, what's the first thing you're going to do, *Mister* Bhandari?"

As he placed his new ID around his neck, Aman opened his mouth to answer Stanley, but the words never left his lips. An explosion engulfed the lobby. A burning cloud of fire consumed Aman and Stanley within seconds. Rocks from the structural columns in the lobby pelted their bodies. Within seconds, three other explosions shook the rest of the building, each on a different floor, causing parts of the upper floors to collapse onto the floor below.

People on the street ducked as they heard the explosion and witnessed the debris falling from the building. Chunks of cinder block, torn pieces of desk furniture, and body parts landed on the cars and sidewalk. When the chaos stopped, the building was leaking smoke from the windows and front door. Survivors immediately called 1-1-2, India's version of America's 911. Little did they know that this was only the first of many detonations across Mumbai and the nearby city of Pune.

Chapter Eighteen

BHUJ, INDIA

Thrasher sat in the agency plane, waiting restlessly for his Indian counterpart to show up to claim the body stored in the cargo hold. He knew that agent Dhoni of the Indian Intelligence Bureau (IIB) was intentionally making him wait and it annoyed the hell out of him. He also knew that he deserved to be kept waiting.

He had tangled with Kedar Dhoni on more than one occasion and while no one experience was the same as the previous, none of them would qualify as being good. It was the last experience with Dhoni that put Thrasher in the CIA's doghouse. The agency had arranged for him to be on stakeout with IIB as part of a joint mission to extract information on Zafar Zaman, a Pakistani ISI agent. The CIA wanted Zaman because he was known to be friends with a colonel in Iran's Revolutionary Guard. India wanted him because of his access to Pakistani military plans regarding troop movements in the heavily disputed Kashmir region.

CIA analysts stumbled upon India's plans regarding Zaman by pure accident when Dhoni blabbed about it to a hooker who was often used in CIA stings. The temptress immediately knew that the information she possessed was worth some extra cash and made arrangements to meet her usual agency contact, Thrasher, in New Delhi. He then arranged for another hotel rendezvous between the hooker and Dhoni. This time, the hotel room was bugged with video surveillance.

A blackmail operation on Dhoni followed. After IIB got what they wanted from the ISI agent, the CIA would take a shot at him and use him as a source inside Iran. In exchange, Dhoni received the sole copy of the surveillance footage so that it wouldn't fall into the hands of his bosses or his new wife.

Thrasher could practically feel the hatred radiating from Dhoni's body during the entire stakeout. He tried to ease the tension with a bottle of Dhoni's favorite liquor, Old Monk, and a trip to the AVN Adult Entertainment Expo in Las Vegas the following month. The gifts didn't exactly level the playing field, but Dhoni was pleased enough so that Thrasher wouldn't have to worry about looking over his shoulder.

The first few nights of the stakeout yielded nothing special in terms of intelligence. Zaman went to work for long hours, came home, and never spoke about his job. Thrasher and Dhoni could have snatched him off the street at any time, but they both agreed that grabbing him in a compromising position would give them additional leverage during their interrogations. Luckily for them, Zaman had a recreational relationship with cocaine, and they were sure it was an itch he would eventually need to scratch. All they had to do was be patient and wait.

On the fourth afternoon, Dhoni was getting some sleep back at the safe house when Thrasher and Dub caught a conversation from Zaman while he was eating a late lunch. He called his drug dealer about a meeting at the Serena Hotel for a "party for three." Thrasher assumed that the "three" referred to himself, the drug dealer, and the cocaine. From an intelligence standpoint, the information was liquid gold. Thrasher had the exact when and where, even the room number. The bad thing was, the meeting was in less than an hour and the safe house in Islamabad was across town. There was no way Dhoni would be able to make it in time, so Thrasher called an audible. He would interrupt Zaman, squeeze him for information, cuff him, and then escort him over to the safe house, where Dhoni would do the same. The events would be out of sequence from what had been agreed to, but each of them would get what they wanted from Zaman.

Thrasher had no time to set up audio and video surveillance in the hotel room where Ali and his drug dealer would meet. The only thing he was able to do was get a room on the same hallway. Zaman was known to arrive early for any meeting, so it was a safe bet that he would get to the hotel first, and the drug dealer would meet him there. All Thrasher had to do was watch the dealer enter the room, wait a few minutes for them to make the deal and snort a few lines before he busted in to catch Zaman red handed. Dub wasn't thrilled about the idea, but given the time constraints, he knew that Thrasher had a point. He reluctantly agreed with his plan and would wait in the van in the alley so that they could make a clean getaway with Zaman in tow.

Thrasher waited in his room, across the hall and two doors down from Zaman. He showed up early as expected. Twenty minutes later, the drug dealer appeared. Thrasher's view through the peep hole of his door was limited. He had thought about cracking his door open to have a look but the latches were heavy and tended to echo in the hallway, which may have spooked the dealer. All Thrasher could do was listen for the door to open and shut.

Hoping that they would sample the nose candy, he waited ten minutes before kicking down the door. But when he did, the "party for three" that Zaman had referred to on the phone was not what Thrasher had assumed. The dealer and the cocaine were present, but so was a near naked, fifteen-year-old Pakistani girl who Thrasher saw in a compromising position on the bed.

The intrusion startled Zaman and the drug dealer, who literally had their pants around their ankles. The good part about that was that they couldn't get to their guns fast enough. But the scene lit an instant fuse inside Thrasher. He told the girl to put her clothes on and run. After she closed the door, the rest was pretty much a blur. Dominated by rage, Thrasher barely remembered beating Zaman and the drug dealer to death. What he did recall was the cracking sound Zaman's neck made when he snapped it one hundred and eighty degrees, which caused him to emerge from his cloud of fury. He surveyed the carnage and knew that what would come next couldn't possibly be good for him.

When he called Dub and told him that they had a problem, the fallout began. The mission had failed, as they had gathered no intel on Zaman's Iran connections. Dhoni was going to go batshit crazy and probably get reprimanded, and Thrasher's career was probably over. Thankfully, Jenkins stepped in to save it. But the event made CIA and IIB relations take a major step backward. IIB's access to Pakistani sources was essential for the CIA because so many of them also had connections to Iran. For six months, the relationship between the two agencies was essentially cut off at the knees. Thrasher was hoping, though, that delivering the body of the terrorist who had connections to the Mumbai attacks would help to smooth things over and rebuild the working relationship.

"Sir, their plane just landed," the agency pilot said.

"Thanks, Tyrell. Sit tight for me. I'm not sure how this is going to go."

The IIB plane circled the runway and parked one hanger away. Thrasher lingered outside the service door to meet Dhoni. When the door lowered, a stocky Dhoni and his handlebar mustache charged down the steps toward Thrasher, who immediately read the man's body language. Dhoni may have made the trip to recover the body, but he wasn't leaving without settling a score with Thrasher. He tossed away his Arnette sunglasses and prepared to fight.

Dhoni tried to kick the side of Thrasher's knee with the heel of his boot, but Thrasher saw it coming and pivoted. He could have easily thrown a punch that would have stunned Dhoni, but he wasn't going to let this become that kind of a fight, not this time. All he had to do was let Dhoni get the aggression out of his system.

"Welcome back, asshole!"

Dhoni whipped a backhanded punch toward Thrasher's face, who dodged it and swatted at Dhoni's wrist to use the man's own momentum to keep him moving to the left. This exposed Dhoni's chest and allowed Thrasher to jab the heel of his hand into his sternum. Dhoni was dazed. The wind had been knocked out of him.

"Let's not do this, Kedar," Thrasher said.

"I've been dreaming of this moment for over six months."

Dhoni was wheezing.

"It's happening."

What followed was a series of well-aimed and well-executed punches, kicks, and elbows from Dhoni, all of which Thrasher either dodged or blocked with no returning blows. The so-called fight couldn't have lasted three minutes before Dhoni finally wore himself out.

"Are we done here?" Thrasher asked.

Dhoni's lungs heaved as he leaned over.

"When I thought about this, I dreamed about you fighting back. Not acting like a pussy."

Thrasher smirked. He had anticipated such a comment and offered no reply.

The tension of the moment was broken when Dhoni's phone rang. Thrasher could tell he didn't want to take it as he was ready for another round of punches, but he reluctantly diverted his eyes to his screen. Ironically, Thrasher's phone rang only seconds later.

"Fuck."

Looking up at Dhoni, he noticed that the look on his face had changed from bitter antagonism to distressed concern. Both phones had messages regarding the bombings of a combined ten global service centers for American companies in Mumbai and Pune. When their eyes met, there were no more looks of contempt. They both knew that they would have to work together on this one.

"Jump in," Thrasher said. "Let's get to Mumbai."

Dhoni nodded and told the IIB's pilot to go back to New Delhi. Thrasher and Dhoni walked up the steps to the plane. Just as the two men were about to take their seats, Dhoni called out to Thrasher, who was in front of him. As he turned around, Dhoni landed a solid right hook to the side of Thrasher's head, which sent him stumbling to his seat.

"Now we're done. And don't ever call my country a shithole again."

Chapter Nineteen

MUMBAI, INDIA

The flight from Bhuj to Mumbai normally took an hour and a half, but Thrasher told the pilot to double time it, so they made it in under an hour. When they landed, Thrasher and Dhoni had the steps to the service door down before the plane came to a complete stop. Traffic in Mumbai was bad enough during any normal day of the week. With the attacks, though, there was no way they would get to the scene by car, so they hustled to a chopper Dhoni had waiting. The nearest landing spot was a field assigned for the Mumbai Cricket Club. It wasn't ideal, but it worked. From there, they fought their way through the crowds to the first bombing site.

Thrasher had expected Dhoni to argue about which site to visit first, but there was no push back. The decision was simple. From Bhuj, Mumbai was a shorter flight than Pune, and the first site available would give them the most immediate feedback, enabling them to compare that scene with the others, and to gauge any consistencies or discrepancies in the evidence.

After pushing and shoving their way through the dense crowd, Dhoni literally stopped in his tracks to the point where Thrasher bumped into him from behind. While the scene looked all too familiar to Thrasher after what he witnessed at the embassy only days before, it made Dhoni's light brown skin go pale and his jaw drop. Thrasher knew Dhoni had experienced the perils of war on many occasions, but even with India's strained relationship with Pakistan, the threats he faced had either been on a military basis or in the tribal regions where laws changed like the wind. Thrasher was reasonably certain that Dhoni must have felt like many Americans did on 9/11. The questions of who, how, and most important, why, must have been spinning through his mind.

"Hey," Thrasher said, "whatever you're feeling is natural, but it can wait. Right now, we have a job to do."

Even behind his Aviator sunglasses, Thrasher could tell that Dhoni blinked away some tears before nodding in agreement.

"Let's get in there and see what we can do," Thrasher continued.

Dhoni quickly dismissed a pudgy, amped up Mumbai police officer who tried to keep them out of the building by showing him his badge, but the firefighters were a different matter. Though they had managed to get the blaze relatively under control, the fire marshal was concerned about its structural integrity and instructed everyone to back away.

Thrasher and Dhoni exchanged looks. If the building was going to collapse, they needed to get inside as fast as possible to make their assessments, and collect any evidence they could use before it was either destroyed or buried.

Thrasher paid the fire marshal no mind and shoved past him before reaching what was left of what was once an icon of the downtown Mumbai skyline. Trying their best to avoid tripping over the debris of glass and cinderblock, the two agents warily entered what used to be the main entrance. Following Thrasher's lead, Dhoni stopped to survey the damage.

"What do you think?"

"I need a minute."

"We may not have a minute. Work fast."

At a bombing scene, Thrasher tended to become a combination of crime scene investigator, intelligence officer, and fire marshal. He managed to shut out all of the ruckus outside, including the firemen who were still yelling at them. He fell into a trance-like state as his mind pieced together all the fragments in front of him to rebuild the scene in his mind so that he could visualize what it looked like only seconds prior to detonation.

Jenkins called his aptitude "spooky good." She had seen other agents at the CIA or other agencies, such as the FBI or ATF, with similar reconstructive abilities, but those people took days or even weeks to put it all back together. Thrasher could do the same in only minutes. It was one of the reasons his confrontational personality was tolerated.

For Thrasher, finding the original location of the bomb in the lobby was easy, but figuring out what had concealed it would take more time. He walked over to where the bomb had blasted a hole in the wall. He was sure that this was the point of origin, but it was doubtful that it would be concealed by a backpack or a briefcase. Considering that the blast started at the back wall, the security guard on duty would have noticed such an object and brought it over to his desk for someone to claim. In that case, the blast would have been at the security desk and not where Thrasher was standing.

"Have you visited this building before?" he asked.

"No, why?"

"Aren't most lobbies decorated with some type of house plant? Even here in India?"

Dhoni had to think about it for a second.

"Usually, yes."

Thrasher continued to look for any remnants that might resemble the pot from a plant, but nothing stuck out to him.

"Didn't the second floor suffer damage as well?"

"I think I heard someone outside say that it did."

"We need to go up."

"Up? This whole place is ready to crumble any minute!"

Thrasher ignored Dhoni and set off to find the stairwell. They could feel the building starting to sway and knew that they didn't have much time. Thrasher's gut told him to keep going, to find what was needed before what was left of the building fell on top of them. When they quickly found the blast hole for the second bomb, Thrasher surveyed the scene. Despite the destruction, he saw that the origin of the blast was close to where a pillar would have been and not in close proximity to any of the desks on the floor. He was starting to feel confident in his potted plant theory.

"Let's go up one more," he said.

On the third floor, Dhoni and Thrasher ran into an unexpected issue. There was no blast hole. All they found was the collapsed fragments from the floor above.

Why would there be bombs on the other floors and not this one?

"Spread out. Check the potted plants."

"Shouldn't we call in the bomb squad? If there is another bomb in here, I don't want to get blown away."

"Then be careful when you look," Thrasher said.

A few minutes into their search, they felt the building move and nearly lost their balance.

"We gotta move!" Dhoni stressed.

"Not yet."

Thrasher's instincts gnawed at him. Something didn't feel right. When he inspected one of the potted plants, he found wires that had no business being there. Tossing out the fake straw, He saw the block of what appeared to be a half pound of C-4 concealed by papier-mâché and gingerly inspected the bomb to ensure that it couldn't detonate. Delicately probing the plant with his fingers, he saw that two of the wires weren't connected to the clay explosive. No one with any bomb building experience would do that.

He felt the building wobble again with much more authority.

"Let's go! Now!"

Thrasher picked up the plant and carried it to the stairwell. Dhoni was gliding down the stairs as fast as he could, and obviously had no qualms about leaving Thrasher behind. It turned out that carrying a large potted plant down a flight of steps wasn't as easy as he'd thought. He could hear the walls beginning to crack like Pop Rocks as he reached the door to the ground floor. Since Dhoni ran out ahead of him, the door to the stairwell was closed, and Thrasher had to hoist the plant on his knee while trying to open the door with his free hand.

That fucking prick.

When he flung the door open, he did his best to run like hell toward the entrance, but the debris on the ground impaired his movement. Because of the damned plant, he couldn't see in front of him, so he made a special effort to walk sideways, but he tripped on a piece of concrete and fell on his face, which caused the plant to fly through the air before landing on its side. Thinking the impact may cause the unconnected wires to touch the C-4, Thrasher covered his head and braced for impact. Miraculously, the bomb didn't go off. Noticing that the fall caused his phone to fall out of his pocket, he snatched it up before grabbing the plant, and getting the hell out of there.

Everyone was so busy running for cover they had no time to notice the idiot carrying a plant as if he needed it for therapy. Dhoni was frantically waving Thrasher forward at the bottom of the walkway, and finally helped him carry the plant to safety. People were screaming everywhere in the streets of Mumbai as the rest of the building crashed down, floor by floor, leaving them being chased by a thick cloud of debris like the fog in a monster movie. Thrasher and Dhoni had no other choice but to take cover behind a parked taxicab and wait for the smog and particle dust to settle. Both men went into coughing fits.

"What the hell is this all about?" Dhoni said.

Motioning Dhoni to bend down, Thrasher held the collar of his shirt over his nose with one hand. He pointed to the block of C-4 inside the potted plant that was still covered in its original wrapping.

"Call your people and tell them to look for the same thing at the other locations here in Mumbai and Pune. We can trace it."

Dhoni's face was covered in soot as he smiled at Thrasher and patted him on the shoulder. But before he could thank him, Thrasher hooked a punch to the man's jaw, which made him double over in pain.

"Don't ever leave me behind again."

Chapter Twenty

Vahid Avesta sat in his private office, a cruel smile creeping across his bearded face, as he flipped through the news coverage of the bombings in India. His confidence in the new Supreme Leader was growing. Not only did the man have the vision for such a plan, he committed to it, and had the guts to try to pull it off. Thus far, everything was going according to plan. The bombings in India had thankfully wiped the incident at the U.S. embassy in Islamabad off the news cycle, but the idiots at the CIA were no doubt still trying to get their bearings.

Both of them screamed components of Pakistan, state sponsored or rogue elements, but the U.S. was erroneously crying about the embassy bombing connecting to Iran. It didn't matter. They would be twiddling their thumbs for weeks, if not months, trying to figure it out. By then, Iran would have everything it wanted and could deny any accusations in the media.

The destruction at the office buildings in India was more than he had hoped. Captain Yazdani and his crew did an excellent job of scoping out the office floor plans weeks before in order to inflict maximum damage. Smoke reigned supreme in the skies of Mumbai and Pune. Employees were scuttling out of buildings, coughing, and hacking, while blood seeped from the various wounds on their bodies. Corpses were being carried out on stretchers or handed down via an assembly line of emergency workers. For Avesta, it was a glorious site to behold. He only wished that he could be there in person to feel his eyes burn from the smoke, and let the stench of carnage and death saturate his sense of smell. He considered these scenes of destruction as art. He understood now why many bombers stuck around the area to relish in the victory of their work.

"Mr. President?"

His assistant's voice called out from the hardline.

"Yes, what is it?"

"President Sharma of India is on the line for you. He says it's quite urgent."

Avesta's malicious smirk stretched further across his sun-spotted face.

That was faster than I expected.

"Put him through, Saeed. And I'm not to be disturbed until I am done with this call."

"Yes, sir."

The line beeped and switched to the Indian president.

"Akshay, given the circumstances, I'm surprised to hear from you. My country would like to offer you our sincerest condolences for the loss of life your country has experienced. We would like to help you in any way that we can in terms of aid."

"Thank you for your kind words, Vahid. It has indeed been a tragic day for us here. I will certainly discuss with you any aid that you can provide, but there is another matter we need to discuss right now."

"Of course. How can Iran assist you?"

"Is the opportunity for the pipeline deal that you proposed still on the table?"

"I'm perplexed. You made it quite clear the last time we spoke that you were, I believe, *prohibited* from moving forward with such a deal. Isn't that the word you used?"

"There's no need to rub salt in the wound, Vahid. I know what I said. But circumstances have obviously changed. Innocent civilians of my country have been assaulted and all indications are that those Pakistani bastards are responsible. The gloves are coming off."

They bought it.

"I never thought Pakistan would go this far," said Avesta. "What do you think prompted them to do this?"

"I can't discuss that, Vahid. You know that. All I am willing to say at this point is that I have taken a very strong stance against Pakistan in the tribal regions during my tenure in this office, so I'm taking this attack personally."

Excellent.

"I can understand that. From Iran's standpoint, we are allies with both you and our friends in Pakistan, so we have a responsibility to remain neutral in this conflict. That said, given the current situation, we are willing to provide you with assistance in regard to the pipeline. What about your agreement with the American pigs?"

"Let me worry about that."

"Fair enough. If you want to revisit the pipeline offer, we'd be delighted. However, I believe that the deal called for India to increase your crude oil imports from my country from fifteen to twenty percent. That number is now thirty percent."

There was a pause on the other end of the line as Sharma digested what he had heard.

"Excuse me?"

"You heard me. Thirty percent. Not twenty."

"Let me get this straight, Vahid. My country has just been attacked and your idea of assistance is to extort me?"

"You had your opportunity at twenty percent, but you decided to side with the American swine. They are the true extortionists. The Americans prod and probe at every country in the world, manipulating and bribing their leaders to get what they want. You know very well what their sanctions have done to my country. This isn't extortion, Akshay. This is business. And what is best for my country is thirty percent."

"Give me a moment to discuss this with my aides."

Avesta said nothing as he calmly waited. He knew he had caught his fish. All he had to do was reel it in.

"Twenty-five," Sharma replied.

"This isn't a negotiation. That time has passed. Thirty. Take it or my next demand will be thirty-five."

There was another pause, but this time, Avesta thought it felt more panicked. He visualized Sharma staring at his aides with an "I don't have a choice" look on his face.

"Fine, but I want you to beef up your security on the border. I don't want any disruptions to the oil flow. If something happens, it's on your watch, at which point negotiations restart. Do we have a deal?"

"Nothing that I can't live with."

"Good. How soon can the oil start flowing?"

"My aides will send over the paperwork of the agreement this afternoon. If you have it back to me by the end of the day, I'll personally make sure that the gateway is opened tomorrow morning."

"We'll get it done."

"It's nice to do business with you again, Akshay. This is how it should be. Two Middle East powers talking to one another without outside influence."

"Save your speeches for the media, Vahid. I'm doing what I have to do for my country, period. And right now, I have to go to war."

Sharma hung up before Avesta could say another word, but it didn't matter. The Iranian president sat back in his fluffy leather chair, giddy as a child who had just eaten his first ice cream cone. He made every attempt to maintain his composure. After all, he was the president. But even leaders of countries have their good days and today was definitely that. Excited, he pushed the button on his phone, which rang to his assistant outside the door.

"Yes, sir?"

"Saeed, get me the soonest appointment you can with the Supreme Leader. It is time to celebrate."

Chapter Twenty-One

THE WHITE HOUSE

For the president of the United States, there are few genuinely good days. Most are simply less bad than others. For Roger Cannon, on a scale of one to ten, today's bad day designation was an easy eight. The problem was that the whole week had been an eight, which made today feel like a nine, and there were no signs of improvement.

For two days, he and his staff had been working round the clock, dealing with the embassy bombing in Islamabad. To his credit, his administration responded promptly. He would be damned if there would be a Benghazi situation on his watch. The issue was, no preliminary intelligence from the CIA had indicated a pending attack. In fact, after reaching out to some of their counterparts at MI-6 and Mossad, there was no such intel from anyone. It appeared as a lone wolf attack by a single terrorist, but Cannon had a good nose for national security. He knew that something didn't smell right. His CIA Director had mentioned a possible connection to Iran, but that was thin, at best. Plus, the terrorist who had actually performed the bombing had a known connection to a Pakistani terrorist organization. The two pieces of information didn't mesh well together.

The larger issue at the moment was the bombing of ten global service centers in India. This put his administration in one hell of a pickle. On the one hand, his country had not been directly attacked. The buildings that were bombed were not on U.S. sovereign soil. However, the companies that owned those buildings and employed the colleagues that worked there were all based in the United States. At the moment, it was hard to tell if the bombings were an indirect attack on the U.S. or a direct attack on India. If it was the latter, it wasn't a matter of whether or not Pakistani militants were involved. It was just a matter of time before it was proven.

If it was an attack on the U.S., whoever was responsible was clever. All of the companies who were hit in the attack were Fortune 500 companies that were publicly traded on the New York Stock Exchange. As a result, all of their stocks were plummeting, and his phone was ringing off the hook with calls from panicked CEOs. He knew most of them personally and had made specific efforts for their companies to have their tasks offshored to Mumbai or Pune. Never mind that the bombings put his country on the playing field. It shined a spotlight directly on *him*. The thought of whether or not this was an attack on him personally had definitely crossed his mind.

He knew that the backup servers at the global service centers pre-vented financial and business data from being lost altogether. In today's technology, if the cloud didn't take care of that, the companies them-selves had put enough money into their IT infrastructure that losing any data was nearly impossible.

Instead, the bombings meant that there was no one on the other end now to do the work, which was a problem. The process improvement teams that had evaluated the procedures for the companies in question managed to divide up tasks, such as billing, payment, the issuing of work orders, handling of phone calls, and the filing of service tickets into smaller single tasks. All of them had their own standard operating procedures (SOP). The colleagues employed by the global service centers were rarely allowed to deviate from what was written in the SOPs. This could create delays for transactions, but it was the compa-nies' way of ensuring that all required approvals or follow-ups were handled by colleagues in the United States.

As then-CEO Cannon and his staff looked at the situation, these were all remedial tasks that Americans didn't want to do anyway. So, until such time as the processes could be automated, the jobs were offshored to India. This made the Indian government happy, allowed American companies to save money by reducing its headcount, and improved their bottom line.

But colleagues in India were now afraid to return to work. With no one there to perform those duties, the required tasks weren't being done at all. The full-time employees in the United States would do whatever they could to cover the work, but with the companies making themselves as lean as possible in terms of full-time employees, it forced the CEO's to have local offices hire temporary employees off the street. This was easily done, but even while paying temps lower wages than full-time employees, the wages were still considerably higher than those being paid in India. Plus, due to the new employees being green, there would be a sharp learning curve. Cannon estimated that it would optimistically take the new hires roughly three months to get the hang of their new tasks and at least another six to nine months for the companies to figure out their next steps as they tried to rebuild. In the meantime, billions of dollars would be lost, which was not a hit that Cannon could allow the economy to take.

An hour after the first attack was reported, the stock market responded accordingly. It was barely 10 a.m. in New York City and the DOW was already down more than seven hundred points and Curbs were in. This meant that because the market was moving too fast in one direction, restrictions were placed on specific types of securities or indexes. For the first time since the October 2008 recession, trading had been suspended on some but not all parts of the market.

The entire situation had understandably caused Cannon's blood pressure to skyrocket. Prior to his presidency, this often caused him to act with an excessive amount of emotion. As president, he was well aware that he could only get away with showing small doses of emotion at a time. Since his presidency began, though, the stress of the job had caused him to start developing migraines, a condition that was known only to his wife, a White House physician, and his chief of staff. In order to keep the physical pain in his head at bay, he entered into a near trance like state, which he was unaware of until the First Lady had mentioned it to him. While the emotions related to his elevated blood pressure could be consciously kept in check, appearing even the slightest bit disconnected was an absolute no-no. Having rumors on social media or news articles written about his emotional responses were bad enough, but they could be weathered. The appearance of being mentally disconnected was not something he could afford, as it would raise questions regarding his capacity to lead the country.

He decided that he needed a breather and asked his secretary and chief of staff for fifteen quiet minutes alone in the Oval Office, where he intended to lean his fifty-two-year-old head back in his leather chair. Hopefully, there were no White House photographers outside on the patio of the West Wing, but it was a chance he was willing to take. Cannon knew that his next phone call was a crucial one and he needed all his wits about him. He was resting his eyes when his assistant buzzed.

"Sir?"

"Yes, Melanie, what is it?"

"You asked me to alert you when it was time for your call with President Sharma."

"Thank you. Is he already on the line?"

"Yes, sir."

"Okay, one second."

Cannon put her on mute. He ran his fingers through his red hair, which was turning increasingly grey. He wiped his eyes, and rolled back his shoulders to get himself ready and back in the game.

"Put him through, Melanie."

The line clicked.

"Akshay, what's the latest news? How are you holding up?"

"If you want me to be honest with you, Roger, I'm pretty pissed off."

"I would be, too, if I were in your shoes. What can you tell me?"

"Hasn't your staff told you?"

"Told me what?"

"Turn on CNN, Roger. See for yourself."

Cannon snatched the remote control from the corner of the Resolute Desk and turned on the TV he had installed over the fireplace to replace the portrait of George Washington. He couldn't believe what he was watching. The CNN feed from New Delhi TV already had security footage of a Pakistani soldier, Lt. Hasan Wasim, moving an unauthorized amount of C-4 explosives from Base Masroor in Karachi.

"Something doesn't feel right, Akshay. How did the India media get this footage so quickly? The bombs only went off hours ago. And how the hell do they know that the transfer was unauthorized? Even though C-4 was used in the bombings, every military base across the world has it in stock."

"Because they obtained a copy of the work order from the base. He was only supposed to take five hundred pounds and instead he took seven hundred. Lab technicians at IIB confirmed that the C-4 that was detonated is a match for what was taken."

"Wait, you have a copy of a work order from a Pakistani military base? Don't you think the timing of all of this is a little convenient?"

Sharma grew frustrated.

"Roger, since innocent civilians of my country have been blatantly murdered, I don't find anything convenient about this. Keep in mind, this wasn't a hit on a military installation. This is a whole new game, and Pakistan just hit way below the belt. Plus, our intel tells us that this Wasim was regularly stationed at one of their nuclear facilities. I'm not waiting. We're going to war with those bastards."

"Hang on, Akshay. No one has heard a peep from Pakistan yet. Let's not rush into anything. Give Pakistan a chance to respond before you make any rash decisions."

"I didn't call you for permission, Roger. I've had *enough* of the Pakistani activities against me and my country. I'm going to put a stop to it, once and for all. One way or another they are going to learn that we are not to be fucked with!"

"Akshay, I understand how you feel. When America was attacked on 9/11, one of my predecessors felt the same way, but let's gather more facts before doing anything rash."

"There is no *we* in this, Roger. I've spoken to the president of Iran, and he's agreed to give me the oil necessary for this war. This is happening whether you like it or not."

"That's not what we agreed to, Akshay, remember? I got your country more jobs at global service centers and found a way to get you the oil you were getting from Iran."

"And you need to remember that my people who worked at those global service centers were the ones attacked. People are afraid to leave their homes and go to work. Not only at service centers, but all across India. This is a direct attack on my country's economy. Our deal is on hiatus until further notice."

"You're putting me in a bad spot, Akshay. I've got a lot of explaining to do to those CEO's and this path you're on isn't going to convince them not to move the jobs out of your country."

"Then I suggest you crank up the dial on that lovely charm of yours. Your companies' businesses can wait! They have enough money."

"Akshay, come on, now . . ."

"Oh, and one more thing. If it comes down to it, I'm not ruling out a nuclear option."

Before Cannon could respond, Sharma hung up the line, leaving him staring into an empty telephone. His migraine was about to get a hell of a lot worse.

Chapter Twenty-Two

ASHEVILLE, NORTH CAROLINA

Delang woke up groggy from a deep sleep, startled by a room he didn't recognize. He noticed that he was hooked up to an IV, but he wasn't in a hospital. He was in a bedroom with spearmint-colored walls that smelled recently painted. The bed was nothing special, a queen-sized mattress within a sleigh bedframe, but he could tell that it had a memory foam topper, which made it damned comfortable. It was no wonder he had slept so soundly.

In the corner, he saw a familiar face, sleeping in a spindled armchair with his fist against his temple and an open mouth starting to drool. He knew without a doubt that he could trust this person. Before deciding to wake his friend, Delang tried to recall the events of the last day.

After getting run off the road and climbing out of the tree, he had trudged through the mountains until he reached a point where a road was visible. His labored breathing was due to a broken nose and bruised ribs. Although his ankle wasn't broken, it didn't feel right as he limped along, so chances were good that it was at least badly sprained. The chilly air made his cuts and lacerations sting like hell.

When he found the main road, Delang made a conscious effort to follow it from a distance in order to ensure that the truck that had run him off the road was not looming, ready to strike again. Unfortunately, the angle of the mountain put tremendous pressure on his ankle. He braced his feet against imbedded rocks and tree stumps and used what-ever hanging branches he could reach to maintain his balance. His movement was excruciatingly slow and it took him over an hour to walk what was probably a half mile.

Eventually, Delang heard a diesel truck slowly climbing up the mountain, heading his direction. At first, he panicked because he remembered that the truck that ran him off the road had a diesel engine. But this wasn't the sound of a Ford F350. The engine sounded clumsy, as if it was hauling heavy cargo and coughing its way through the mountain. Though he knew it was risky, Delang trusted his instincts and gingerly climbed his way down toward the road.

Delang saw that it was a logging truck and flagged it down. One glance at the wandering hitchhiker's disheveled appearance and the burly truck driver could tell he was in trouble. While he offered to take his new passenger to the hospital, Delang asked if he could ride with him down the mountain.

After thanking the driver for the lift, Delang cautiously made his way back to his cabin. He had no idea what could be waiting for him, but he knew that he had to make the arduous climb through the woods up to his cabin to make sure his wife, Abby, was not in danger. Perspiration was soaking through his shirt and dripping down his face. He could feel an aching sensation trickle down his arms and into his hands. It was hard to tell if he was having a heart attack or if it was residual effects from his busted ribs, but he pushed forward and managed to reach the Sig Sauer P320 that he had fastened under his back patio.

Peering over the patio, he saw no one and nothing suspicious. He dared not enter through the front door. If an enemy was inside, there was a good chance it was boobytrapped. He peaked through the rear patio window and into his living room, but the curtains obstructed his view. All he could see were two feet on the couch, and they weren't moving. A tidal wave of concern for his wife made his chest ache even more.

I have to get inside.

In case he and Abby ever needed to get out of the house in a rush, Delang had arranged for an architect friend to build an escape tunnel that ran from his private office to underneath the patio. The tunnel door was obscured by a stack of firewood. The kindling was real and had to be occasionally replaced to keep up its appearance, but a closer look showed that it was stacked on a shelf with lipped edges, which kept it from moving when the door swung inward. All Delang had to do was push the button that looked like a knot in the cedar wood.

As he entered, Delang flipped the emergency lighting that lined the tunnel and ten-foot shaft. The last thing he needed was to fall on his ass and injure himself any further. He had to climb the wooden ladder on one foot to protect his damaged ankle. Even so, the movement was rigorous, and he felt a burning sensation rake up his leg.

After hitting the button on the side of the ladder, the door latch released. Delang carefully lowered it toward him so that gravity didn't cause it to fly open. Once inside, he held his gun in front of him and scanned each room in the back of the house for anything unusual. He didn't see anything suspicious and tip-toed across the hardwood floor, carefully avoiding the squeaks he knew by heart, and proceeded to the living room. He saw the top of a brown head on the couch and rushed over to Abby to make sure that she was still alive.

"Abbs?"

Abruptly awakened and startled by the sight of the gun, Abby screamed.

"Whoa, whoa! It's me!"

Catching her breath, she wondered what was so wrong that it would cause Tom to wake her in such a way. As she came out of her nap, she scanned her husband up and down, and knew something was wrong.

"What the hell happened?!"

Delang leaned over to hug her and passed out in her arms. A few hours later, he was awakened by a familiar voice, which yanked Delang from his album of memories.

"You look pretty good for a dead man."

Delang opened his eyes slowly and looked at the figure in the corner chair.

"Hey, Kirk," he said. "Wait. Dead man?"

Delang had once been the handler for Kirk Kurruther's grandfather, Cameron, who had helped the CIA in the 1953 coup to depose Moham-med Mossadegh and reinstall the Shah. He fled to America, where legendary agent Kermit Roosevelt kept him hidden. After Roosevelt died, Cameron's file was handed down to other agents until it finally hit Delang's desk. While Cameron wasn't an active asset, he was useful to Delang in terms of Iranian matters and always offered his opinion without expecting to receive anything in return.

The two men had a special friendship. After Delang was kidnapped by the Iranians, he failed to show for a meeting with Cameron, which caused the old man to start looking in all the wrong places and eventual-ly got spotted by the IRGC, who proceeded to send a man to murder him. When Kirk found out that the Iranians were involved, he ignored all the advice not to go, and hopped on a plane to Iran to find the man responsible. He would later be held at the same secret prison as Delang, where the two risked a daring escape out of the country.

"You don't remember?"

"No, tell me. What?"

"You passed out at home and were mumbling something to Abby about a "cemetery plan." You were smart to have a back-up plan in case someone came for you here again in the States. She called your friend at the news station and had them report your death. She didn't know where else to take you, so she stuffed you in the car and made the trip here. You were pretty out of it, but we got you upstairs."

Delang raised his eyebrows. He remembered being in the car, going in and out of consciousness, but little else.

"I guess my body gave out when the adrenaline rush subsided. Who did the IV?"

"I did!"

Delang heard another familiar voice coming from the door.

"Hey, Simin. When did you get so good at this? And where'd you get the materials?"

Simin Dehghani was Kirk's Iranian girlfriend. Somehow, during the chaos of their escape from Iran, Farhad introduced them. Simin aided them in their escape from the facility where they were being held but was nearly killed when the Revolutionary Guard found out about her. She and Kirk were smitten with each other from the beginning, and Delang knew he couldn't break them up, so he made arrangements with the State Department to have her brought Stateside. Considering what they'd done for him, it was the least he could do.

"I just got my certification as a paramedic, remember?" said Simin. "After Kirk got shot outside the embassy in Turkmenistan, I couldn't stand the thought of being so helpless by his bedside. I needed to take care of my man."

Kirk grinned and his eyes began to water.

"Hey, babe," Kirk said.

"Hi, honey."

She leaned down to give him a kiss.

"Nice to see that you two are still disgusting together. Where's Abby?"

"She ran to the pharmacy to get more bandages and aspirin. You're going to need them."

Simin checked his pulse.

Delang took note of numerous scrapes and scratches and huffed.

"Roll up your sleeve for me. It's time for a shot," Simin said.

"What for?"

"Tetanus."

Delang reluctantly exposed his triceps and grimaced as the needle went in.

Kirk leaned forward.

"You wanna tell me what the hell happened?"

Delang proceeded to give Kirk and Simin all the details. All things considered, they were less shocked than he expected.

"I always knew that they'd try and get you again," Kirk said. "Too many loose ends."

"There's no way to know if it was them or not. Once I exposed myself at the Congressional hearings, I made myself an open target to any one of my enemies with a grudge."

"If you say so," Kirk said.

He didn't believe his statement.

"Well, while you've been asleep, the world is going to hell," Simin said.

"Huh? What do you mean?"

Simin and Kirk filled him in on the embassy bombing in Pakistan, and the subsequent bombings in India. Delang remembered hearing about the incident at the embassy right before the truck first slammed into him, but he knew nothing about what happened in India.

"It's trending all over Twitter and Instagram. You should see what everyone is saying," she said.

Simin was a connoisseur of social media. While Kirk and Delang hated it, she loved it because it was a freedom she could never enjoy in Iran.

Delang threw his covers off and unhooked the IV.

"Come on, help me downstairs. I need to get in front of a TV."

When they got downstairs, Delang stood shocked.

"There's no way that two incidents like that can happen two days apart and be a coincidence."

Kirk pursed his lips and shook his head. As Delang turned his head back to the TV, the image that had appeared on screen had changed, but he got a brief glimpse.

"Where's the remote? Can you rewind it?"

Kirk backed up the broadcast to the image of the Pakistani soldier that the news was claiming to be the bomber.

"What is it?" Simin asked.

"I know that kid," said Delang. "I know his family."

Chapter Twenty-Three

NORTHWEST PAKISTAN
NAGAR DISTRICT

When he had gone to bed the previous night, Pakistani president Ameer Raja could barely contain himself with excitement. Normally a sound sleeper, he laid awake in his king-sized, four-poster bed inside the Aiwan-e-Sadr Presidential Palace, staring up at the ruby colored canopy, daydreaming about the endless possibilities that the next day's deal would bring to his country. He knew that he needed a solid night's rest to charge his batteries for the ceremony, but his brain was "all systems go," which meant that sleep could wait. It took a while for the adrenaline to subside, and he barely managed to get four hours of sleep.

The construction trucks and equipment were already in place and ready to go. The meeting was more symbolic than anything else. General Secretary of the Chinese Communist Party Zhang Xu was flying into Islamabad to meet the head of state for a short welcoming ceremony before they drove together to a village outside Chilās, where they would officially break ground on Phase Two of the Khunjerab Railway. This was part of the Chinese-Pakistan Economic Corridor (CPEG). Pakistan already had a railway running from southern Karachi to northern Islamabad, but this route to the northwest would connect with the Southern Xinjaing Railway in Kashgar, China.

While the railway was the cornerstone of the deal, other parts were also essential. The original announcement of the railway last year electrified members of Parliament, who passed a spending bill to allow a pipeline for natural gas to flow from Nawabshah to the Baluchistan district on the southern Iranian border. Dubbed the Peace Pipeline, it was completed six months ago, but the U.S. had laid down the hammer and imposed its strictest sanctions against the Islamic Republic after a drone strike in Basra, Iraq was traced back to the Iranian Revolutionary Guard. This forced Raja to back out of the deal at the last minute, preventing the pipeline from being used. His decision made President Avesta so unhappy that he refused to take his calls for two months.

Pakistan was forced to double its production in the Sui gas fields. Raja had hoped that Iran's new Ayatollah would bring a softer attitude towards the U.S. that would inevitably loosen the sanctions, thereby allowing the Peace Pipeline deal to come back to the table.

Regardless, the Khunjerab Railway opened up immense possibilities for his country. It meant opening up an unprecedented trade corridor with the country that was essentially the world's banker. Between building the railway connection and its economic effects downstream, the railway would be responsible for creating thousands more jobs and increase Pakistan's GDP by at least five percent. Numbers such as that were enough to make any president lick their lips.

However, when the day he eagerly anticipated finally arrived, his dream quickly morphed into a nightmare, making him wish that he had gotten the sleep that his wife kept reminding him he needed. After receiving word regarding the U.S. embassy bombing, he was told by the Director-General of ISI that the bomber was a rogue member of a Pakistani terrorist organization. While his government had no official connection to this group, he knew that it wouldn't take much for the CIA to make a loose connection to either ISI or other members of his government.

Unfortunately, it wasn't the only call he would receive from the Director-General that day. Hours later, he was made aware of several global service centers owned by American companies that were bombed in neighboring India. President Raja hated Sharma as much as Sharma hated him, but he knew that he'd given no such order for India to be attacked, especially on a day when the Chinese General Secretary was flying in. Either one of the incidents could have caused China to walk away, but to his surprise, the meeting remained on schedule.

Raja sat on the outdoor stage at the end of a row of chairs filled with his aides, with the General Secretary and his aides on the opposite side. He had hoped that the intense heat on what would have otherwise been considered a gorgeous day would chase away his fatigue but to no avail. He did his best to hide his yawns by fiercely clenching his jaw or discreetly covering his mouth, but knew that the press core had caught him on more than one occasion. If he was lucky, they would think that he was bored by his Foreign Secretary's opening remarks. That he could handle. But being bored at either the bombings or by the presence of China's head of state was not an image he could live down.

When his Foreign Secretary finished his statement, Raja and the General Secretary stepped forward to shake hands before sitting at the main table, where they would sign the document signifying the beginning of phase two construction. Once the signing ritual was complete, they each held up the finalized documents, and gave an approving smile for the flashing cameras. Afterward, they donned hardhats and stepped offstage, where their respective aides handed them a shovel. General Secretary Xu played to the press corps and gave them three fingers signaling that he wanted them to give the two leaders a count before they sank their tools into the dirt. As expected, the media laughed before the two men embraced the momentous occasion by placing their arms around the other's shoulder. Before Raja knew what happened, Xu spoke, and his translator snuck up behind him.

"This is a wonderful moment for our two countries," the aide said, as he translated into Raja's ear.

"Indeed. Let this be the first of many future agreements that will benefit us both."

"I'm not sure what's going on with these bombings, but make sure you get a handle on it, or these photos will be the only memory of China's presence here."

On the outside, Raja had no choice but to continue to hold his smile as Xu's translator whispered the threat into his ear, but on the inside, he felt a bolt of troubling electricity shoot down his spine.

Chapter Twenty-Four

NEW DEHLI, INDIA

A thousand miles away, President Akshay Sharma stood in his private office of the presidential palace, watching his Pakistani counterpart. He couldn't stand seeing him smile for the cameras with such reckless disregard for what he'd just done to India.

"He's mocking you," his chief of staff said.

Sharma nodded. The more he stared at the CNN broadcast, the more he could feel his blood pressure rise.

The batteries from the remote control came flying out when Sharma threw it on the tan carpet. He swiped up the phone from his desk and rang for his secretary. He didn't wait for her to respond before barking his order.

"Get me the Defense Secretary. Now!"

Chapter Twenty-Five

SA'DABAD PALACE
TEHRAN, IRAN

"Mr. President?"

Avesta wiped the sleep from his eyes and woke to see the dense mustache of one of his aides, Navid Dorri, standing over his bed.

"What time is it?"

"It's nearly five a.m., sir. You have an urgent call from President Raja of Pakistan. I told him you were sleeping, but he insisted."

Avesta placed his forearm over his eyes and groaned. Even as a lifelong politician, he still hated early mornings. He knew that his fifty-eight-year-old body should be used to it by now, but his body wasn't wired that way. He much preferred staying up late to getting up early. Having gone to bed only five hours ago, it was not the start to his day that he wanted.

"Alright. I'll take it in my private study."

"Yes, sir. Of course."

Avesta threw off the covers and put on his flannel robe. His knees and ankles cracked to life on the Persian rug as he made his way into the study. He was still picking crust from his eye when he picked up the phone.

"Ameer?"

He yawned.

"He fucked me!"

Avesta snapped to attention at Raja's intense comment.

"Wait. Who are you talking about? What happened?"

"Sharma. He set his dogs loose and his air force dropped a ton of bombs over the Nagar District. The construction trucks, the building materials . . . all gone!"

Now fully awake, Avesta grasped the situation. Everything was falling into place.

"Well, what did you expect, Ameer? A Pakistani soldier was caught on tape setting up the bombs at businesses in Mumbai and Pune. It sounds like a measured response to me."

"I had nothing to do with that, Vahid. He may have been one of our soldiers, but I gave no such order."

"Too bad that's what President Sharma thinks. If I were in his shoes, I would've done the same thing. You should be grateful that nothing more was done. If you're calling me at this hour, it means that he showed discretion and had the pilots drop the bombs at an hour where there would be minimal loss of life."

"You don't understand. They didn't just bomb the land where we broke ground. Miles of land extending to the northwest has been totally destroyed. The incident caused the Chinese to back out of the railway deal!"

"How could the Chinese know about this already?"

"Because some of the bombs were dropped within five miles of the China border. The agents working the border station called it in to the commanders. It didn't take long for the information to reach Secretary Xu."

Avesta held his palm over the microphone and tapped his feet back and forth in a little dance. He knew that China would back out of the deal, doing it so soon exceeded his expectations.

"I'm sorry to hear that, Ameer. But why call me and tell me all of this? Sounds like your plate is full of decisions that you have to make. What do you need from Iran?"

"If Sharma wants a war, I'm going to give him the fight of his life. But in order to do that, I need oil from the Peace Pipeline."

Avesta couldn't help but smile at Raja's request. The Supreme Leader's plan was working out perfectly.

"Sorry, Ameer, but if you recall, you made it crystal clear the last time we spoke that you were siding with the American Zionists in their economic sanctions against us. Based on that decision alone, tell me why I shouldn't hang up this phone right now."

"Vahid, our two countries have a deep history of cooperation. When Iran experienced the massive flooding in 2019, did I hesitate to send supplies? No. Thousands of Iranians are still alive to today because of our assistance."

"That was a humanitarian effort, Ameer. You're talking about us aiding you for a war."

"The pipeline to China would have given my country thousands of jobs and advanced the supply of goods in and out of our country by at least a decade. My country's economic well-being has been put at risk. Do you still think my request isn't based on humanitarian reasons?"

"Sounds like you rehearsed that line before calling, Ameer."

"Let's not be childish, Vahid. I am asking you for help as the president of my country. Will Iran help us or not?"

Avesta took a long pause. It was one of the business tricks he had learned over the years. Pausing kept the person on the other end hanging in suspense while Avesta already knew his decision, without any doubt. He was placing a big chunk of bait on the hook, hoping that Pakistan would do anything to bite into it. At the least, he wanted Raja to sweat. He was still pissed at him for not coming to his aide when they requested nuclear materials.

"Hello?" Raja asked.

"I'm still here, Ameer. Okay, you can have your oil, but I have two conditions."

"Those being what?"

"First, your oil imports from us go up twenty percent not ten percent."

Now it was Raja's turn to pause, though his was not intentional. He hated that Iran was sticking the screws to him over this deal, but he also knew that he had little choice in the matter, as the deal was a seller's market.

"And the second?"

"You step up your security and allow Iranian soldiers into the Balochistan region. I don't want any insurgents on the border blowing anything up."

"Fine, but I have a condition of my own."

"You really think you are in a position to make any stipulations?"

"I don't care. If you want our money, you will do this for me."

"What is it?"

"Don't sell any oil to India. I want to starve them out and crush them."

This time, Avesta hesitated before responding. He had no intention of telling Raja that Iran was double dipping on the war and supplying both sides, but Raja's condition caught him off guard. He could lie but doing so could damage the deal in the long-term and he wanted to keep the oil flowing. With the type of media coverage he expected from the war, he couldn't lie about it because it wouldn't be long before the secret came out.

"I'm afraid I can't do that, Ameer."

"Why not?"

"Sharma called me a few days ago, asking for the same thing. Because of the sanctions the U.S. placed on us, I had no choice. My country needs the money. Iran will have to stay neutral in this conflict between you and our friends in India."

Though he knew Raja had covered the phone with the palm of his hand, Avesta could still hear the string of obscenities he was letting loose.

"But I can do one thing for you."

"Such as?" Raja said.

"Well, it being a new pipeline and all, I'm sure that there are certain bugs that need to be worked out. You never know what kind of glitch could cause the oil flow to slow down."

Raja beamed on the other end. He could read between the lines.

"It would be rather unfortunate if that happened. Especially if it took time to fix those issues."

"Naturally."

"When can I expect the first volumes of oil?"

"As soon as I have your signature on the paperwork. Have your aide send it over."

"You'll have it within the hour. Thank you, Vahid."

As Raja clicked off, Avesta rested the phone on his shoulder. A smile spread across his face, so wide that it would have made a man with a hundred virgins feel jealous. The Supreme Leader was a genius with unparalleled vision. Under his leadership, Iran would become the mega power of the Middle East.

We will crush Israel and America, once and for all.

After putting the phone back on the receiver, Avesta peeked out the door for his aide and motioned him over.

"Yes, sir?"

"I want you to contact the Supreme Leader's assistant as soon as morning prayers are concluded. I need to meet with the Ayatollah as soon as possible."

Chapter Twenty-Six

ISLAMABAD, PAKISTAN

Dub remained by Jenkins's hospital bed. Griffin had been kind enough to take turns with him long enough that he could get some sleep, but he was adamant about logging whatever hours it took. But the time was weighing on him. It wasn't in his nature to sit still. He needed to be out in the field, kicking ass and finding answers, which he certainly couldn't do sitting in a chair.

His concern for Jenkins was growing. The doctors had placed her in a medically induced coma to help relieve pressure on her brain. By all accounts, they should've been able to bring her back to consciousness by now, but the swelling in her head was not subsiding as quickly as they hoped. It was gut wrenching to see Jenkins comatose with such a pale complexion and tubes and IV's sticking out of her. Dub knew that he could spare himself some of the agony by asking one of the others from the safe house to take an additional shift, but Jenkins had always been loyal to her agents and he felt he owed her nothing less in return.

As he was thumbing through his text messages and emails, Dub's weariness was taking a toll on him. His eyelids felt like massive bags of wet sand that were steadily drooping shut. He could feel himself floating over the edge of consciousness when a vibration from his pocket startled him awake. Dub's eyes darted back and forth across the room to ensure that no one had slipped by him and then he checked on Jenkins, who hadn't budged. When his pocket buzzed again, he realized that it wasn't his phone; it was Jenkins's. The call was coming into her secure line, but the caller ID indicated an 828 area code and wasn't one of her main contacts. Dub debated answering it, but anyone who had the number to her secure line had to be someone important, so he flipped the switch for the secure line and answered it.

"Hello?"

The person on the other end wavered as if they didn't expect a man to answer.

"I'm looking for Raven."

The voice sounded familiar, but Dub couldn't quite place it. Definitely American, though.

"Identify yourself."

"This is *Merlin*. Do you know who I am?"

Delang cited his code name. Dub had met him on two prior occasions, but never had the pleasure of working with the legendary agent.

"I do. This is *Sandpiper*. Our lady friend has introduced us a couple of times in Langley. Most everyone calls me Dub. Ring any bells?"

"Your father is Korean, right?"

"Affirmative."

"Yes, of course, I remember you."

Delang was relieved to be talking to a fellow company man.

"Where's Beth?"

"Tom, I don't know what kind of deserted island you've been on for the last few days, but a lot of shit has gone down."

Dub proceeded to fill Delang in on everything that had happened at the embassy as well as Jenkins's condition. Delang then updated Dub about his mountain experience.

"What are the doctors telling you?" Delang asked.

"Not much, but I don't think there's much they can say at this point. Until the swelling in her head goes down, it's safer for her to stay in a medically induced coma."

"What about the connection to the bomber?"

"Thrasher was trying to nail that down, but then he got stuck in that shitstorm over in India. But, Tom, the bomber received a call from a Tehran phone number shortly before he launched the RPG at the embassy."

"Something doesn't fit. If Iran wanted to bomb the embassy, the whole point of doing it would be for us to know they did it. Then, these bombs go off in India, which wipes the embassy story off the headlines. At the least, Iran should be shouting from the water tower so that their headline isn't forgotten, but they haven't said a peep. This whole thing doesn't pass the litmus test."

"How so?"

"The Pakistani soldier that they caught on tape stealing the C-4 and planting in the India offices, Hasan Wasim, I know that kid's family. I used to do business with his uncle, Izad Hyat."

"Wait. Izad Hyat? He was the guy that met with Beth before the RPG hit the building."

"You're sure?"

"Well, I wasn't there to witness it, but that's what another colleague told me."

"This is too much of a coincidence, Dub. I may not be well acquainted with this Hasan kid, but I'm telling you that his uncle Izad was as much of a stand-up guy from ISI as you're going to run into. Is it possible his nephew went rogue? Yes. But do I believe it? No."

"Whaddya wanna do?"

"Where's Thrasher?"

"I haven't heard from him in a while, but last I checked, he was in Mumbai with one of his so-called buddies from IIB."

"His 'so-called' buddies?"

"You know him. He has a unique way of making friends."

"Right. Well, I'm not in position to tell you what to do, but if I were you, I would be getting on the phone to Langley and making arrangements for Thrasher to get his ass inside Iran ASAP and find out what the hell is going on."

"What makes you think Iran is involved in this?"

"They came after me, didn't they? We may not have much to go on at this point, but if we don't get someone on the ground, pronto, we're gonna be too far behind the eight ball to ever figure any of this out."

"Good point. I'll see what I can do, but I've gotta stay here and keep an eye on the boss. What about you?"

"As far as the Iranians know, I'm dead, and I'd like to keep it that way. I'll have to do some digging on my end to see what I can find. In the meantime, do you mind keeping me up to speed with any intel you receive on your end?"

"You got it."

"Sounds good, thanks. But, Dub, one more thing."

"What's that?"

"If it was Iran that came after me a second time, then it's not a far stretch for them to come after Beth again, too. Keep your eyes open and stay locked and loaded."

"Way ahead of you."

Dub double checked the magazine in his Sig Sauer P226 9mm from his belt and slammed it back in. Just as he put Beth's phone on his belt, Dub's own rang. He rolled his eyes at the annoyance until he saw that it was a Tehran phone number.

"Yes?"

"Is she still alive?" the voice said.

Dub drew a short breath and sat straight up. He recognized the voice immediately.

"You know better than to call me at this number. Don't contact me again."

He hung up.

Chapter Twenty-Seven

QOM, IRAN

The official residence and workplace of the Supreme Leader of Iran is located in the heart of downtown Tehran, only four miles from Azadi Tower. For security purposes, it is walled off from the street, but the structure is nothing special. If it weren't for the Revolutionary Guardsman patrolling the perimeter, the bland and humble two-story building would be easy to miss. The only formal acknowledgement indicating that the most powerful man in the country inhabited the dwelling was a gold plaque outside the main gate, which read *House of Leadership for the Supreme Leader of the Islamic Republic of Iran*.

Each of Shir-Del's predecessors spent most of their time inside the building either doing what needed to be done in various capacities or praying in the courtyard outside, which was filled with Black Alder and Persian Ironwood trees. While no one would dare argue with the Supreme Leader if he decided to sleep or conduct business anywhere he chose, they traditionally left the grounds only when called upon to do so. This served two purposes: it gave them the homefield advantage on anyone that wanted to see them and protected them from assassination against any Mossad agents who found their way inside the country's borders.

In keeping with tradition, Ayatollah Shir-Del intended to conduct the majority of his business at the House of Leadership as there was no point in upsetting the norm. However, he found the building's design and lack of décor too boring for his taste. Most of the rooms consisted of nothing more than carpets with four walls, prayer rugs, a few windows, and the occasional picture of Ayatollah Khomeini to remind those inside who their government was built to represent. Shir-Del wasn't a naturally opulent man but he considered himself to have a high degree of taste for architecture. He'd spent years perfecting his home in Qom to appear stylish but not overly extravagant on the outside, and highly elegant on the inside. The slight echo of his feet traipsing across the red, chestnut-stained hardwood floor, and through the three-pointed archways project-ed the sounds of a leader consistently on his march for destiny.

His favorite room in the house was his library, modeled after the Ab-bey Library of Saint Gall in St. Gallen, Switzerland. The room was filled with wall-to-ceiling books, supported by mahogany shelves that were only broken up by a walkway on the second floor or the occasional painting that had been purchased on the black market.

One of those paintings was Rembrandt's only seascape, *The Storm on the Sea of Galilee,* which had originally been stolen in 1990 from the Isabella Steward Gardner Museum in Boston. It was estimated to be worth $100 million. Even the ceiling was artistically painted with replicas of famous Persian artwork, surrounded by lush borders. The entire room cost him a crisp two million to build, which he conveniently siphoned from one of the Revolutionary Guard accounts that was put together from the drug and sex trafficking trade along the border with Iraq.

Shir-Del treasured the time in his library. He basked in each moment he could spend inside it, like a man feeling the warm sun on his skin after a lifetime of darkness. It was not only his sanctuary for quiet time to think, pray, and reflect. It contained his most coveted possessions from Iran's rich history. For this reason, few knew that the room even existed and even fewer had been allowed inside.

This would have to change, though. As the newly appointed Su-preme Leader, Shir-Del knew that he was entitled to his own secrets, but if he was determined to continue to spend portions of his time in the library, he would have to make the sacrifice of trusting a select few of the country's leadership inside his personal temple. Reluctantly, but necessarily, he had to increase the size of his inner circle.

He was sitting in his favorite club chair toward the rear of the room, watching news footage of the raging war between India and Pakistan on his eighty-inch, flat screen TV. He felt more invigorated than a child bouncing on his first trampoline. This euphoria, though, had the downside of increasing his blood pressure, which ultimately led him to break out into a series of blotchy, brown skin rashes, and irritated his optic nerve. Given that he wanted to relish in the war he'd created, his visual impairment couldn't be tolerated. Since he had used all of his medicine, he called his private doctor, who no one knew about except his house servant and wife, and instructed him to come over immediately. The cramping in his retina was morphing into a piercing headache when he heard the welcome knock at the library's oversized wooden door.

"Get in here!"

His doctor, Shahid Aslam, scampered across the floor with his medical bag in tow.

"I'm sorry, Supreme Leader, I got here as fast as I could."

The doctor knelt beside his patient and pulled the vile of Carbamazepine from his bag and stabbed it with the syringe.

"No excuses! Do you know how much I've been suffering while I've been sitting here waiting for you? Hurry up and give me the shot before I decide you're no longer needed."

Shir-Del pulled up his sleeve and extended the underside of his forearm.

Dr. Aslam dared not make another comment. In his current condition, the Supreme Leader's outbursts could get worse and he could become violent. As he plucked the bubbles out of the syringe, he had no doubt that the man would make good on his word to kill him if he didn't get the medicine into his system right away. With the smack of two fingers on his patient's forearm, he slid the needle into the pronounced vein and depressed the plunger. The Supreme Leader's eyes rolled back into his head as he felt the drug swimming through his bloodstream. When Shir-Del let out a subtle moan of relief, the doctor relaxed as he pulled out the needle.

"Feeling better now, Supreme Leader?"

"Much."

"I'm relieved to hear that. Do you need anything else?"

Shir-Del gave the doctor a look of contempt before backhanding him across the side of the face. After falling on his backside, the doctor put his hands up in defense.

"Don't you *ever* make me wait that long again. For twenty minutes, I sat here waiting for you, unable to see properly. You need to move your family closer to my house. I'm not going to endure that experience again."

"But, Supreme Leader, I can't afford to live in this area. I can barely afford the place we have. And I'm working the extra hours you want me to at the Hashemabad Air Base with Captain Yazdani. It's . . ."

Shir-Del stood from his chair and wasted no time kicking the man in the stomach.

"Consider that notification of your raise. The next time we see each other you'd better be prepared to tell me that you found a place no more than five minutes away. I will handle Captain Yazdani, but don't you ever mention him or his work in this room again!"

"Yes, Supreme Leader."

Dr. Aslam persisted with his hacking cough on the bare floor.

Before Shir-Del could threaten his doctor further, his phone on a nearby table rang. It was his house servant, Emran. His guests had arrived earlier than expected.

"Wait a moment for the doctor to leave and then send them in," he replied.

Shir-Del turned back to the doctor.

"Be sure to leave me a spare vial and a few syringes. I don't want to be caught without my medicine and have to wait for you ever again."

"Yes, Supreme Leader."

"Now, get out of here. Leave the vial and syringes with Emran on your way out. Then, take the door leading outside to the courtyard and don't you dare let anyone see you."

"Yes, Supreme Leader."

The doctor collected the belongings that had spilled from his bag and walked hunched over to the door. Moments later, the heavy oak door to the library moaned open and President Avesta and General Lajani walked towards their leader with roaming eyes.

"Gentleman, thank you for coming on such short notice."

Lajani smiled.

Like we had a choice.

On the top shelf of one of the bookcases was a human skull that he had no doubt belonged to Rahim Shirazi. It confirmed what he feared. The Supreme Leader was serious about handing out punishment for failure.

"Supreme Leader, this room is quite amazing. When did you build this?" Lajani said.

"Many years ago. And I'm glad you like it. There's something that I want to show both of you. Come."

Shir-Del walked the two men toward the center of the room where they stood between two bookshelves stacked with his most cherished collection.

"Part one of my plan is going well, wouldn't you agree?"

He motioned his head towards the news coverage of the India-Pakistan war.

"Yes, Supreme Leader," said both men.

"Good. Now, it's time to make you aware of phase two. Vahid, would you mind grabbing that purple box from the shelf to your right. Be careful as you open it. Its contents are fragile."

Avesta did as asked. The box was book-like but not a book itself. Rather, the edge of its cover served as a magnetic seal. When he saw the contents inside, his eyes bulged like saucers. He looked at Lajani, whose curiosity demanded that he join the president at his side.

"Is this real?" Lajani whispered.

Avesta slowly nodded.

"I thought this had been destroyed, Supreme Leader."

"Hardly. My father saw to it that it was kept in a safe place."

Shir-Del couldn't help but pick up the framed, autographed picture of Hitler from the protected box and held it in front of them to savor.

The inscription read: *His Imperial Majesty- Reza Shah Pahlavi- Shahanshah of Iran- Best Wishes, Adolf Hitler- Berlin 12 March 1936.*

"Forgive me, Supreme Leader, but I thought all traces of the Shah were to be removed from our country's great history," Avesta said.

"Many of them were, and for good reason, but the Shah is irrelevant to my point. The section of books surrounding you are twenty-five hundred volumes of literature, pro-Nazi publications, speeches, and lectures detailing the kinship of Iran and Nazi Germany prior to its demise. The rest of the world is totally unaware that these documents exist. I have spent my entire adult life studying them and preparing for this moment."

"What moment is that Supreme Leader?" Lajani asked.

"First, we must look at the greatness of Hitler-Shah. His vision to eradicate the Jews from this planet was a bold one: one that had never been dared to be implemented before his time. Others before him had thought of it, but Hitler-Shah was most courageous to try. Unfortunately, his ego consumed him. He tried to make Germany do too much on its own. As powerful and mighty as his military was, to think that it could fight a two-front war against the Americans and Europe in the west and the Soviets in the east was absurd. We all know how it turned out. To succeed, one needs friends to battle alongside you."

"Hitler had Mussolini fighting alongside him, Supreme Leader," Lajani said.

Shir-Del glared at Lajani in contempt. He hated being interrupted.

"Mussolini was a fool and Italy's army was weak. Those aren't the types of friends I'm talking about."

"Okay," Lajani said.

"We are going to take the lessons of the Nazi past and apply them logically to our current time. Vahid, does the oil on the Peace Pipeline continue to flow to our friends in India and Pakistan?"

"Yes, Supreme Leader."

"And how many barrels of oil per day are we producing for them? Both countries combined."

"We can produce roughly six million barrels per day."

"Which equates to how much?"

"At the current rate, estimated sales are between three and four hundred million per day."

"Excellent. You are to let the war between India and Pakistan continue for at least a week, but in the meantime, you will begin mediating the truce between the two. Be sure to take your time about it, though."

"Truce? Supreme Leader, shouldn't we let it go on for as long as possible to reap the profits of the oil sales?" Avesta asked.

Shir-Del placed his hands behind his back, and slowly nodded.

"You're thinking like Hitler-Shah, Vahid. You're not thinking long-term. Never get too greedy. It leads to desperation and desperate men make careless mistakes. You must remember that the language of the oil deal on the Peace Pipeline stays in place no matter what, correct?"

"Yes, Supreme Leader," Avesta said.

"Then we have nothing to worry about with regards to our economic sanctions that the pigheaded Americans have placed on us. Some are still there, but the money from the flowing oil not only gives us options; it has started to crack the glass ceiling. By being the country that mediates the truce between India and Pakistan, it projects a different image of Iran. The world will think Iran has become a country of peace under my new rule. Discreetly, though, we will be taking a page out of the west's playbook."

"How so?" Lajani asked.

His curiosity had piqued.

"Article five of NATO indicates that an attack on any one of the members is an attack on them all. This agreement was designed to keep Russia at bay during the Cold War but was invoked after 9/11. I propose we form a similar coalition with our other friends in the region, such as Syria, Yemen, Libya, Lebanon, and Pakistan. I want Oman and Iraq to join as well but convincing them to join will be difficult. For now, we stick with those five countries and expand from there."

"A coalition to do what?"

"For years, the Jewish swine have fought an underground war against our Islamic brothers with car bombings, assassinations, and thwarting our attempts to acquire a nuclear arsenal. Our fight against our Sunni friends will never diminish, but for sake of all of our security against the Jews, we must take the bold step of putting those issues aside during matters of national security. This new coalition will propose that any attack by Israel on any of our members will be an attack against us all. Once any attack occurs, and I'm certain it will, we can dismantle the Jewish state once and for all and let our Muslim brothers rightfully reclaim their holy land."

A wicked grin crept onto Avesta's face. His Supreme Leader continued to amaze him.

"What if the Jews use their nukes against us, Supreme Leader?"

"That's why Pakistan will play a key role in the coalition. Should that occur, the terms of their membership will dictate that they are forced to share their nuclear arsenal."

"What about India? What role will they play?"

"Unfortunately, India and Israel have too close of a relationship. Israel supplies India with too many weapons, which is why they'll win this war against Pakistan sooner than later. It's also why we must broker a truce before events transpire that cause our Pakistani friends too much damage. As for India, we got what we needed from them. The oil flows."

"Supreme Leader, your plan is divine. Allah will most certainly reward you."

"Not just me, Vahid. Allah will reward Iran, and we will steadily become the most powerful country in the region. Before Hitler-Shah used the swastika as the symbol of his Nazi regime, it was a symbol of good fortune in our region of the world. But we can't rely on the element of chance or wait for good fortune to be bestowed upon us. Now is the time for us to make our own luck."

As Shir-Del, Avesta, and Lajani shook hands, Dr. Aslam absorbed what he'd overheard and tip-toed away from the outside door and off the property without being discovered.

Chapter Twenty-Eight

U.S. CONSULATE
MUMBAI, INDIA

Thrasher was aggravated to the point of squeezing the dried gel out of his spikey hair. The embassy in Pakistan had been attacked, his boss was in a coma, and India and Pakistan were at war. He knew that all of this was connected but couldn't make his brain connect the dots.

After escaping the building in downtown Mumbai, he and Dhoni removed the C-4 from the office plant, and headed to one of the IIB's satellite offices on the outskirts of the city. It didn't take long for the IIB analysts to determine that the C-4 originated in Pakistan. Upon hearing the news, logic went out the window, and burning emotion overtook every IIB agent in the room. Pakistan had stepped over the line, and they would pay for it.

Thrasher tried pleading with them not to jump to any conclusions, that something didn't feel right, especially since there were plants with C-4 that hadn't exploded in the other office buildings. It was as if someone had deliberately sabotaged some of the devices to prevent damage. But his theory only made matters worse. Since many of them had experienced family losses at the hands of the Pakistani military, their displeasure for Pakistan was strong. Thrasher quickly matched those emotions with his own, and didn't hesitate to step into someone's face. It became a seven-on-one shouting match before Dhoni hooked him by the arm and escorted him out of the building. Once outside, Thrasher jerked his arm away, and was ready to throw a punch at Dhoni when the agent surprised him.

"I'm not saying you're right, but these bombings don't scream Pakistan to me. It's too cute for their taste. Let me know if you find anything."

Thrasher nodded. Dhoni may be a pain in the ass, but he wasn't an idiot.

When he reached the consulate, he went straight to the station chief's office. Kathy Petal was of Indian origin but born in Virginia. Her adopted father was a career navy man, so the idea of government service rubbed off on her with ease. She joined the CIA two years after Jenkins, and the two created a strong bond together after working an op in Islamabad, where they successfully tracked down an American who was recruiting for ISIS.

Jenkins had wanted to have one of the special operatives find a way for him to meet his maker when he arrived home, but Patel's more gentle nature found a way to sabotage the man's car so that it broke down on the highway, which allowed CIA personnel to gobble him up and take him back to the States for prosecution.

Her solution wasn't the CIA's organic way of doing things, but Jenkins knew that she was right, and earned her respect immediately. She and Patel kept in touch and the two always made an effort to have breakfast together whenever possible. Patel had heard of Thrasher's antics and did her best to prepare for the man, but he made his usual unwelcome impression when he burst into her office without so much as a knock or a hello.

"You know Beth, right?"

"Let me guess. You're Thrasher."

"Congratulations, you've earned yourself a prize. Did you hear what happened to her?"

Patel emerged from behind her desk to close the door.

"Sit," she said.

She pointed to the seat in front of her desk.

Thrasher crinkled his lips. He knew that the standard dressing down was coming. Patel chose the authoritative position of standing over him.

"Beth was right about your personality."

"Did she also tell you how lethal I can be when provoked?"

"You can cut the rottweiler act, Thrasher. We're on the same side, but I'm not gonna let you throw your weight around my office."

Thrasher stood. His six-foot-two frame towered over Patel's five-foot-five, but she didn't back down.

"Look, I don't have time for this. Beth's in a coma, and she's there because I didn't get to the embassy in time. If you're the friend that she says you are, then I need an office with a computer so I can hook up my people."

Patel exhaled, obviously annoyed.

"My second in command is on vacation in Sicily. You can use his office. Down the hall. Second door on the right. But let's you and I get off on the right foot, okay?"

Patel formally extended her hand to shake Thrasher's. He accepted it with a nod.

From the unoccupied office, Thrasher logged into the CIA's remote secure server and pulled out his phone to call Dub and Griffin, but he didn't recognize the phone in his hand. The screen was cracked to shit, and its casing was different but otherwise looked intact. When he reached back into his cargo pants pocket, he retrieved his. He had two phones.

Where did I get another phone?

Then he remembered. As he carried the plant containing the C-4 from the office building, he'd fallen. There was a phone on the ground that he'd thought was his but wasn't. So, who did it belong to?

After borrowing the correct charging cord from Patel, Thrasher connected it and impatiently waited for it to recharge. With each passing second, he tapped his finger more forcefully on the desk. When he couldn't wait any longer, he tried to turn the phone on. But because it was passcode protected, and he didn't know who it belonged to, he was forced to sync the phone with his computer and call Dub for assistance. Thanks to his expertise in cracking into electronics, the hack took only thirty minutes.

Because the screen was so cracked, he couldn't make out much, so he transferred everything from the camera roll to the computer's hard drive. The last entry was a video. It appeared to be a kid starting a new job and documented his first day in the building. At first, he found nothing of substance. But his instincts told him to replay it. He found what he was looking for on the third playback. At the start of the video, there was a van in the background with four people exiting. When the kid came into the building to talk with the security officer, he saw them again. They were bringing in office plants.

Bingo.

Whoever this kid was, Thrasher was going to send some money to his family because his video may have just given him the lead he desperately needed.

He called Griffin and sent her a copy. From her side, she isolated and enhanced the faces of the workers who were bringing in the office plants. It took her less than an hour to run their faces against the agency's recognition software and ping him back. One belonged to the Pakistani soldier who stole the C-4 from the base in Karachi. Either this guy went rogue to start his own little war or IIB was right, and Pakistan had crossed a fine line. Two of the men he didn't recognize. Griffin needed to do some more digging because the software didn't find a match. The fourth and final man, though, Thrasher knew as soon as he saw his enhanced picture. His unibrow was unforgettable.

"Son-of-a-bitch."

Mahmoud Yazdani. Farhad was right. The Iranians *were* involved.

Thrasher's moment of shock was interrupted when his phone rang. It was Dub.

"Whatcha got for me?"

Dub sighed on the other end.

Can't this guy ever say hello?

He told Thrasher of Delang's phone call and his doubts about the soldier's guilt in the bombings. Once he was finished, Thrasher texted him a picture of Yazdani.

"Looks like the Iranians have their fingers in a lot of pies," Dub said.

"Yeah, well, one of them better be humble pie because I'm gonna nail someone's ass to the fucking wall!"

"Be sure to call me before you do because I want a piece of the action."

"Count on it, but there's another call I have to make first. I'll get back to you."

Thrasher hung up without saying goodbye and flipped to another number on his contact list. It was about to kick to voice mail when the recipient picked up.

"You got something?" agent Dhori asked.

"You're gonna love me forever when I give it to you."

"Hmph. I doubt that. What is it?"

"There's a van you need to track down."

Chapter Twenty-Nine

THE WHITE HOUSE
A WEEK LATER

A visibly infuriated President Cannon was watching a press conference on Al-Jazeera. The staff in the room knew to stay a safe distance away. Whatever blow-up the usually mild-mannered president was about to have, none of them wanted to be first in the line of fire. The intelligence agencies had their heads on the chopping block.

The CEO's from Microsoft, GE, JP Morgan, Bank of America, and Cisco, who usually enjoyed a chummy relationship with the president, weren't so friendly at the moment. They were freaked out, pissed off, and continued to ring the president's phone off the hook. Their buildings in Mumbai and Pune were so badly damaged by the bombs that no one could return to work. With civilian dwellings being targeted, construction crews were more eager to collect hazard pay during the country's declared state of emergency than they were about working at the companies' alternate sites.

The limited staff in India who remembered to take their laptops on their way out of the buildings were constrained by their inability to either find a network connection or accomplish an ever-increasing number of tasks. Service centers that weren't directly affected by the bombings were ordered to work from home, which decreased productivity due to network issues.

Sharma had also suspended all flights in and out of India, so the companies couldn't send any tech support into the country to assist with network connections. The CEO's had their local U.S. offices hiring temps off the street to assist with the backlog, but the results were microscopic at best. Their customers weren't getting the assistance they needed, and their vendors weren't getting paid.

Adding insult to injury, Iran had slithered its way out of the shadows and into the limelight by managing to play the role of peacekeeper between India and Pakistan. The country that had for decades shouted from the mountain tops about wiping Israel off the map and ridding the world of America's iron hand was now being seen as a country that had turned the corner on its diplomatic agenda under the regime of the new Supreme Leader.

The nauseating image of a beaming President Avesta, standing between Presidents Raja and Sharma, with his arms wrapped around their shoulders, was going viral. Those in the world who knew nothing about geopolitics (but thought they did) were claiming that it was a new era for Iran. Governments that knew all too well what Iran was capable of but had no balls to say otherwise would ride this wave of positivity, and find it in their hearts to renegotiate their terms of the economic sanctions against them. And although Cannon hadn't spoken to him in a few days, he felt that the prime minister of Israel was meeting with his defense staff to discuss offensive scenarios should the western world come to Iran's side.

Israel wasn't alone in their concerns. The leaders of Egypt, India, Jordan, and the United Arab Emirates were also tugging at his coat tail. From their perspective, America was being seen as a clumsy, bumbling fool for never having seen this coming. For the rest of the viewing public, America was seen as a power that was irrelevant in the Middle East that shouldn't butt its oversized nose into the business of the Muslim world. Unfortunately for Cannon, it was all happening on his watch.

Without diverting his eyes from the screen, Cannon motioned for his chief of staff, Ryleigh Tibbetts, to join him. Trying not to look nervous, she pulled her dirty blonde hair into a ponytail, but approached with caution.

"Yes, Mr. President?"

"I'm not seeing anything about the attack on our embassy in Pakistan. Why?"

"Sir, the press sees it as old news. It'll still get coverage, but on the back page. The raging war between India and Pakistan suffocated the story enough as it was."

"How's that possible? A week ago, Iran was in our cross hairs about being behind the bombing. We even got them to the point where they issued a denial."

"Yes, sir, but nothing stuck, and there was no additional evidence. To the media, with Iran playing the successful mediator, those claims are substantiated. Iran's role in these accords is butter for them."

"So, how do we play this?"

"Sir, my advice is to not respond, and certainly not provoke the situation until we have evidence to the contrary indicating Iran's role. Otherwise, the media is going to ride this train for weeks."

Cannon covered his eyes.

"I don't believe this," he said.

The president eyed the rest of his staff, but the person he was specifically looking for wasn't there. Instead, he stared at his number two in command, Jeremy Molinar, the CIA's Deputy Director, which signaled him to approach the president.

"What about your agent in the coma?" Cannon said. "Any word?"

"She's still out of commission."

"Where's Henry?" he asked, speaking of CIA Director Henry Wallace.

"He stayed at Langley. One of the agents has caught a scent and is following it."

"Yeah, well, I smell something, too. *Bullshit!*"

The president's outburst startled everyone in the room. All of their shoulders hopped up. Despite being a good five inches taller than the president, even Molinar took a step backward.

"I need *something*, Jeremy. I don't care if it's a theory or not. I'll be hung up by my thumbs before I let Iran toss us aside like a rag doll on the international stage for everyone to watch! No one with half a brain who knows anything about Iran can possibly believe that they're a peacekeeper. Yet, look at *this*."

Cannon pointed at the image of Iran's president, standing gleefully between his counterparts in Pakistan and India.

"This image will be burned into the minds of millions across the world. It doesn't matter if it's not true. I know damned well that they've got something up their sleeve, and I'm not going to bluff at the table. We're gonna beat them at their own game, but I *have* to know what cards they're holding."

Molinar hesitated. His twenty-year experience of walking the high wire act between intelligence and politicians told him that he needed more information before he told the president what he wanted to tell him. On the other hand, the president was on point. The CIA had been caught with their pants down once again, but rather than the incident resulting in thousands dying, like on 9/11, the president had been publicly embarrassed. He had to throw the president a bone with a little meat on it.

"Mr. President, one of our agents survived the aftermath of one of the bombings in India, and recovered a piece of evidence that points in Iran's direction."

"Spill it."

"Sir, he recovered a video that showed the Pakistani soldier planting the bomb and a captain in the Revolutionary Guard with him."

"Wait, so Pakistan and Iran are working together against India? Or are you saying that these two characters went rogue and are working together?"

"It's unconfirmed, sir, but the working theory is that the Pakistani soldier caught on camera was set up by Iran, and used as a pawn to start the war between India and Pakistan."

"Why am I just now hearing about this?"

"The evidence is thin at best. All we have is a video of the two of them at one of the GSC offices at the same time. After that, they disappeared. There's nothing to link them to."

The president took a deep breath before he flew off the handle. He could see in Molinar's face that there was more to the story, but the man was unable to explain anymore because he wasn't willing to put his ass on the line for a gut feeling. But sitting idly by and hoping for the best wasn't an option.

"How do you figure the kid's being set up?"

"One of our former agents has a hunch."

"Which agent?"

"Tom Delang, sir."

The president paused. After Delang testified before Congress, Cannon had invited the veteran agent to the White House to welcome him back to the States, and thank him for his service. What was supposed to be a fifteen-minute meeting at the end of the day wound up being an all-night discussion. He found Delang likable, credible, and extremely plugged in to the Middle East.

"Make your request."

"Our best option is to track down the Pakistani soldier. Our analysts are working with Indian intelligence to trace his movements after he left the office building."

Teamwork between intelligence agencies. I like it.

"This agent of ours. The one you said caught a scent. Is he American?"

Molinar nodded. Careful to protect his people, he didn't like discussing his operatives' backgrounds.

"Can I count on him to get the job done? No matter what the cost? Even if it means his own life?"

"Sir, Jaybird may not be the best guest to invite to happy hour, but he's one of our brightest. The idea of letting anyone down sours his guts to the core."

Cannon diverted his eyes back to the TV screen, which was now centered on Vahid Avesta.

"Do what you have to. Pronto."

Chapter Thirty

UNITED ARAB EMIRATES

Though Thrasher's request to come back to IIB was vehemently rejected, Dhoni surprised him by following up on the video footage like a drug sniffing police dog. He called in every favor available to him to cut through bureaucratic red tape, and meticulously pieced together every piece of traffic cam, body cam, and ATM footage to trace the van's movements. As Thrasher predicted, the van made stops at other office buildings with the same catastrophic results. Then, in a smart move, instead of catching a plane in Mumbai or Pune, where the chaos caused authorities to close the city, the van drove north, and entered Surat International Airport.

The thought of Thrasher being right made Dhoni nauseous, but he knew that the man he called a "flagrant jackass" had a sharp radar, so he pulled all twelve flights departing Surat airport for Iran. Narrowing it down wouldn't be easy because the security cameras outside the main terminal were mostly limited to the cargo areas to prevent theft. But Dhoni hit a stroke of luck. When the van pulled into the airport, it headed directly to the hangers reserved for private flights. Per government protocol, all private flights in and out of India are required to be checked in by federal sky marshals, who were also equipped with body cameras. When Dhoni pulled all the body cams, there was one flight bound for Bandar Abbas, where he saw that the passengers were making a conscious effort to hide their faces from the cameras. After the sky marshal cleared them for their flight, one of the passengers tripped and fell into the marshal's arms. The camera got a clear look at his face. It was Pakistani soldier Hasan Wasim.

If Wasim was a pawn, as Thrasher insisted, how did he have a passport ready for his flight? As he replayed the video footage, it appeared to Dhoni that Wasim's "trip" into the sky marshal was blatantly fake. It was like the kid wanted to be seen on camera. If so, Thrasher's theory inched closer to being correct. Dhoni had no choice. Thrasher needed to know.

As soon as he answered, he greeted Dhoni with his usual pleasantries.

"I fucking told you! When are you gonna start listening to me?"

Jackass.

"Your boss called mine. We're going to Iran, together."

Though they used their standard covers, India intelligence officers flying into Iran raised no flags among its customs officers. Americans didn't have the same luxury. United States citizens were allowed to visit Iran only if they were part of a sponsored company with a group visa or the person in question had an authorized chaperone for the duration of their trip. Those chaperones were often undercover agents for the Ministry of Intelligence or the Revolutionary Guard. Neither was an option for a U.S. intelligence official like Thrasher. Americans were watched and followed throughout their trip, and since they were considered enemies of the state, if a CIA agent was exposed, he or she would be held, imprisoned, and tortured. To get around this, Thrasher turned to the recent environmental laws regarding the Persian Gulf.

The Strait of Hormuz is a ninety-mile stretch of water in the Persian Gulf off the coast of Bandar Abbas and the northeast tip of the UAE. In recent years, it has become a boiling point of tension between Iran and its enemies, especially the United States. Iran's navy patrols the Strait like a great white shark protecting its habitat, and has threatened to close the waterway many times during the past few years. Since doing so would threaten the world's oil supply, Iran has bowed to international pressure, but they have put the world on notice that they can hold anyone hostage if they so choose.

Twenty five percent of the global oil supply passes through the Strait of Hormuz each year. Although it is high in resources, the Strait has suffered from a lack of government regulation, which has strained its natural deposits. Overfishing by commercial companies has caused fish stocks to fall to critical levels. More important, traffic from oil tankers and shipping lines has created pollution extending into the Persian Gulf.

Because of the country's sandstorms, naturally low precipitation levels, population growth, and years of environmental mismanagement, Iran's natural lakes have dried up, creating a worsening water crisis. To counteract this, the Iranian government passed a bill to run a pipeline inland from the Strait of Hormuz, and built desalinization plants to get clean water to its people and crops. Given that the Strait of Hormuz is only twenty-one miles wide at its narrowest point, Iran can't afford for it to be polluted.

With few environmental scientists as its disposal, Iran turned to its Arab neighbors for assistance. The first on their call list was the UAE, renowned for its environmental advances, thanks to its embrace of the western world. Twice a month, Iran allows the UAE to send its scientists into the Strait of Hormuz to test the purity of the water, and call in any crews they deem necessary to assist with the cleanup efforts. Iran agreed to split the bill.

This was Thrasher and Dhoni's ticket in. Thrasher posed as a Belgian scientist with Dhoni as his assistant, a role he wasn't happy about, and knew Thrasher did on purpose to be a smartass. UAE scientists on board showed them all the testing procedures that needed to be done so that they could pass as legit should they be questioned by the Iranian navy. They normally departed from the port of Mina Rashid, performed their relevant water tests, and docked at Qeshm Island off the coast of

Bandar Abbas. Because twenty-five percent of Iran's bird population migrates to the island's marine forests, this only enhanced Thrasher's cover as he added ornithology to his scientific resume. After they docked and grabbed a quick bite to eat, the two operatives quietly walked away, never to return to their boat.

With its carved rock formations, Chankooh Canyon served as the perfect location for two would-be tourists who were dying to pose for photos to post on their Instagram accounts. While beautiful in its ancient way, the rock formations made it appear as if giant insects had burrowed into the rock. Thrasher thought that the canyon looked like the inside of a wasp's nest. If they were caught, he wouldn't be far off. With so many sightseers around, it was difficult for Thrasher and Dhoni to converse. The echoes bouncing off the canyon walls added another degree of complication.

They waited impatiently but their contact didn't show.

"I thought you said that this source of yours was reliable," Dhoni said.

"I don't know what to tell you. He said he'd be here."

"We can't wait much longer. If we need to abort, our window to get back to the boat is closing fast. We've already wasted an hour."

"Shut up, he'll be here!"

Thrasher's outburst drew the attention of the others in the canyon. The sightseers looked at each other before walking toward Thrasher and Dhoni, and encircling them. Nervous and surrounded, Dhoni reached for the gun under his vest.

"Wait," Thrasher said.

He placed his hand over Dhoni's.

With the sun to his back, Thrasher's source emerged from the lower part of the canyon, wearing his beloved *Star Wars* t-shirt.

"Sorry we're late, fellas," Farhad said. "Welcome to Iran."

Chapter Thirty-One

ASHEVILLE, NORTH CAROLINA

Delang was starting to go stir crazy. For days, while staying with Kirk and Simin, all he did was take a page from Thrasher's book on impatience. Checking the web and watching the news. Repeat. He couldn't stand not being in the loop about what was happening in the world. Simin felt like she had become his unofficial social media secretary. Unfortunately, none of the sources he used were yielding any desired results. On top of everything, pretending to be dead was a pain in the ass because he couldn't leave the house. He wasn't even supposed to answer the door when his food was delivered for fear that all the recent news coverage might cause him to be recognized.

He kept bouncing so many ideas and thoughts about Iran off of Abby, Kirk, and Simin that they decided to take a break from him, and headed out to Wicked Weed, a local brewery downtown. Not that Delang blamed them. His mind hadn't jumped around with so many "what if" scenarios since he'd first been kidnapped by the Iranians. He thought about calling his Saudi friend, Tariq al-Masari, to get his opinion, but decided that would be pointless. Saudi Arabia wasn't involved in the crisis and there was nothing that Tariq could do.

In one of their recent conversations, he'd told Tariq that bad things happen in the world when good men do nothing. So, sitting idly by wasn't an option for Delang. He had to get back into the game. Somehow. The way to do that was to start with himself.

That's what his father always told him.

"If your house isn't in order, then don't expect to be able to help someone else with theirs."

He needed to continue to lay low, but Delang decided that he had no choice but to alter his plans and call someone who could help him. Since his phone had burned up in the crash, and Abby had taken her phone, Delang picked up the landline but hesitated before he pressed the final number. Diverting from his own protocols was not in his nature. He'd disciplined himself enough over his years as an agent to know that the safeguards he put in place were there for a reason.

After careful consideration, knowing that he had to make an effort to change the situation or it wouldn't get any better, he pressed the final button.

"Highlands Police Department, Sergeant Torres speaking."

"Hey, Cowboy."

In some ways, Miguel Torres was the epitome of a small-town cop. He knew everyone by name, and made it his business to stick his nose in everyone else's business. The ladies at the local hair salon loved him for his chiseled physique and dimpled smile, but even more because he brought them scented candles or flowers once a week. This allowed him to keep up with the town rumors that swirled around the salon, which made his job easier.

Delang met him three years ago when he was a rookie. The young officer instantly impressed him with how dialed in he was to the area. When Delang introduced himself, despite only being in town for a few hours, Torres already knew that he was the man looking to buy the house formerly owned by the Babb family. As they got to know each other, Delang learned that Torres was a diehard Dallas Cowboys fan, and used his nickname whenever they spoke.

"Tom?!"

"Yes, it's me, Cowboy, but keep your voice down."

"Holy hell, man, where are you? What happened?"

"Listen, I can't tell you where I am, but you should know that I'm safe, and that there's a good reason why the news said I was dead. As for what happened, I need your help."

"Sure, you got it. Anything. Name it."

"When I left the Lakeside Restaurant a week ago, someone in a truck was waiting for me, and ran me off the road. But before I got in my car to leave, I noticed that one of your other cops was issuing a parking ticket on Leonard Street. I need you to pull the vehicle footage and the body cam videos from that day, and see if you can get a picture of the driver in the Ford F350."

Torres hesitated.

"Due to all the backlash against the police these days, the chief has been riding us pretty hard about logging evidence in ongoing cases without delay. As you can imagine, we don't get many cases like yours around here. If I log it, it's going to get noticed."

"Delay it for as long as you can. I need everything you can find on that truck."

"You got it. Can I reach you at this number?"

"For now, yes, but don't use it unless you have to. I'll get a burner phone, and send you the number when I can."

"Ten-four. I'll get back to you."

When Torres hung up, Delang didn't know whether he should feel good about the call. Breaking his own rules meant potentially exposing himself, and his wife and friends, too. He should have been patient and waited for them to get back so that he could have used one of their phones. If his enemies were out for the ultimate revenge, the game just reset and was about to be taken to a whole new level.

Frustrated with himself and his situation, Delang tossed the cordless phone aside and turned on the TV. Instead of the news, he chose something mindless to dull his brain and put him at ease. A pop culture channel showed a familiar face under the headline:

FILMMAKER TO HONOR
FALLEN CIA AGENT AND FRIEND

"And now to Los Angeles where Kandice Douglas has the story," host Nicole Yarbrough said.

The screen flipped to a formal interview with Delang's picture and his life history displayed on a dark backdrop. Vik Wheaton sat front and center in a director's chair.

"Mr. Wheaton, from all the reports we received, Tom Delang spent some of his last moments with you. Can you confirm this?"

"Yes, it's true. We were friends for many years, and although I didn't know that he was CIA, he agreed to meet with me to discuss the terms of the movie deal that will depict his terrible ordeal in Iran. When he left that meeting, I was sure I would be speaking with him again soon, but events took a turn for the worse."

"Is it your belief that the Iranians came for him in an act of revenge?"

"There's no doubt in my mind."

"So, when will we see the movie?"

"I'm still working on the screenplay, but in light of the events regarding my friend Tom's death, the studio has decided to fast track it. We'll begin the casting process within the month, and it's my hope that the public gets to see it in theaters before the end of the year."

"Any secrets you can share with us in terms of what to expect?"

"Tom Delang was a hero. More importantly, he was my friend. And I intend to make a film that reflects that."

Wheaton turned his eyes directly to the camera. He had a cryptic grin on his face.

"Friends look out for one another."

Delang turned off the TV. In all of the commotion about the embassy, India, and pretending to stay dead, his movie deal with Wheaton wasn't even on his radar. Had his meeting with Vik been a setup? His death would definitely hype the movie and return Wheaton back to his Hollywood glory. Delang rubbed the grey stubble on his chin, but his thoughts were interrupted by an incoming phone call. Seeing that it was Kirk, he picked up.

"Hello?"

"Hey, we're getting ready to head back. You want anything? I remembered you saying that you like the sour craft beers."

"Sure, grab what you think is good. But I have another favor to ask you. It's a big one."

"Shoot."

"Ever been to Los Angeles?"

Chapter Thirty-Two

At a hotel down the street from the Biltmore Estate, Ward, listening on the other end, was blindsided by what he'd just heard. It was only the second time in his fifteen-year career that he'd failed a client. He was enraged at himself for not paying closer attention to detail.

He called Chang to give her the bad news. She flat-out refused to call the third party. It was his screw up, so he could be the one to deliver the bad news. When she told him who it was, his oversized gut dropped through his shoes. Few people intimidated Ward, but this wasn't the usual Hollywood slimeball who liked to appear like a tiger but had paper claws. Former Senator Vivian Walsh had some serious teeth and knew how to use them. Regretfully, he had to let her know about this development. He banged his fist against the wall before dialing the number.

"Yes?"

"There's a problem and there's not just one."

At her request, after running Delang off the road, Ward had switched cars and headed to Asheville where he was supposed to bug Kurruthers's entire house, hoping to learn his routine so it would be easier to bump him off. Unfortunately, his girlfriend came home earlier than expected and interrupted the job. He managed to sneak out undetected, but was only able to bug the land line. The plan was to go back in the next day, but each time he did, someone was home. This had been the case for the last week. Whether he liked it or not, the bug planted in the landline was his only lifeline to what was going on inside the house.

The good news was that the bug finally yielded some results. The bad news was the results were shitty. Ward proceeded to inform Walsh that Delang was not only alive and well but was sniffing around the movie deal. Anything he found out would lead directly back to her.

"You're paid to eliminate problems. Not create them."

"I'll clean this up."

"You damn well better or going back to selling real estate in the suburbs will be the least of your problems!"

"Don't worry. There's an opportunity here I can't miss."

"Which is?"

"Delang is sending Kurruthers to L.A. to talk with Wheaton. At that meeting, I'll kill them both. Do you have a problem with that?"

"No. Lisa will find another director. Do it. And when you're finished, be sure to get your ass back to North Carolina, and finish Delang. No slip ups this time. Oh, and I'm cutting your fee."

"Excuse me?"

"I'm not paying you to fuck up. Clean this up and do it right this time. Or else the next mess that gets cleaned up will be your own."

Chapter Thirty-Three

OUTSIDE ISFAHAN, IRAN

While Dhoni offered up a pleasant greeting, in typical fashion, Thrasher was all business when Farhad and his PMOI colleagues picked them up from Bandar Abbas though he did at least say hello.

"I hope you have something for me," he said.

"We have a lead on Mahmoud's whereabouts, and we think he has the Pakistani soldier with him," said Farhad.

"How good of a lead is it?"

"At the moment, it's the only one we have."

"So, where are we headed?"

"Isfahan."

"The info better be worth the trip."

Thrasher made a beeline for the car.

"Is he always like this?" Farhad asked.

"I don't think he has another gear," Dhoni replied.

From Bandar Abbas, Isfahan is an eleven to twelve-hour drive, depending on traffic. Thrasher, impatient as ever, wanted to commandeer Farhad's car, but knew better. In his travels across the world, none of his orders called for him to go into Iran, so he knew nothing about how often or where the Revolutionary Guard had a tendency to set up roadblocks to harass travelers and line their own pockets or to perform inspections for fear of spies. Whether he liked it or not, Farhad was the lead dog in the pack, at least for now.

After they stopped for a restroom break at the Izad Khast Castle, their newly found PMOI colleagues made fun of Thrasher and Dhoni standing guard behind while the other peed. Operations officers in the field were trained to never have their backs turned while urinating in public. Without a fellow colleague watching over them, it provided an opportunity for an enemy to sneak up behind them for a kill.

Though he could have made an issue of Farhad's slow driving, Thrasher decided that it wasn't worth it. His recent country hopping had taken a toll on him, and he needed some shut eye.

"Keep an eye out. And don't shoot me in my sleep," he said.

"Don't tease me," Dhoni said.

It was an hour past sunset when a large pothole made the car lurch, which woke up Thrasher, and allowed him to catch a glimpse of a lavish scene outside his window.

"Stop the car."

"What? We're almost there."

"I wanna stretch my legs. Stop the car."

Farhad pulled over. Thrasher opened the door and was in mid-stride before the car came to a complete stop. He lit a cigarette and offered one to Farhad, which he accepted.

"What is that?"

Thrasher pointed to a bridge in the distance.

"That's the Si-o-se-pol bridge. It was built during the Safavid Empire in the seventeenth century, I think. It used to connect some of the old mansions, but those are gone now. Now, we mostly use it as a place to hang out. The parties there keep me in the booze running business because everyone there brings their own. But we can't get too rowdy, or the Revolutionary Guard will show up."

"I love the way all of the arches below light up and twinkle against the ripples in the river."

Farhad raised an eyebrow at Thrasher. He couldn't figure this guy out. One minute, his rude personality was barking orders, and the next it seemed like he had a soft side for appreciating the finer aspects in life.

"It's not all camels and sand here, ya know."

Thrasher glared at Farhad as he exhaled. The trail of smoke flowed into the crisp night air.

"That's not what I was saying. I just didn't realize that some of the architecture here was so beautiful. Don't you know a compliment when you hear it?"

Farhad paused. Jaybird may be naturally coarse, but he should've taken the compliment.

"Well, if you like that then you're gonna love where our next meeting takes place. You ready to roll?"

"Let me finish this and enjoy the view for a minute. R&R doesn't come easy for me."

"Okay. So, what's your story?"

"My story?"

"Yeah. How did you get into the agency?"

Thrasher debated answering this question. He knew never to discuss his bona fide personal background to any source in the field because it was a good way for him and anyone he cared about to end up dead. During his time in the doghouse, Delang had taught him to be more guided by his gut on this issue. Certainly, he shouldn't go baring his soul to complete strangers. That would be stupid. But Delang made his bones in the field by making and keeping friends he could depend on. Thrasher was quick to remind him that such a philosophy is what ended up getting him ratted out by one of his so-called trusted friends.

"Nothing's guaranteed in this business. All we have is what's in front of us today, and we're all defined by our judgment calls in the field," Delang said.

As he twisted out his butt on the ground, Thrasher looked around to see how many of the other dozen PMOI colleagues were close enough to hear him.

"Let's take a walk," Thrasher said.

As they walked further away from the others, it occurred to Thrasher that the rocks crumpling beneath their feet were symbolic of the grinding decision of whether or not he should share what was on his mind. When they were far enough out of earshot, Thrasher ultimately decided to establish some trust with Farhad, and tell the tale of how his career began with an innocent trip to the Black Hills of South Dakota to see the famous American landmark. After all, if Tom Delang trusted this kid then so could he.

"I guess our stories aren't all that different," Farhad replied.

He explained the original email from Kirk Kurruthers that set him on his current path. "We both answered the door when destiny came knocking."

"I don't know about destiny, but I guess we were both in the right place at the right time."

Thrasher let the words hang in the air as they stared at the stone elegance of the Si-o-se-pol bridge under the beaming half-moon.

"Any time you're ready, ladies," Dhoni shouted.

Thrasher raised his hand to signal that they'd be right there. Farhad turned to go, but Thrasher held him up.

"You know that I don't tell my story to just anyone, right? By telling you this, I'm trusting you more than I trust most people. Don't make me regret it. I'll go down in a blaze of glory before I end up in the same situation as Tom."

"I get it. Your info's locked away in my vault."

"Good. Now how far to this next site you were talking about?"

"Fifteen minutes, tops."

"Let's hit it."

Chapter Thirty-Four

NAQSH-E JAHAN SQUARE
ISFAHAN, IRAN

When they arrived, Thrasher quickly realized that Farhad was right about loving the destination. Naqsh-e Jahan Square was a site to behold, a gem of Persian architecture. During ancient times, it was a stop along the Silk Road, which connected a network of trade routes. Each day, tradesmen set up their tents to sell food and coffee. At night, they packed up and gave way to an assortment of entertainers, including snake charmers, jugglers, acrobats, performing actors, and prostitutes. Today, the Imperial Bazaar that lined the Square was filled with much of the same, only the shopkeepers kept their businesses going well into the night. Prostitution wasn't exactly a thing of the past, but to keep the Revolutionary Guard at bay, it was more secluded. One just needed to know where to look or who to ask.

Thrasher was impressed as he gawked at his surroundings. It reminded him of the National Mall in Washington, D.C. But whereas the Mall was open and promoted tourism to the sites surrounding it, the Square was lined by a wall of nearly two thousand feet of three-pointed stone arches where the vendors operated their businesses. The endless trading in the square made Isfahan friendly to foreigners. Thrasher figured that the IRGC probably had their spies lurking around, but given the volume of people they couldn't be everywhere, which allowed him to blend in more easily, especially when he made a concentrated effort to slump his shoulders and look less conspicuous.

"What's with you?" said Dhoni. "You look like a baby slurping down his favorite food. The way you're ogling this place, I feel like I should offer you a bib."

Thrasher scowled.

"Before working . . ."

Thrasher paused, knowing the danger of uttering the initials C-I-A aloud in his current environment

"Before working as an environmental scientist, I was an art history major in college."

"Seriously? You?"

"Don't knock it 'til you've tried it. There's a lot more to me than you think."

"You're one big enigma, you know that? Home base should have coded you *Riddler* instead."

Thrasher scowled again.

As they neared the reflecting pool and its line of spurting water fountains, Thrasher saw three buildings towering over each side of the bazaar, which Farhad informed him were the Sheikh Lotf Allah Mosque, the Shah Mosque, and Ali Qapu Palace.

"Please tell me that we're headed to the Palace. I'm well-versed in Islam, and I may not look terribly pale, but I'll stick out like a sore thumb in a mosque."

"None of the above. Keep your head down and follow me."

Before reaching the entrance to Shah Mosque, Farhad headed toward one of the arches and into the vendor area. He walked straight toward a candle shop where a squat heavy man with a mirror shine to his bald head was waiting. All but three of Farhad's PMOI friends waited outside as he entered the shop, nodding to the owner, who waited for Thrasher and Dhoni before pulling down the aluminum gate to close his shop for the day.

When the gate slammed shut, Thrasher's appreciation for art décor instantly switched off, and his lethal side clicked back into place. He and Dhoni instinctually pulled their guns and swept the room, careful to keep everyone within range. Dhoni snuck behind the shop owner and grabbed him around the chest, using him as a shield. By the squeamish look in the man's eyes behind his Coke bottle glasses, Thrasher thought he was about to piss himself.

"Farhad!" the bald man said.

"Whoa, whoa! Guys, it's cool," said Farhad. "He's with us!"

He raised his hands, trying to calm the situation.

"Farhad, we don't like being locked in," Thrasher said.

"No offense, kid," said Dhoni, "but there's more of you guys than us and for all we know, there could be something waiting for us when we get where we're going."

"You guys have an odd way of showing your appreciation."

"Gratitude doesn't exactly come with the job description," said Thrasher.

Farhad kept his hands raised and slowly walked toward Thrasher until the barrel of the agent's Sig Sauer P226 was inches from his forehead.

"You trusted me with your story. I need you to trust me that we're here to help you."

Thrasher's eyes narrowed. Farhad's intel was their only lead when it came to his theory about Iran's involvement in the current predicament. Either he trusted him now or he and Dhoni were on their own. Thrasher lowered his weapon then nodded at Dhoni, indicating that he should do the same.

"I'll lower it, but I'm not putting it away," Dhoni said.

"We good?" Thrasher said.

He noticed Farhad smirk.

"What?"

"Nothing. This reminded me of a moment I had with Kirk. I'm good if you're good. Come on, this way."

The shop owner's hands shook as he removed three padlocks connecting the drink machine to the concrete wall and swung it open. Behind it was a narrow stairway illuminated by a series of portable LED lights strung together by orange extension cords leading to a thirty by forty basement. Thrasher and Dhoni exchanged glances.

"You know that we're breaking every rule in the survival handbook, right? Basements are rat traps for guys like us."

"I know, but what other choice do we have? Keep your weapon handy just in case."

"Then what?"

"Never mind. Keep moving."

Once inside the belly of the bland stone basement, as amateur as it was, Thrasher was impressed with the operation he saw in front of him. Farhad and his PMOI colleagues had maps spread on the large oak tables and butcher paper hung on the walls with tons of colorful Post-It notes stuck to it like paper feathers. There was only one computer in the room, and a pimple-faced teenage boy who looked overdue for a haircut was pounding away at the keyboard with his eyes fiercely glued to the screen.

Farhad tapped the shoulder of a tall, lanky woman in a black burka with a ruby red chador lowered to expose her dark brown hair with auburn highlights. She had the sharp jawline of a hardened Marine commander.

"Donya, these are the agents I was telling you about."

Donya said nothing as she approached, looking them up and down.

"They're handsome, but do they have names?"

"Actually, I don't know. This one," he said, pointing to Thrasher, "Calls himself Jaybird. And the other one never gave me his name."

"Well, I'm not calling anyone by a bird name. What do you call yourselves?"

"Jay Jacoby."

Thrasher extended his hand, citing his cover name in the field. Dhoni did the same.

"Ketan Jadhav."

Donya rolled her eyes, well-aware that both men were lying.

"Okay, if you say so. Tell your agencies they should come up with better names."

Thrasher and Dhoni grinned at each other. They liked the feistiness behind her honeyed voice.

Donya asked everyone to stop working and called the meeting to order. Everyone gathered around a table in the center of the room. Farhad, Thrasher, and Dhoni were at her side.

"Farhad's friend at the cell phone company traced Mahmoud's last known burner phone here," she said, thumping her finger on the map. "Hashemabad Air Base. It's about forty-five minutes northwest."

"Give me the good, the bad, and the ugly about it," Thrasher said.

"The good part for us is that this base is rather small compared to the others. It's not exactly a secret facility in the middle of nowhere, though, and has security around the perimeter, in the two overlook towers, and each of the facilities on ground. But if you two are the caliber of agents that we hope you are then this shouldn't be a problem."

"Have you been able to visually confirm that Mahmoud is there?"

"I was on stakeout two nights ago. I briefly saw him walking from one facility to the other," Farhad chimed in.

"Briefly? You're sure it was him?"

"No doubt. He's there."

"What about this Pakistani soldier, Hasan Wasim? Any eyes on him specifically?" Dhoni asked.

"No," said Farhad.

"Then, how do you know he's really there?" Thrasher said.

Thrasher noted Farhad and Donya trading concerned looks. They were holding back on something.

"Let's hear it," he said.

"There's something you need to know about Mahmoud," Donya said. "Before he joined the IRGC he went to college and got his degree in chemistry. Since then, he's been focusing on pharmaceuticals."

"What kind of chemistry? Do we need to be worried about chemical weapons in there?"

"No, I don't think so, but I think you do need to be worried about where he went to college as much as you do about the type of chemistry he's been working on."

"Which is?"

"Germany. He's been focused on creating drugs specifically used in altering brain chemistry."

"Excuse me?"

Donya sighed.

"Germany still has more than its fair share of underground Nazi groups. During his time there, we think that Mahmoud got involved with some of them because he began to dig around to find any and all documentation relating to the experiments that the Nazis did on the Jews during the Holocaust. At the time, most of these experiments centered around how they could test the Jews as it related to helping Nazi soldiers in battle. You know, testing them for hypothermia and ways to make seawater drinkable. That kind of stuff. They also used them as lab rats for infectious diseases such as tuberculosis and malaria. But we think that Mahmoud is trying to take the next step."

"Which is what?"

"If what I've read online is true, scientists in America have been studying Navy Seals for years, trying to determine what it is about their backgrounds that makes them so elite. The idea being that if they found one common denominator amongst them then your government would know how to better recruit them."

"Right. It's the age-old question of whether soldiers are made or born."

"Precisely. But Mahmoud saw how anti-depressant drugs allows the people taking them to perform better on their day-to-day tasks because they're more focused. Now, what type of profession does the Ayatollah government want more of than anything else?"

"Nuclear scientists." Thrasher said.

Donya nodded.

"If Mahmoud created a drug that will exponentially allow people with scientific backgrounds to have a greater focus on their profession, then they will not need to find nuclear scientists."

"They can be grown. . ."

"So to speak. But to do that you need test subjects."

"Like perhaps a Pakistani soldier who knows how to get in and out of a state-run nuclear facility," Dhoni said.

"It's a stretch on Mahmoud's part because we don't know much about Wasim, but all indications are that he's no scientist," said Donya. "I think Mahmoud figures that he has nothing to lose by trying, especially since he already used him to get the C-4 out of Pakistan. It's a better use of his time than killing him."

"Essentially, Yazdani is Iran's version of what Josef Mengele was for the Nazis," said Thrasher.

Every PMOI member in the room nodded.

"Only Mahmoud isn't just a scientist. He's a highly trained soldier who is every bit as dangerous on the battlefield as he is in a chemistry lab," Farhad said.

"How do you know so much about this guy?" asked Thrasher.

Donya reached into her burka, pulled out a photo of a barely conscious woman with drug ridden eyes, drooling from the mouth, and smacked it on the table for Thrasher to see.

"He was married to my sister, Mehry. She suffered from depression, which he saw as a mental disorder and used her as his first guinea pig."

"So, this is personal for you," Thrasher said.

He worried that the personal angle for her threatened the credibility of the mission.

"Yes, but there's more to him than what he did to my sister."

"Such as?"

"I've never been able to prove it, but I think Mahmoud was once a student of the new Ayatollah."

"Excuse me?"

"Years ago, when Ayatollah Shir-Del was starting out on the Guardian Council, he was known to give secret classes about what Shia Islam can learn from the Nazis."

"Shit."

Dhoni whispered aloud.

"Exactly. I was never there to see him attend, but my sister told me about it. Not long after, I found a bunch of Nazi books in Mahmoud's office. He could have gotten them from his time in Germany, but I doubt it. It's rumored that Shir-Del has a private collection of Nazi memorabilia. I think Shir-Del has kept in touch and gave them to him."

"In other words," said Thrasher, "you can't knock him off because the Ayatollah will come after the PMOI with hell's fury, so you want us to do it."

"I don't want him dead. I want him alive."

"Listen, I'm not a kidnapper for hire, okay? I kill enemies of the state."

"He *is* an enemy of the U.S. government. Look at what he's trying to do! If he succeeds in his experiments, don't you think that the U.S. will be in the Ayatollah's crosshairs?"

"We're here for Wasim. That's all. End of story," Dhoni piped up.

"Then we don't have a deal. Get out!"

Donya stomped her foot and pointed toward the door. An awkward silence hung in the air like a dark cloud that was ready to release a downpour while Thrasher and Donya exchanged sizzling glares.

Farhad studied the map on the table.

"I think I may have an idea that can work for both of us," he said.

Chapter Thirty-Five

"Show me the layout of the facility," Thrasher said.

As they hovered over the map, Farhad laid out the specifics of the air base. One of the little-known facts about Hashemabad Air Base was that it served as a central conduit for moving provisions, drugs, and ammunition to members of Hamas and Hezbollah. Mossad and other intelligence agencies had been trying to break the supply chain of this operation for years, but for once, Iran was smart about how they did it.

The size of the air base helped camouflage their enterprise. It had only two major runways, barracks for soldiers, and a large storage facility. The planes toting cargo were owned by the Iranian elite and always flew into Jordan or Egypt. From there, it was the responsibility of Iran's jihadi brothers in arms to get the cargo into the hands of those who needed it—by any means necessary.

Thankfully for the Iranians, the Jordanian and Egyptian intelligence services had not caught on to their logistics in the six years they'd been running it. The tab for Iran to pay off the right people in those governments amounted to a snappy five million dollars a year for each country, but in the previous Ayatollah's eyes, it was worth it. The new Supreme Leader had no desire to put a halt to his well-oiled machine.

The soldier barracks were on the northeast side of the base along with the commissary, reception hall, and a newly constructed bowling alley to which the younger soldiers had acquired an athletic addiction. The munitions storage was located on the western side. While it varied by country, general regulations for any army base called for ammunitions facilities to be situated at least five hundred yards away from a barracks area, but Thrasher's eye caught something. In his opinion, it was closer to the barracks than it should be. Considering that he was looking at a hand drawn map, it probably was.

"Where is Wasim being kept?" Dhoni asked.

"I think he's here," said Farhad. "This slender building about two hundred meters south of the barracks. Mahmoud was going back and forth between this building. It used to be a classroom and indoor training facility for the soldiers before they built the new one on the other side of the complex. It's old, but it would be the perfect place to set up a science lab and holding area for prisoners."

Thrasher studied the sketch of the base and looked at Dhoni.

"Are you thinking what I'm thinking?"

Dhoni nodded.

"How's your weapons situation look? Are you stocked up?"

Without saying a word, Donya walked across the room to the area where the pimple faced teenager was sitting, and motioned him to move. When he got up, Donya moved his chair out of the way, and flipped up the rug. Underneath it was a trap door that concealed an assortment of guns and assault rifles, including AK-47's, Norinco CQ's, Heckler & Koch G3's, Bushmaster XM-15's, and M-16's, plus a few dozen grenades. She picked one up, and tossed it up and down like a tennis ball.

"You think this will do?"

Dhoni let out a low whistle.

"For sure," Thrasher said.

He grinned, always happy to see an arsenal of quality weapons.

"There's one wrinkle," Farhad added.

"What's that?"

"We'll help you get your man out, but we want what's in here."

He pointed to another facility on the map.

"What am I looking at?"

187

"This is where they keep their drug supply to Hamas and Hezbollah. Mostly cocaine and opioids. We need it."

Thrasher gave the Iranian a dirty look.

"I didn't come here to help you become a drug lord, Farhad. Plus, it's on the opposite side of the base. We can't be in two places at once."

"Fuck being a drug lord!" said Donya. "This is about our survival as a group. We have to eat, and we need a cash flow that can keep our resistance going. Whether we like it or not, we can't do that without the drug trade."

Thrasher grimaced.

"I can't get the CIA involved in this. In case you can't tell, we're trying to help the Iranian people break free of the Ayatollah's grasp, not get them hooked on narcotics."

Donya stepped forward and stared up into Thrasher's eyes. Despite being a foot shorter than him, she was a force to be reckoned with, and he felt it.

"Don't you dare patronize me. Everyone here knows what the CIA is capable of. It was your agency that started this mess with the Ayatollah when you removed Mossadegh from power back in the fifties. Then, you started trafficking cocaine with the Central American Contras in the eighties. From what I understand, it contributed to the creation of the crack cocaine epidemic in the United States. So, you might want to hop down off your moral high horse."

Thrasher was cornered. Donya knew her history, and this was a case where he had no choice but to toe the company line. He glimpsed over to Dhoni, who shrugged.

"Don't look at me. You know she's right."

Thrasher let out an audible, frustrated breath. As an orphan, he should've remembered his days of having to scratch and claw to survive in the world.

"Fine. We'll help you get the facility open, but your people can load the drugs up and drive them out of there."

He pointed to Dhoni and himself.

"*Our* priority is getting Wasim out before he's an invalid. Got it?"

"Deal," Donya said.

She gave Thrasher a firm handshake.

"How many of my people do you think that we will lose on this mission?"

"It depends on how quickly we can get in and out, but loading the drugs up is going to slow you down. The more time you spend doing that, the better chance you have of losing people. You'll probably need a dozen."

"Farhad?" said Donya.

"I'll work on it," he replied.

"What about Mahmoud?"

"What about him?" said Thrasher.

"I want him, alive."

"No guarantees. As I told you, Wasim is my priority."

Unsatisfied with the answer, Donya clenched her jaw.

"Then at least inflict some pain on him, and tell him it's from me."

"That I can do."

Chapter Thirty-Six

FOOLADSHAHR, IRAN

It took a few hours for Farhad to track down reinforcements, and most of them didn't begin arriving until almost midnight. As he and Dhoni helped them unload their gear, Thrasher became more and more impressed with the PMOI members. They brought additional weapons beyond what Donya had hidden in the cryptic basement, but more important, they brought spare IRGC uniforms, which would help them enter the base. Thrasher knew that these weren't easy to come by, and when he asked Farhad where they'd gotten them, he received an odd answer.

"Unless I'm the one getting the contraband, I've learned not to ask. All of us smugglers have our own secrets. Plus, if one of us gets captured, it won't put the others at risk."

"I feel like there's a 'but' coming," Thrasher said.

Farhad smirked and leaned over to whisper in Thrasher's ear.

"A lot of them came from dead IRGC soldiers killed by Mossad. If you look closely, you'll see bullet holes in the uniforms. We'll just have to roll with it, and hope that no one at the base looks too closely."

"Mossad is doing business with you guys? Since when?"

"That I don't know. It was before my time in the group. They're not the easiest people to work with, but someone over there is sympathetic to our cause so they usually help us out a spoonful at a time. Donya has become a good politician when it comes to dealing with them. This time, though, all she had to do was mention 'Nazis' and 'Iran' in the same sentence and they didn't hesitate to pitch in."

While they managed to scratch disguises off the list, the one thing they were short on, though, was money. Because of the low global value of the Iranian rial, IRGC soldiers were suckers for being bought off, especially inside the lower ranks of the food chain. The true believers weren't all that different, but their cooperation came with a higher price tag. Either way, Thrasher didn't cross the Iranian border with a suitcase full of cash, and the U.S. didn't have money laying around inside Iran, so he texted Dub for help.

THRASHER: How's our lady doing?

DUB: She's awake but in and out. The blood is starting to drain from her brain. Not stable yet.

THRASHER: OK. Keep me posted. Need some cash.

DUB: POTUS has given us top priority. How much?

THRASHER: $25K should do it. Euros.

DUB: To who?

Donya gave Thrasher the names of five different couriers that the PMOI used when banks were needed to move money. The low amounts split among five banks allowed them to stay below the radar, and Donya was careful enough to use people she trusted not to shave any off the top for personal reasons. She also kept the couriers in a three-week rotation to prevent the in-country banks from becoming suspicious, and alerting the IRGC to wanted PMOI members.

When Farhad received word that everyone was in town, the team left the Naqsh-e Jahan Square and drove thirty minutes southwest to the city of Fooladshahr, where the group inhabited an abandoned cement factory. Everyone was eagerly awaiting Donya's arrival with her guests in tow so that they could design a battle plan to get in and out of the base as quickly as possible. After brief introductions to some of Donya's top lieutenants, Payman and Shahab, Thrasher dove right in.

"First things first. Do we have a military vehicle that can get us in?"

"I took care of that. I called one of the assets that I've used before inside the Guard. He's a third lieutenant who makes regular night runs for cargo in and out of the military bases, and he agreed to help us for a price," Dhoni said.

"How reliable?"

"None of these guys are reliable, but lucky for us, he's loyal to the money. We pay, he helps. That's his track record and I've never had a problem with him. He'll meet us in Jahadabad, ten miles outside the base. We load up and go from there."

"How's he going to get us past the gate?"

"His friend there owes him a favor. We had to pay him off, too, but he agreed not to search the truck on our way in."

"What do we owe these guys?"

"IIB is picking up the tab."

Thrasher looked surprised.

"Since when are you so generous?"

"I couldn't wait for your cheapskate ass to pony up the dough."

Dhoni smiled and gave Thrasher a slap on the shoulder.

Thrasher detested being touched and wasn't pleased that Dhoni embarrassed him in front of the PMOI, but the laugh from the room lightened the mood, so he let it go.

"Okay, here's the plan. Once we get through the gate, your man drives us to the storage facility. Assuming that the guards think we are dropping off another payload, we can pop 'em but we gotta keep it quiet."

He pointed to Payman and Shahab.

"From there, you two boys stand guard outside while we go in and clear the building. Donya, how many guards inside?"

"Three that we know of."

Thrasher rolled his eyes. He fucking hated guesswork.

"We'll have to move fast," Dhoni said.

Thrasher grunted.

"Farhad, while your buddies load up the truck with your product, you're coming with us to the ammunitions facility. We'll need you to smooth-talk the guards so we can take them down. After that, you know what to do. When chaos ensues, the three of us go in, hit Yazdani where it counts, and grab Wasim."

"Understood," Farhad said.

"Donya, when your team sees the signal, they've got no more than five minutes to get their asses back in the truck, and come get us. And if you leave us hanging, you better make sure that I'm dead, because if not I'm coming back to kill every single one of you sons-of-bitches. That clear enough?"

Thrasher gave Donya a sharp look to let her know he was serious.

"You don't need to threaten us. We're here for you, aren't we?"

"For all I know, you're here for the drugs."

"The drugs ensure our survival. I'm here for Mahmoud."

"If you want him, then you better make damn sure your band of misfits bring us back."

"Can I talk to you for a minute?" Dhoni said.

He dragged Thrasher away by the elbow. Once out of range from the others, Thrasher yanked his arm away.

"What the hell are you doing? We're supposed to be going in for one guy. Now we're taking two?"

Dhoni held up two fingers.

193

"I don't like it any more than you do," Thrasher said, "but this may be the only way we ensure that we get out of there. I'm not getting killed over a drug deal. If she wants this Mahmoud psycho as much as she says, then he's our guaranteed ticket out. But if you have any better ideas, I'm all ears."

Dhoni chewed his lip and studied Thrasher. He knew he was right.

"I hope you know what you're doing," he said.

They walked back to the group.

"So, Donya, do we have a deal?" said Thrasher. "Everything clear?"

Donya looked to her lieutenants, who nodded.

"What else do you need from me?" she asked.

"Got any vodka?"

Chapter Thirty-Seven

HASHEMABAD AIR BASE
RESEARCH & DEVELOPMENT BUILDING

Yazdani was frustrated and encouraged. Most of his test subjects were showing dramatic improvement in their ability to focus on the fragmented nuclear documents they'd been provided. However, based on the high doses of the drug concoction he'd administered, the subjects were either not eating, which decreased their energy and functionality, or were developing blood clots or tumors. The answer was to be found somewhere in the formula he was working on, which he could feel but not yet see.

Yazdani had become fascinated with the prospect of mind control in his late teenage years when he saw the original, Frank Sinatra version of *The Manchurian Candidate* while on holiday with his family in Turkey. While he loathed the Americans and their ideals, he was fascinated by the idea of having complete control over a person's thoughts and actions, making them do things they otherwise would not do. When he saw the revamped version of the film with Denzel Washington while attending college in Germany, he felt it was a sign directly from Allah, telling him to go forth with his mythic pursuit. He knew that Allah wouldn't fail him. Creating a drug that produced slaves obedient to his will would be one of the greatest human accomplishments of all time.

But the journey toward his goal was an uphill battle. At the insistence of Shir-Del, he started by reading the Nazi documents provided to him by his revolutionary friends in Germany. Of course, they were not exactly his friends, but the underground Nazis and revolutionary Iranians had an unspoken agreement since they shared a common hatred for what they called, "the Jewish problem." Neither side trusted the other, but they agreed to assist each other whenever possible as long as they didn't interfere with each other's success.

Impressed by his intellect and dedication to the cause, Shir-Del then provided him with documents from his private library. Yazdani couldn't believe his eyes when he saw that they were scientific notes personally written by Josef Mengele.

During World War II, Joseph Mengele had the gumption to first dabble in the field of mind control by using mescaline. Its hallucinogenic effects were derived from the peyote cactus and were similar to those of LSD. Mengele started using the drug on children under the age of thirteen at Auschwitz. He thought the drug would easily take over the mind of children who were already impressionable and whose brains weren't fully developed. From what Yazdani could find, the results were terrible because Mengele had a hard time determining the correct dosage to give his test subjects. Most of them died of cardiac arrest because their young minds couldn't handle the psychedelic effects. They essentially panicked to death.

Little else is known about other drug experiments Mengele performed with the drug because the Nazis covered their tracks well by burning the rest of the data when it became clear that an Allied victory was imminent.

Mahmoud hit the research jackpot when he learned about the CIA's experiments with LSD under their MK-Ultra plan during the 1970s. As much as he despised the corrupt American agency, he dared not divert his eyes from their relentless ambition. Though the agency's director ordered the project's documents to be destroyed in 1973, tens of thousands survived and were submitted to Congress as part of the Freedom of Information Act. For Mahmoud, this made it difficult to hate America because its stupidity at the hands of it's politicians was laughable and served him the information he needed on a silver platter.

The program's leader, Sidney Gottlieb, had a two-step theory when it came to mind control. First, demolish the old mind's way of thinking. Second, install the mind preferred by him and his band of scientific misfits. All the research that Yazdani could find indicated that the doctor had made tremendous progress on the first part of the theory but not so much on the second. Documents from that time that were recently made public indicated that they had success installing electrodes into the brains of dogs to make them perform a variety of motor skills. Yazdani found this intriguing because all of this was done with 1960s technology, which could be easily applied through modern advancements, even in Iran. But when he raised the issue to his bosses at the Revolutionary Guard, he was told that the Supreme Leader turned down the idea because it was too expensive, and Iranian surgeons did not have the necessary skills.

Yazdani was disappointed but not discouraged because he knew the Supreme Leader was right. It would also be too time consuming. He was convinced that pharmaceuticals were the quicker path forward. Given his passion for chemistry, this gave him a surge of confidence.

While he found the Americans' research notes enlightening, he decided to approach the task from a different angle. Rather than wipe the brain totally clean and try to replace it with new thoughts, Yazdani decided that it was best to utilize test subjects that had a base knowledge of certain subjects and an eagerness to learn more.

Since the Mossad had made it their mission to prevent any foreign nuclear scientists from setting foot in Iran, and other friendly countries had refused to provide any nuclear materials and technology to build the bomb, Yazdani started with kidnapping physicists still working on their degrees. All he would have to do is find a way to give their brains a nudge in the right direction, which would allow them to learn nuclear science on their own.

To do this, he concentrated his efforts on the positive effects of chemicals used in anti-depressants. When a person feels sad, the brain naturally consumes serotonin. The selective uptake inhibitors from anti-depressants block this reabsorption and make serotonin more available to improve the transmission of signals between the brain's nerve cells. As the chemical increases in the blood, it fills energy holes in the brain, which results in less emotion and increased focus.

Early on in his marriage to his first wife, Mehry, Yazdani noticed that she tended to fall into fits of sadness that would last for days on end when she rarely spoke or ate, and had no interest in sexual relations. He became impotent when he forced himself on her, which he'd never encountered. Enraged that she'd stolen his sexual power, he tried beating the sadness out of her on more than one occasion. When that didn't work, he dismissed her as mentally disabled.

While most Iranian men would simply choose to bring a new wife into the picture, Yazdani decided to go a different route. He used Mehry as his first test subject, and slipped eight hundred milligrams of his home-brewed drug with a high amount of serotonin and dopamine into her morning tea. This caused flu-like symptoms, dilated pupils, confusion, and diarrhea. When he cut her off from the drug cold turkey, she was more despondent than ever, and barely decipherable when she spoke. The woman's sister begged him to do something, but instead of taking her to a hospital outside the country, he resumed giving her the drug at an increased dosage with epinephrine mixed in. With her body already in crisis, this reintroduction caused muscle stiffness and a loss of agility before a massive heart attack ultimately killed her.

Yazdani was indifferent to her death. He was sick of her depression constantly souring his mood, and she was no good to him if she could not be intimate. Her death was a small price to pay along the road to his ultimate goal.

From her death, though, it became apparent that anti-depressant chemicals alone weren't the solution. It also occurred to Yazdani that his project was less about control and more about mind focus. His chemicals needed to be mixed with something.

It dawned on Yazdani that artists, such as painters and musicians, who take hallucinogenic drugs like LSD often have creative experiences that allow them to flourish. If he could find a way to isolate the part of the drug that latches itself to the part of the brain responsible for creativity, the frontal cortex, and mix it with selective serotonin inhibitors, then his new drug might allow the brain to make unprecedented neuron connections and increase the test subject's intelligence. He was going to build his own version of *The Manchurian Candidate* and use America's ideas against them.

The problem was getting the correct documentation on nuclear bombs and their corresponding facilities. The Science and Technology department from the Ministry of Intelligence supplied what they could from their operators' successful missions, but it continued to be received in small pieces. The pressure was squarely on Mahmoud to build his band of academic zombies to fill in the gaps.

If he achieved this success, the issue would be whether the subjects were going to be compelled to share this information. If not, he hoped that a dose of a truth serum, such as sodium amytal, would loosen their tongues, but there was no telling how it would interact with his potion or how their bodies would respond. His plan was to utilize the brain matter from army cadavers or test subjects who died under his watch, and examine the effects under a microscope with the biology team. Since he didn't have a drug that worked, he would have to cross that bridge when he came to it.

The test subjects were housed and observed inside a standard jail house. Each prisoner was brought in daily from their individual cells in the opposite wing. The reason for keeping the sleeping quarters away from the test rooms is that there was no telling what effects his drugs would have, so Mahmoud wanted to ensure that the patients maintained total focus while in their workspace, and not take naps if they saw a nearby bed. Allowing them to spend time next to each other in their row of cells promoted a brotherhood. With listening devices installed in the cells, he could also eavesdrop on any of their conversations.

The observation cells contained a chair and desk behind sheets of locked, reinforced plexiglass. Both were metal and bolted to the floor to prevent patients from using them as weapons against themselves, their jailers, or as tools to break out. Every day, Yazdani and the doctor appointed by the Supreme Leader walked the hall outside each of their five cells, observing and scrutinizing their every move.

Yazdani approached Dr. Shahid Aslam.

"Do you have the latest round of test results?"

"Yes, sir. I think we need to stabilize patients one, three, and four for a while. According to their latest angiograms, they are developing heavy blood clots. They will need to be given blood thinners to help stop the clotting, and I will need to give them a stress test to determine whether or not they require heart stents."

"Are they making progress on the schematics? Connecting the dots from what we gave them to what we are hoping they will learn?"

"It's slow going, but all of them show a tremendous amount of concentration when their energy levels are high. When they don't eat, though, the lack of nutrients slows their brain stimulation, and they're not worth much."

Yazdani grunted.

"Give them the pills and the stress test. I'll see if I can tweak the formula a bit to prevent their loss of appetite. In the meantime, tell the guards to force feed them if they have to. What about subjects two and five?"

Dr. Aslam adjusted his glasses and paused. He thought that he knew what the captain was going to say, but as a medical professional, he didn't like hearing it.

"Subject two's cancer has spread to the bone. It won't be long before he's dead."

"Have you saved his work?"

"Yes, sir."

"Then go ahead and give him the Pancuronium bromide and put him out of his misery. If he's no longer any use to us then I don't want him here. We'll find someone else to pick up where he left off. What about my new toy? Subject five."

"He's resting in his cell, but his muscles are stiff, and he can't seem to make sense of anything. All he does is mumble and drool. I think you may have missed the mark on this one."

Yazdani eyed the doctor harshly.

"I didn't miss anything, Doctor. Wasim makes deliveries to and from Pakistan's nuclear station in Karachi twice a month. He may not be a scientist, but I want to see if he can put what he sees there together with his engineering degree to help us build the facility we need to become a nuclear power. If Israel keeps sabotaging the ones we have in place, we'll never get there."

"To do that, he needs to be in a functional state."

Yazdani had heard enough back talk. He pulled the Browning 9mm pistol from the holster on his belt and pressed the barrel against the doctor's forehead. Aslam dropped his clipboard and froze while a nervous sweat formed on his brow.

"Then I suggest you figure out the correct dosage to give him. Am I clear?"

"Yes, sir."

As Yazdani pulled the gun away from the doctor's head, he was rocked by a blast from outside the building.

Chapter Thirty-Eight

Yazdani ran up the stairs and thrust open the main door to the jail house. He was instantly hit by the blistering heat from the fireball cloud rising from the nearby ammunitions compound. He raised his arm to shield his eyes as the next burst rocked the grounds harder than the first. The concussive force of the blast knocked him off his feet, but he shook it off and regained his wits.

Three soldiers under his command tried helping him to his feet.

"Take your hands off me! I'm fine. Go see if you can help!"

"Yes, sir!" they responded.

As he pushed himself onto his elbows, Yazdani got his first look at the carnage before him. The night sky above emanated with the squealing pitch of a fireworks display as the gunpowder from the bullets projected itself outward. Soldiers were running toward what was left of the building, fire extinguishers in hand, while others stopped short, due to the intense heat. They were waving their arms at the on-base fire truck screaming toward them.

Yazdani grabbed the radio from his belt.

"Captain Yazdani to Watchtower. What the hell is going on? Is the base under attack?"

"Watchtower here. This is Sergeant Siasar. Sir, we're trying to figure that out. But the explosion didn't come from the sky, so it's not from a missile or drone. It definitely came from the ground. Do you have any visuals?"

Yazdani climbed to his feet and surveyed the damage. He saw no unusual or alarming activity, only soldiers moving to help or standing frozen, wondering what was happening.

"Negative. Nothing I can report."

"Oh, I don't know about that."

Yazdani heard a voice behind him. Startled, he whipped his head around but saw nothing but a fist headed straight toward his cheek. With no time to react, the sucker punch sent him falling backward, where he was caught by another individual he hadn't seen.

"Nice punch," Dhoni said.

Thrasher held up his fist to display a set of brass knuckles.

"Never leave home without them," he said.

Dhoni read the name on the uniform.

"One down. One to go."

"Let's get him inside," Thrasher said.

Dhoni grabbed the limp body by the arms while Thrasher took the legs. As they carried Yazdani through the door headfirst, they were met by a man in a white medical coat, attempting to squeeze past them. He paused as he saw Yazdani.

"Oh my God. Is he okay? What happened?"

Dr. Aslam began checking the captain's vital signs while he was still hanging from their arms. He had no reason to doubt Thrasher and Dhoni, who were dressed in IRGC fatigues, but they were unable to grab their weapons since they had Yazdani in their arms. They stared at each other, tongue-tied until they heard a familiar voice behind them.

"Hey, I just got a text."

Dr. Aslam turned, and saw a man he hated with a passion.

"You!" he said through gritted teeth.

Dr. Aslam forgot about Yazdani for a moment and lunged at Farhad. Dhoni dropped Yazdani's legs and struck the doctor in the gut before he could reach his target. The doctor stumbled backward, but before he could make another move, Dhoni snatched him by the front of his shirt and slammed his head into the wall.

"Two for one special!"

Dhoni caught a hint of a smile on Thrasher's face, who quickly tuned to yell at Farhad.

"What the hell was that all about?"

"Long story," Farhad said. "I'll have to tell you later. I just got a text from the guys at the other facility. They're halfway done filling up the truck with the drugs, so we need to find Wasim and get moving."

"Seems like the Molotov cocktails worked."

"After you guys took out the guards, it was a piece of cake."

Thrasher saw a roll of duct tape on top of a filing cabinet and tossed it to Farhad.

"Tie up the doctor and Yazdani. Make sure to cover their mouths, we don't need them screaming."

"Got it."

"You ready?"

Dhoni pulled the Sig Sauer P229 9mm from his holster and nodded.

Time was of the essence, so Thrasher and Dhoni made their way down the decrepit hallway, carefully checked each room to make sure they weren't going to face a hail of bullets from any unknown soldiers.

One room made them pause.

"Check this out," said Dhoni.

After sweeping the room, Thrasher gazed in wonder at the chemistry lab. He saw chemical formulas written on whiteboards and multiple computers running data analysis. Beakers of colored chemicals were everywhere. An antiseptic smell hung in the room and filled their nasal passages, which sent both men into coughing fits.

"I guess this is where the magic happens," Dhoni said.

When Thrasher spotted grey respirator masks scattered along the main table, he motioned to Dhoni, and began backing away. There was no telling what type of airborne poison was in there, and he didn't want to risk it any further.

"Let's get outta here and find our man," Thrasher said between coughs.

Thrasher snapped his fingers at the stairway door marked "Observation." They descended the staircase with guns extended, ready to shoot anything that got in their way.

Great. Another basement.

"It looks deserted," Dhoni said.

"Doubtful. Keep an eye out."

To be safe, Thrasher shot out three of the overhead surveillance cameras as he continued to search for any threat that might be lurking. Other than the observation deck above, the area downstairs was fairly compact with rooms walled off with Plexiglass between two staircases. An empty room at the end of the hall housed what looked to be surveillance monitors with a control board to lock and unlock the rooms. Thrasher saw Dhoni stop dead in his tracks with his weapon hanging helplessly at his side.

"I think we're in the right place. Look."

"Holy hell."

The two veteran agents had each witnessed horrible tragedies during their time in the field, but this was different. They tried to comprehend what their eyes were seeing as they scanned each of the prisoners in their individual rooms.

Three of the patients were hovered over their schematics with books of data scattered across the room and markings all over the wall. They appeared immune to the explosion that shook the grounds only minutes before. One was methodically twirling his black hair at his desk as he stared at the material in front of him. Another was talking to himself as he made changes to the markings on the walls, speed walking back and forth from one side of the room to the other. The third man sat in his chair with his arms crossed, lost in thought, looking at papers taped to the wall. None of the men could have been older than twenty-five and all of them were wearing brown uniforms.

The prisoner in the second room looked the worst. His hair was nearly gone and what was left was thin and stringy. At one point, he'd been sitting in the chair, but had fallen. His muscles were so stiff that they had maintained the chair's seated position while on the ground. He was bleeding from the ears and eyes. Vomit was leaking from his open mouth. Thrasher could see that the man was barely breathing.

He pulled out his phone and slid open the camera lens cover.

"What're you doing?" Dhoni asked.

"We've gotta document this."

Thrasher walked down the line of rooms and filmed what he saw. The folks back in Langley weren't going to believe this. Everyone knew that Iran was desperate and crazy, but this was next level stuff.

In the last cell, Thrasher and Dhoni came upon Hasan Wasim, who was constrained in a chair behind a desk in the middle of the room. His eyes seemed to have rolled up into the back of his tilted head. He was still dressed in his Pakistani uniform, which was soaked in drool. Thrasher couldn't tell if he was aware of their presence, but Wasim was muttering to himself.

"See if you can find the release button," said Thrasher.

He pointed Dhoni to the control room. When the door buzzed and unlocked, Thrasher yanked it open and went to help Wasim. He gagged from the stench and at the puddle of drool that he was forced to step in. After cutting the ties to the chair with the karambit on his belt, he tried to hoist him up and get him walking. It was tough going. The soldier's muscles were stiff as a surfboard. He'd either been sitting for an extended period of time or whatever drugs he was on impacted his motor skills. Thrasher had to grab him around the back of his belt and use his own leg to bounce the man forward.

Getting up the stairs is going to be a bitch.

"Watch out!"

As Thrasher made his way through the doorway with a vegetative Wasim, gunshots rang out and Dhoni shoved the two men back into the observation room.

Chapter Thirty-Nine

Thrasher pushed Wasim off of him and pulled Dhoni into the observation room. A trail of blood streaked across the floor. He ripped open his partner's uniform to inspect the damage. It wasn't good. Blood was pooling on the white undershirt from two gunshots to his chest. Red fluid oozed from his mouth. Thrasher had no doubt that Dhoni's lung had collapsed, but that was the least of his problems. One of the bullet holes was near the heart and it looked like an artery had been hit.

"Hang on, man," Thrasher said.

Dhoni gurgled something indecipherable and pulled Thrasher's arm to bring him closer.

"Gadhe," Dhoni said in Hindi.

"Yeah, I know," Thrasher said. "I'm an asshole."

Dhoni yanked him closer and clasped his partner's hand in a brotherly handshake. Thrasher wasn't sure how to respond. He and Dhoni had tangled with each other more times than he cared to remember, and at one point he had wished that the man would take a long walk off a short pier. Now that his Indian counterpart was knocking on death's door, Thrasher was tongue tied. He decided to tell him what he would want to hear if the position was reversed.

"Don't you fucking die on me. You hear? I'm gonna get us out of here."

Dhoni's grip loosened and he slowly released his last breath.

"Kedar!"

Thrasher checked for a pulse but didn't find one. Dhoni was gone. Thrasher's dismay quickly changed to rage. He pulled the slide back on his gun and peeked around the open door.

"You might as well come out," said Yazdani.

Thrasher closed his eyes, trying to determine his next move.

"There's no way out of here except past me," said Yazdani, sporting a black eye.

As Thrasher emerged from inside Wasim's observation room, he saw that Yazdani had one arm wrapped around Farhad, and a gun pointed at his temple. Thrasher had his gun extended and steadily walked toward his enemy.

"Stop right there or the weasel gets it," Yazdani said in Farsi.

He cowered behind Farhad's head, using it as a shield.

"Fuck you," Thrasher said in English.

He continued forward.

"An American. I should have guessed."

Yazdani strengthened his grip on Farhad and turned the gun sideways so that Thrasher could see it pressing firmly against his hostage's head.

"Jay," Farhad pleaded, "he's serious."

Thrasher stopped but didn't lower his weapon. His trigger finger begged for even a sliver of an opening so he could get off a shot.

"So am I," Thrasher responded.

Farhad didn't know if he should be more afraid of the lunatic chemist who had a gun pressed against his head or the rabid American standing before him. He'd seen more than his fair share of enraged people in his lifetime, most of them zealot IRGC soldiers, but the hot-blooded rage in Jay's eyes scared the shit out of him. He looked like a wild animal, ready to pounce. A chiseled vein protruded down the center of his forehead. Blinded by his temper, it looked to Farhad like the American didn't really care if he lived or died.

Yazdani whispered to Farhad.

"Azam was right about you. He should've killed you when he had the chance."

"Donya was right about you, too, you psycho," said Farhad.

"And when I'm done with you, she'll be next on my list."

Yazdani walked forward with Farhad and stopped fifteen feet short of Thrasher. Neither man backed down.

"Put it down. I have the leverage," Yazdani said.

Thrasher caught a glimpse of movement from the side.

"Do you?" he said.

Thrasher gripped his gun tightly as the doors from the other observation rooms opened. He had no idea how it could have happened and wondered if Dhoni had accidently opened *all* of the doors before he died.

The thin-haired Bahraini patient from room two appeared first. Even in his weakened state, his bloodied eyes opened wide when he recognized Yazdani. With all the energy he could muster, he bull rushed the man who'd used him as a lab rat.

Yazdani fired with reckless disregard and patient two's head exploded in a cloud of pink mist. But shooting him meant that Yazdani pointed the gun away from Farhad's head. As soon as he got the shot off, Farhad elbowed him in the stomach, ducked under his arm and tried to shove the deranged chemist toward Thrasher, but Yazdani saw it coming. He pivoted and cold cocked the side of Farhad's head with the butt of his gun. Farhad never saw it coming. He stumbled backward and smacked the side of his face onto the stairwell railing.

Yazdani grinned. He was looking forward to doing what Azam Aslani didn't have the guts to do and rid his country of the drunken booze hound. He aimed his gun at the side of Farhad's head, but before he could pull the trigger, he was jumped from behind by Patient One. When their bodies hit the cement floor with an unyielding thump, Yazdani's gun slid along the floor in the opposite direction. With the hallucinogens in full effect, Patient One was relentless with his punches, kicks, and knees to his captor's body. Somewhere within all of the chemicals clouding his brain, the man's natural defenses appeared and paired with the torturous memories of the man who had kidnapped him.

Yazdani tried to avoid the blows and recover his gun. But he knew that he couldn't kill Patient One. That would destroy all the progress he'd made on the man. His advancements on the nuclear documents were astounding and proved that his formulas were working. He needed the man alive so his work could proceed.

With no other choice, Yazdani struck Patient One in the throat with the tips of his fingers. The chubby Jordanian man reached for his neck, which allowed Yazdani to land a punch to his gut. When he fell to the side, Yazdani stood, pulled a heavy flashlight from his belt and wacked the scientist in the back of the head, rendering him unconscious.

While Yazdani was busy with Patient One, Thrasher had his own problems. Patient Three surprised him by jumping on Thrasher's back, but as soon as he felt it, Thrasher threw him over his shoulder, slamming him onto the floor. The man bounced right back up as if he'd felt no pain. Before Thrasher could make another move, Patient Four jumped into the mix and kicked Thrasher behind his knees, which swept him off his feet. He winced as he fell on his tailbone.

After yanking Thrasher's gun away and tossing it aside, Patient Four bent over and grabbed his skull between his hands and screamed in Arabic. "We have to stop them! We have to stop the birds! They'll kill us all!"

Thrasher noticed the man's pupils morphing colors. He had no idea what kind of psychedelic experience the Saudi man was having, but there were no signs of it subsiding any time soon. The strength of his vice-like grip was overwhelming as he compressed his cranium. He only let go when Patient Three grabbed Thrasher by the collar and dragged him into his room.

Thrasher grabbed Patient Three's wrist and twisted it until the man yelped in pain. It was the first sign that he was still human. Thrasher maintained his grip on Patient Three as he sent a hefty punch to his balls and a backward mule kick to Patient Four's kidney. When Patient Three doubled over in pain, Thrasher gave him a sharp knee to the nose and heard the unmistakable crack of cartilage. With no more strength left, he tipped over like a domino and passed out on the floor. Thrasher caught a glimpse from the door's reflection. Patient Four charged at him from behind. He quickly stepped aside and swung the door directly into the man's head, which put him out cold.

Thrasher and Yazdani were gasping for air as sweat from their brows dripped on the floor. They turned to stare each other down. Both men saw that their guns were too far away to retrieve. The look in each man's face said that this wasn't going to end in a gunfight and neither man wanted it to. Yazdani pulled a seven-inch trench knife from his belt and flashed it at Thrasher, who pulled his custom made five-and-a-half inch karambit and flipped it open. His blade may have been shorter but he knew how to use it.

Yazdani wasted no time approaching Thrasher. Once he was within striking distance, he made a broad slash in the air toward Thrasher's midsection. The two knives collided with a pronounced ping in the air. Thrasher's curved blade caught Yazdani's at an awkward angle, which allowed him to land a punch to the man's gut.

The chemist stumbled back. With the knife tucked in his right hand, he swiped left and right at Thrasher's face. After the second missed wide, the American stabbed at Yazdani's abdomen, but he caught Thrasher's arm with his left hand and followed with a swipe to his forearm while landing an elbow to the chin. It was a classic one-two move. Thrasher grunted in pain, which was music to Yazdani's ears. He grinned, pleased that he'd drawn first blood.

Thrasher covered the wound on his right forearm with his left hand, but he was careful not to drop his blade when the elbow to the face sent him wobbling. Turning back, he watched the corners of Yazdani's mouth curl upward.

Keep smiling, fucker.

What Yazdani didn't know was that Thrasher was ambidextrous. He was just as good with a knife in his left hand as he was with his right. The "bring it on" motion his opponent made with his free hand sent a surge of violent adrenaline through his bloodstream. Thrasher was more than happy to grant the Iranian's request.

This will be his last.

Thrasher let loose with a series of stabs, swipes, and slashes toward Yazdani, who reciprocated as best as he could. The perennial clinks and tings of the metal crashing into each other danced in the air. He blocked Thrasher's last swipe with his trench knife, but it caught high on his blade. Thrasher saw this immediately and twisted his wrist so that the pointed edge of his knife penetrated the underside of the Iranian's forearm and sliced downward, opening the veins. Yazdani cried out in agony. The sight of so much blood spurting out of his arm turned his complexion pasty.

Knowing he had the advantage, Thrasher wasted no time finishing the job and delivered a blunt front kick to his sternum, sending Yazdani bouncing off the plexiglass wall. Thrasher charged forward and plunged the pointed edge of his blade into the middle of the Iranian's throat, and met him eye to eye.

Yazdani's eyes widened as he stared back into the raging abyss that were his opponent's. Thrasher wasn't finished. He slid the knife further into the man's neck. When Thrasher felt the curved blade grab the larynx, he twisted his hand and yanked the insides out of the throat.

Thrasher felt nothing but disdain as he stepped back to watch the man die. For reasons unknown, the Iranian was able to stay on his feet and quivered forward, spitting blood. His lips were moving but no words came out. When Yazdani got close enough, Thrasher sent a crippling sidekick to his chest, which propelled Yazdani backward with such force that he broke the plexiglass wall behind him.

Even as Yazdani laid on his back, barely alive, Thrasher's rage was unsatisfied. He snatched the Iranian's knife from the floor, sat on top of the dying man, and stabbed him repeatedly in the chest, neck, and eyes. Each jab was coupled with a therapeutic scream as blood splattered everywhere. Thrasher had no idea if Iranians believed in open casket funerals, but Yazdani sure as hell wasn't going to get one.

Out of breath, Thrasher stood, covered in blood, and admired his work.

Then, he heard a voice behind him.

"Oh my God. What did you do?"

Chapter Forty

When Farhad saw Thrasher soaked in blood and realized what he had done, his bruised face went ashen. He looked past Thrasher to identify the victim, but inside, he knew.

"What did you do?" he asked.

"What's it look like?"

"Donya's gonna freak about this."

Thrasher glanced at him sideways before taking a picture of the ravaged corpse. It was then that he noted the small swastika tattoo on the side of what was left of Yazdani's neck.

"Where's your pal?" Farhad said.

"In there, dead."

Thrasher pointed to the next room.

"I'm sorry."

Thrasher nodded and continued with his business. He grabbed a nearby rag and wrapped the wound on his right arm. After removing Patient Two's clothes, he glanced back at Dhoni.

"I shouldn't do this, but I can't leave him here. Can you carry Wasim?"

"I'm a little woozy, but, yeah, I think so."

It wasn't easy for either of them, but they managed to carry both Dhoni and Wasim up the stairs and toward the exit. As they neared the front door, Thrasher noted that a body was missing.

"Where'd that doctor guy go?"

"Cut loose. He tried to convince Mahmoud to let him give me a sedative, but Mahmoud told him leave."

Thrasher thought to ask what the deal was between Farhad and the doctor, but decided against it.

No time for stories.

The scene outside was more chaotic than before. Thrasher had been right about his estimates. The barracks was too close to the munitions building and was now consumed by flames. Soldiers were scrambling outside while others tried to put out the flames with fire extinguishers and hoses. While two of the on-base fire trucks were busy with the raging mess at the ammunition building, another pulled up to the barracks as Thrasher and Farhad made their way outside. A blast of heat hit them instantly as black smoke saturated the air, making both of them cough.

"Where's the truck?" Thrasher said.

Farhad looked around but saw nothing.

"It should be here. . ."

"Dammit, I knew it! Come on. We'll have to find our own way out."

Carrying Dhoni and Wasim on their shoulders, they double-timed it to the transportation depot. Soldiers running in the opposite direction assumed that Farhad and Thrasher belonged there and were carrying injured men to safety.

When they arrived at the warehouse to steal a truck, they ran into Payman, one of Donya's lieutenants, who was startled to see them.

"Well, I'll be damned," Thrasher said.

He gently lowered Dhoni's body to the ground.

"Give me one reason why I shouldn't shoot you dead right here."

Payman froze. He knew from the pre-mission discussion that the American was serious.

"I'm sorry, sir. The drugs, they took up too much room in the other truck," he said. "Donya told me to get a new one and pick you up."

"Yeah, I'm sure she did," said Thrasher.

"I promise you, boss. She did."

"Whatever. Grab the truck and let's go. Farhad, put Wasim in the back with me. You sit up front and make sure this guy gets us through the gate."

They loaded up quickly and headed toward the exit. At the main gate, they were met by several armed guards.

"No one leaves. Base commander's orders," Sgt. Emran Bameri said.

Farhad was momentarily distracted by the large gap between the man's two front teeth.

"You don't understand. We've got a severely injured man and two of Captain Yazdani's vital patients," Farhad said. "The Supreme Leader told him specifically to save these two. You know what Captain Yazdani was working on, don't you?"

The guard hesitated. It was a guess on Farhad's part, but everyone at the base not only knew what Yazdani was working on, but where his orders came from.

"Let's take a look in back," Bameri said.

He found one soldier badly injured, maybe dead. Another was stiff as a board and drooling on himself, but clearly alive. The man was dressed in brown scrubs like one of Yazdani's patients. He was rocking back and forth, talking to himself as he repeatedly combed his hair with his fingernails.

"The fire lights the sky to the way home," Thrasher said in Farsi. "I see it. Can you see it?"

Bameri was conflicted. The base commander had called down to the gate only minutes before. He didn't want to get into trouble for disobeying orders, but the base commander didn't have this information and, ultimately, all soldiers reported to the Supreme Leader.

"Open the gate. Let them through!"

Payman and Farhad saluted the guards and sped away from the destructive scene.

Chapter Forty-One

WEST HOLLYWOOD, CALIFORNIA

Though Simin begged him not to go to Los Angeles, Kirk knew he had to. Delang was the last connection to his grandfather. He also knew that Delang would do the same for him if the situation was reversed.

"I can't risk losing you again," she said.

"A man's gotta do what a man's gotta do, little lady," Kirk said, in his John Wayne voice.

Simin couldn't help but smile. Kirk's voice impressions were cheesy, but it was one of the things she loved about him. There was no point in debating. Kirk was going. All she could do was give him a deep, wet kiss that would make his knees so weak it would ensure his return. When she finished, she gave him a modest punch in the gut.

"You come back to me! And keep me posted, okay?"

"You got it, babe."

"Oh, and one more thing. When this is over, you owe me dinner at a fancy restaurant."

Kirk smiled as he made his way to the airport. Simin had become more American than she realized.

After landing at LAX, Kirk stopped by a local gun store. The owner, Gus, was an ex-SEAL and owed Delang a favor. He took Kirk into the back and slapped a Springfield 9mm into his hand, and only asked to get it back before he left town. Kirk agreed.

The ride to Wheaton's house was somber. The Uber driver was friendly and tried to strike up a conversation, no doubt looking for a good tip, but Kirk wasn't in the mood. With each passing mile, he became more aware of his precarious position. It wasn't that Delang's request was unreasonable. Kirk had wrestled with his fair share of slimeballs in his time and had no problem setting any of them straight. He'd done so on numerous occasions in his previous job with a private security company, called the Gregory Group, located in Charlotte, North Carolina. Some of them were loons who were only bad asses in their own minds while others were the actual clients. In each of those cases, he'd been armed.

But that was part of the job. Doing so as a favor to a friend, especially in a state like California, with its high penalties for gun possession, was another. Why he would even need a gun was a bit of a mystery. If push came to shove, he should be able to handle Wheaton without it. He knew that he couldn't turn down Delang's request, though. He had been such a good friend to his grandfather, and they'd been through too much together in Iran.

Some people you just don't say no to.

During the ride, Delang called and provided him with an update. His cop friend in the Highlands did him a solid and would be sending him a copy of a surveillance picture that clearly showed the face of the man who ran him off the road. Delang's instincts were tingling, and Kirk knew it was best not to ignore them.

It was nine p.m. when he arrived at Wheaton's house. Only a single light was on inside the single-story, hacienda style home. Kirk wondered whether the Hollywood weirdo was even there, but he remembered that Delang had told him that Wheaton often worked out of his basement. Kirk waited a few minutes until he saw a man with a ponytail peek his head outside the door.

"Can I help you?"

"Vik Wheaton?"

"Yes?"

"I'm friends with Tom Delang. We need to talk."

221

Wheaton's eyes narrowed.

"What's this about?"

"That kind of depends on your answers. Are you going to let me in, or do I need to convince you?"

Kirk pulled up his shirt and exposed the handle of the gun from his waistband.

Wheaton froze. He was no stranger to guns. They'd always been on his movie sets, but this was the first time someone had shown up his house intending to use one. But if the Asian looking man standing in front of him really was friends with Delang then it was essential that he heard what he had to say. Wheaton stepped aside as his guest pushed his way in.

Kirk evaluated the living room. It's hanging accent lights, vinyl wall paneling, and perfectly rectangular marble coffee table gave it a modern look, but other than a brand-new full-length couch, it didn't look like anything special. In Kirk's opinion, it could have just as easily been a room inside a nice home in the South Park area of Charlotte. It was proof that money didn't go as far in California as it did in the southeast.

"Anyone else here or just you?"

"Only numero uno. Who are you?"

"Kirk Kurruthers. Ring a bell?"

Wheaton's eyes popped open. He didn't know how this man had tracked him down and he didn't care. The film Gods were surely on his side.

"Close the curtains," Kirk instructed.

Wheaton gave him a puzzled look but slid the curtains shut to cover the front window. He politely offered Kirk a glass of tequila, but Kirk declined as he tapped away at his phone. Wheaton grabbed a notepad from one of the end tables, pulled a pen from behind his ear and took a seat on the couch.

"So, what can you tell me about Tom? His death was such a surprise. I've been trying to find someone who can help fill in the blanks on his experience in Iran."

"It's not what I can tell you. It's what I can show you."

Kirk turned his phone around to show Wheaton on the other end of the FaceTime call.

"Hello, Vik."

"Tom?! My God. I thought you were dead. It's so good to see you!"

"Is it?"

"What's that supposed to mean?"

"It means that I find it convenient that I got run off the road and stuck in a tree right after I met with you. Meanwhile, I see you hyping the movie and acting like a bigshot on TV. The studio fast-tracked the movie after the news broke about my death, didn't they?"

"Of course they did, Tom. With a story like yours, as long as the town is buzzing about it, they're gonna ride the wave all the way to the bank."

"Kirk, shoot him in the leg."

Kirk pulled out his gun and aimed it at Wheaton.

"Whoa! Whoa! Wait!"

Wheaton leaned back and held up both hands.

"Got something that you want to share with us?" Kirk said.

"I swear to you, I had nothing to do with running you off the road. The first time I heard anything about it was in the airport on my way back to L.A."

"Uh huh," Delang said.

Wheaton leaned up to look directly into the phone.

"Tom, you've gotta believe . . ."

Before he could finish his sentence, a nickel sized piece of cotton stuffing fluttered out of the couch.

"Gun! Get down!"

***

Dammit!

Ward had trailed Kurruthers from the airport and intended to either run him off the road or shoot him as soon as he got to Wheaton's house. That way, he would not have to kill Wheaton. He knew the client had given him the green light to do so, but if he could avoid it, he would. The problem was, Kurruthers was smarter than he expected. Using an Uber driver meant having another witness, and Ward wasn't about to have the death of an innocent person on his hands. He'd killed in the name of business before, but he wasn't going to pop an uninvolved guy who was just doing his job. There weren't many moral lines he wouldn't cross, but that was one of them.

When Kurruthers entered the gun shop on Magnolia Boulevard, it only meant one thing. If Ward wanted to shoot him outside Wheaton's house, he would have to get the drop on him but there was something about the way he moved that Ward didn't like. He could tell that Kurruthers had been trained. His eyes were on the lookout for anything out of sorts, so unless he wanted a wild west shootout in the suburbs, confronting him in the driveway was out of the question.

Back to plan A.

Though the front drapes had been closed, he could see through a side window. He crept along the edge of the house and watched the two men interact. When he saw Kurruthers pull a gun on Wheaton, he thought it was good news. Bumping off Wheaton would save him a step and then he could shoot Kurruthers to make it look like a perfect murder-suicide.

But when Kurruthers didn't shoot, Ward knew he had to do the dirty work himself. The windows were filthy so he couldn't see what was happening but it didn't matter. Wheaton had leaned back enough on the couch, which gave Ward an unobstructed view, so he wasted no time taking the shot.

When he saw white stuffing float through the air instead of red blood and brain matter, he knew he'd missed. He was going to fire again but Kurruthers came to the rescue and dove onto Wheaton, knocking them both over the couch. Ward cursed his luck. It seemed like the mission was destined to be a pain in his side. He had no choice but to get inside and finish the job.

The back door leading into the kitchen was unlocked and creaked as he pushed it open. Peeking around the side, he saw that the lights had been turned off, but the room was empty. The door to his immediate left was closed. He crawled past the stove, an eat-in table, and peeped around the corner where he saw a bright spotlight in the room. As he crawled forward, he saw a phone sitting on the coffee table. The video was on, and positioned directly at him.

"Hi there. Remember me, big man?" Delang said.

Ward extended his gun and was about to shoot the phone when he felt the barrel of another gun pressed against the back of his head.

Busted.

"Hand it over," Kirk said.

Ward could've chosen to fight, but there was no point. As big as he was compared to Kurruthers, he knew that muscles don't stop bullets. Frustrated, he stuck his arms outward, allowing Kurruthers to take his gun.

How did this guy sneak up behind me?

What Ward couldn't have known is that the door next to the kitchen led to a bathroom. Had he made it down the hall, he would have seen that the first bedroom on the left contained said bathroom that circled back to the kitchen. It was an odd design, but not uncommon for houses in that area built in the early 1980s.

Kurruthers led him over to the blue wing chair in the living room. Wheaton turned the lights back on.

"Chad?" Wheaton said.

"Wait, you know this asshole?" Kirk asked.

He stiffened and took a step back in case the two men were working together.

"Chad Ward. We aren't friends, but we've met. He's a Hollywood regular that runs around doing dirty work for the studio. I've seen him on more than a few movie sets."

"Is that your guy?"

Kirk asked Delang by way of the video call.

"That's him," Delang said, confirming that Ward was the man in the photo sent from Sergeant Torres. "Time to spill your guts before my friend does it for you. Who hired you to take me out?"

Ward hesitated. Screwing up a job was one thing but giving up the privacy of a client was another. Kirk watched him deliberate, but he didn't have the patience to coax the information out of him in a professional manner. He aimed Ward's gun at his foot and pulled the trigger. The husky man cried out in anguish, but Kirk didn't wait for the pain to subside. He took the hot barrel of the silencer and pressed it against the top of his hand.

"The next shot takes off a finger," Kirk said.

"You don't have what it takes," Ward scoffed.

Kirk switched the gun into his left hand and held up his right to show a missing pinky. He'd lost it during a torture session in Iran, but Ward didn't know that. The look on his face said it all. The only way out of this was to give up the goose.

"Don't take it personally, Delang," he said. "Just the job I was hired to do."

"Who was it?" Kirk said.

His gun was pointed at Ward, but he looked squarely at Wheaton.

"Walsh. Former Senator Vivian Walsh."

Wheaton froze. Delang and Kirk stared at each other.

Ward spent the next few minutes explaining how the case hit his desk. Based on Delang's expanded closed-door testimony to Congressional leaders, the Senator was made aware of Kirk Kurruther's involvement in Delang's escape. While she played no part in Delang's original capture by the Iranians, it was his testimony on live TV that ruined her Congressional career and flushed her power down the drain. She planned to clean house. Anyone attached to Delang was to be eliminated, and Kurruthers was next on her hit list.

When the movie deal became a genuine possibility, she pulled one of the few remaining IOU cards from her depleted arsenal, and happily dealt it to Lisa Chang, with whom Ward conveniently had a retainer on file.

"Now what?"

Kirk looked at Delang, who didn't answer.

Chapter Forty-Two

TEHRAN, IRAN

Shir-Del, Avesta, and Lajani were gathered in the Supreme Leader's private office at the House of Leadership. For the past three-and-a-half hours, Avesta had been holding video conferences with the leaders of other Middle Eastern countries. Lajani was listening in and occasionally handed him notes. While other leaders eagerly accepted Avesta's invitation, his current phone call with President Raja of Pakistan was going mind numbingly slow. Raja's analytical mind kept flip-flopping on the merits of the proposal, and his inability to commit was making Avesta and Lajani more annoyed. Shir-Del diligently observed but rarely offered insight. His presence served as little more than motivation for his president and IRGC chief, as he wanted to evaluate their skillset.

"Ameer, this back and forth can't go on. You need to decide," Avesta persisted.

"This isn't a light decision, Vahid. We aren't fans of the Jews either and we've maintained our position not to recognize Israel until they agree to the establishment of a Palestinian state."

"Then why is this such a hard decision? With other countries joining us, we now have the power to keep Israel in check, but Pakistan is the only one with a nuclear arsenal. Without you, the rest of us are simply another Middle East club. Your nuclear arsenal is the key to making this agreement work."

"I can see that, Vahid. While Pakistan has never been part of the Non-Proliferation Treaty, we do have agreements with the International Atomic Energy Commission about keeping our weapons secure."

"What agreements?" Lajani chimed in.

"General, let's not play games. Bandits in the region have been trying for years to gain access to our warheads and fissile material. You know this because some of your own people tried last year. Don't bother to deny it."

Avesta covered the mouth of the phone and whispered to Lajani.

"You didn't tell me he knew about that."

Lajani shrugged.

"We wouldn't have to perform covert actions if you'd be willing to share with us," said Lajani.

"What do you think my country is, a nuclear flea market? No. Everyone knows why you want the parts, and I'm not interested in being publicly flogged by the international community for supplying you with the material after you take it upon yourself to blow Israel off the map. It could start a worldwide nuclear war, and I'm not going to be responsible for that!"

Avesta looked at Shir-Del. The displeased Supreme Leader was aggressively twisting the whiskers on his face so tightly that he could hear the course hairs crunch together from ten feet away. He needed to get the conversation back on track.

"Ameer, what you're talking about is using your weapons for offense. At one time or another, Israel has conducted their own operations against each of our countries in the name of protecting what their so-called national security. Now, we can debate their right to exist another time, but each day we do that, they get stronger. What we're talking about here is being able to use your nuclear weapons for defense only. If they hit any of us first, we have the fundamental right to respond."

"I can hardly consider Mossad assassinating a bombmaker or one of your scientists to be worthy of a nuclear response."

Avesta knew that the conversation was going in circles. He looked to Shir-Del, who nodded and extended his palm to Lajani as if to say, "the floor is yours."

"Mr. President, you leave us no choice. I take it that you recognize this man?"

Lajani pulled out his phone and showed his screen to the computer's camera lens. It displayed a picture of a helpless soldier, tied to a chair.

"That's Hasan Wasim. We've been looking for him everywhere! Where is he?"

"One of my soldiers sent me this picture a couple days ago. He's in our custody. Don't worry, he's fine."

Shir-Del smirked at Lajani's lie.

"General, we must have this man back. He has some serious questions to answer and is the key to proving that he didn't act on any direct orders from our government."

"I don't think so, Mr. President. We don't know why Wasim did what he did against India, but as of this moment, he's ours, and we can do what we want with him. The only way that you're getting him back is if Pakistan joins the coalition we are proposing."

"That's extortion."

"That's politics."

"This is not how friendly nations treat one another."

"You're right. Friends share their toys with another. You should have thought about that the other dozen times we've asked you for nuclear assistance."

Raja's eyebrows twitched.

"You set us up, didn't you?" he said. "Wasim works for you."

"We did no such thing!"

A thunderous voice shouted from behind the computer. Seconds later, Shir-Del shoved Avesta out of his chair and sat down.

"Was it not Iran that came to your aid, gave you the oil that you needed to fight India, and then helped negotiate a truce so that your countrymen's blood wasn't smeared on TV? You talk about our countries being friendly nations; yet you insult us!"

Raja settled into his chair. Rarely did the Grand Ayatollah make any type of appearance in political conferences. It was also the first time the Supreme Leader had ever spoken to him.

"Supreme Leader, please forgive me, but Iran didn't give us any oil. We paid for it. And might I add, we paid a higher price on it than was previously agreed."

"The terms of any deal are always in motion until they are agreed upon. Don't expect us to apologize for getting the best deal for our country. The oil continues to flow into your country, does it not?"

"Of course, it does."

"And your country is prospering from it, is it not? My understanding is that the Chinese have renewed their interest in the railway that was destroyed in the war, correct?"

Raja squirmed. He didn't know how the Supreme Leader knew, but the Chinese General Secretary had called him earlier in the morning to discuss terms for the railway as construction resumed.

"They've reached out to me, yes."

"Then it seems like Pakistan is on its way to the top. And the journey back is owed to Iran."

"In part."

"In large part," Avesta said.

Shir-Del noted the interruption in the back of his mind. He would address it with Avesta later.

The Pakistani president tapped his fingers on his leg. He wasn't convinced of Iran's innocence, but he had no evidence to prove otherwise.

The only available proof was tied to a chair in their custody. He had to try another tactic.

"Supreme Leader, no matter his value, I can't trade one soldier for access to our nuclear arms."

"It's not just him that you're trading for. You're also ensuring that Iran's oil keeps flowing in Pakistan's direction."

Raja paused.

"You wouldn't dare," he said.

"Not only would we, but in addition, we've spoken with other leaders in the region this morning. They've agreed to sanctions against Pakistan unless you agree."

"What?!"

"You heard me correctly. You can expect our friends in Libya, Syria, Yemen, and Lebanon to restrict their trade with Pakistan. They are aware of the economic risk to their countries for doing so, but they've agreed that it's a risk they are willing to take."

Raja was stunned. He'd heard that the new Supreme Leader had a chilling combination of guts and brains, but he never dreamt of him turning other countries to unite against his.

"Of course," Shir-Del said, "all of this can be avoided if you agree to join our coalition against the Jews. It is, after all, in everyone's best interest. It will guarantee our safety against the Zionists. But the choice is yours, Mr. President."

Shir-Del sat up and crossed his arms. It was the moment of truth.

Raja was cornered like a rat against a snake but tried not to make it appear that way. He chewed on his cheek as he debated the circumstances in his mind. It was a monster play by the Supreme Leader, but he liked the idea of his fellow Muslims being protected from the Jews.

"I want something more. I want a twenty-five percent discount on the price of oil per barrel. What I am giving up is worth at least that."

Shir-Del looked to Avesta. He nodded.

"Done," said Shir-Del.

"When would I get our soldier back?" Raja asked.

"We'll have him ready for you as soon as the deal is signed," said Lajani.

"I want guarantees from Iran and the others in the coalition for assistance against any future attacks by India. No neutralities."

"I'm sure we can arrange that," Avesta said.

Raja sighed. He'd put off assisting Iran with their nuclear build up long enough.

"Send me the details. Our staffs can work on it."

He signed off without saying goodbye. As the screen went black, Shir-Del turned to Lajani.

"General, see to it that Hasan Wasim has no memory of the events he took part in."

"Supreme Leader, didn't we just agree to hand him back over to Pakistan?"

"We agreed to give him back. We never said what shape he would be in."

Lajani glanced at Avesta, who grinned. Shir-Del made his way to the door.

"Come. We must give thanks to Allah."

Chapter Forty-Three

FOOLADSHAHR, IRAN

Back at the cement factory, Donya's team was unloading the drugs when Farhad and the others pulled up. Thrasher rebandaged the knife wound on his right arm then carried Wasim from the truck to a cot set up in the corner. He stared down at the poor bastard and wondered if he would ever get his brains back enough to tell him what the hell happened in India.

Donya took one look at Thrasher's blood-spattered appearance and knew something was wrong.

"What happened?"

"Kedar's dead."

"Who?"

Thrasher had to correct himself. Dhoni had given her an alias when he introduced himself.

"My colleague."

"How?"

"Mahmoud got the jump on us. He got hit."

"I'm sorry."

Thrasher nodded.

"And where's Mahmoud now?" she said.

Thrasher pulled the karambit from his pocket and handed it to her.

"Here," he said.

"What's this?"

"That's the knife I used to rip out his throat."

Donya saw the blood stuck to it.

"He's dead? I told you I wanted him alive!"

Thrasher sneered.

"And I told you that was never my priority. The son-of-a-bitch killed my partner."

"He experimented on my sister."

"You mean like that?" he said.

He pointed to Wasim.

"Only she didn't live. He poisoned her to death with his homemade chemicals."

"Then he got what he deserved. You're welcome!"

Thrasher walked away but turned back when he heard Donya flip the blade open.

"Don't even think about it," he said.

She looked at the blood dripping from the blade.

"Is this really his blood?"

Thrasher pulled the phone from his pocket and showed her the picture of Yazdani's throatless corpse. Her eyes start to well up.

"It should've been me who did it."

"No. The world needs good people like you. That's why it has people like me."

Thrasher's phone buzzed. The caller ID said RAVEN.

"Hey, how you feeling?"

"Like my head just went through a meat grinder," said Jenkins. "Dub filled me in on everything that's been happening. How are things on your end? Was the Pakistani soldier there? Did you get him?"

Thrasher winced. He didn't want to tell her the bad news, but now that she was awake, he couldn't avoid it.

"Yeah, I got him, but there are some complications."

Thrasher told her about Dhoni, and what happened at the base.

"So, not only do I have to break it to the Director that the agency is now involved in the Iranian drug business; I also have to call Indian Intelligence that we got their man killed?"

"It's not like I had a variety of options. The PMOI wouldn't help us if we didn't help them. As for Dhoni, it was a mission. Shit happens."

"Your compassion is overwhelming, Ben."

Thrasher sighed.

"What about this chemist? Mahmoud, something. Can we flip him?" Jenkins asked.

If you didn't like the other news then you're gonna hate this tidbit.

"No," he said.

Jenkins caught the emotional change in his voice.

"Ben, what did you do now?"

Thrasher told her about what he saw at the base and lost his cool when he came to the part about Dhoni and killing the bastard.

"Again, Ben? He could have been the key to proving Iran's involvement and we could've hung them out to dry over human rights violations. Now, we've got nothing!"

"Not nothing. We've still got the soldier."

"Then, you sure as shit better figure out how to make him lucid again!"

Jenkins hung up.

That went well.

Jenkins was normally level-headed. Thrasher figured that for her to lose her cool meant that her head was more damaged than he thought or that she was one step away from issuing a burn notice on him. It was hard to tell which was true.

Farhad noticed Donya wiping tears from her eyes and Thrasher rubbing his temple.

"Is everything okay?" he said.

She nodded. He turned to Thrasher.

"What about you?"

"No, I'm not okay. Look at Wasim. He's the only link I have to this whole conspiracy, and he can't tell an orange from an elephant."

"Think he'll snap out of it?"

"How the hell should I know? There's no telling what kind of crap that lunatic put into his system."

Farhad sighed. He knew he had no other choice.

"What if I know a way to maybe snap him out of it?"

Thrasher perked up.

"I'm all ears."

"The doctor."

"The one at the facility who wanted to wring your neck?"

"He and I have a history."

"I kinda figured that. I'm guessing it's not a good one."

"He thinks I killed his daughter."

"Thinks?"

"A few years ago, I sold her some vodka and bourbon on her birthday. No big thing. It was business as usual. But she was eighteen, barely over a hundred pounds, and didn't know how to handle it. She got behind the wheel and couldn't control her car along the curvy roads along Chalous Road outside Tehran, and she drove over a cliff."

"So, he blames you."

Farhad nodded.

"You know where he lives?"

"I know where he used to live. Whether or not he's moved since then, I don't know."

Thrasher looked to Donya.

"You're a hacker, right? Can you find out where this guy's house is located?"

"Probably," she said.

"Get on it. We hit the road as soon as we get the address."

"What about him?"

Donya pointed to Wasim.

"He's coming, too."

Chapter Forty-Four

PARDISAN, IRAN

As Farhad drove Donya's van on the four-hour trip from Foolad-shahr to Dr. Aslam's house in Pardisan, Thrasher kept an eye on Wasim. He alternated between checking the poor man's pulse and wiping his drool but made sure to keep one hand on his gun in case Wasim suddenly woke up and decided to go nuts on him. Despite being pulled away from Yazdani's lab, it didn't appear that his condition was improving, which added to Thrasher's worries.

Pardisan was an academic area of Iran on the outskirts of Qom, populated mostly by students attending the city's universities. In any other country, this would cause Thrasher to lower his guard a bit because partying students tend to pay less attention to his covert activities, but this city was not filled with typical college students. It was a major hub for the country's clerics of the Islamic Seminary and a breeding ground for zealots of the Shiite faith who spread the word of their distorted version of Islam and the western world.

Thrasher's impatience and concern about Wasim was already in overdrive, so he didn't welcome the added stress of keeping his radar on high alert for anything out of the ordinary. In a city filled with men who aspired to make it to the Guardian Council or become Supreme Leader, all it would take was running a stop sign to arouse the curiosity of the clerics.

He and Farhad could be caught that easily. If he was lucky, Farhad would only be sent to the notorious Evin Prison. Thrasher didn't need to think about his fate. As a CIA operative in Iran, he knew he would be gutted and hung from the nearest light pole.

Farhad could see that Thrasher's internal surveillance antenna was hypersensitive. Like a shark in the water, his eyes slowly glided from side to side as he surveyed their surroundings.

"How much longer?" he asked.

"We're almost there," Farhad replied.

Thrasher's eyes stopped darting back and forth long enough to lock on Farhad in the rearview mirror.

"How much is 'almost'? Ten minutes? Five?"

Farhad sighed. He should have known better than to give such a vague response to a man with patience the size of a gnat.

"Less than five minutes."

When they made the turn onto the main street, Thrasher told Farhad to drive slowly by the house and then go around the block so that he could see the back of the house. Once they came around and parked several units down, Thrasher checked his watch. It was five a.m. and sunrise was coming soon. They needed to act fast. Thankfully, all the lights in the house were off, as were those of the neighbors.

"The doctor looked to be in his fifties. Is his wife roughly the same age?" Thrasher asked.

Farhad hesitated.

"She died. Couldn't handle the grief after her daughter died. She killed herself."

"You might've mentioned that earlier."

"Look, I didn't do anything wrong by selling that girl the liquor. I can't tell you that everything that happened doesn't still bother me. Not exactly an easy thing to talk about, alright?"

Thrasher nodded, conceding the point.

"Any dogs I need to know about?" he said.

"Not likely. Dogs are pretty much considered vermin in Iran."

"Have you been in the house before?"

"No."

Great.

Thrasher scanned the outside of the brown house. It looked like a run-down duplex, just like the other houses on the street.

"It doesn't look that big from the outside. Maybe a thousand square feet. Do these types of houses have a basement?"

"Doubtful. Not many houses around here have those."

Thrasher noted the second-floor balcony and what looked to be a sliding glass door.

"Is that the bedroom?"

"Most likely."

"Do you know what kind of car he drives?"

"It used to be a red Samand, but I don't know if he still has it."

Thrasher looked up and down the street. There were several Samands, but none of them were red and there was no vehicle parked in front of Aslam's home.

"I think we missed him."

"Okay, so what now?"

"Time to go in. Go around back again."

As Farhad drove around back and parked, Thrasher looked around the car for any tools he could use to break in. There wasn't much to work with, but he found an old, twenty-ounce claw hammer and a Phillips head screwdriver that would do the job.

"Keep an eye on him. I'll be right back."

After surveying the area once more, Thrasher quietly made his way to the doctor's rear entrance, which also had a sliding door. He took out his boot knife and wedged the blade between the base of the door's handle and the door. He needed enough separation to get the claw into the open space. Since Dub was the better burglar, it took Thrasher a little extra elbow grease, but he got it done. From there, he pried the handle off the door and inserted the screwdriver into the installation hole to disengage the mortise lock. Three minutes later, he was in the house. He searched to make sure no one else was there. It looked like the daughter's room was undisturbed. The dresser was covered with dust, but there was a package with a yellow bow sitting on top.

Once he confirmed that the house was empty, he grabbed one of the doctor's white medical coats from a coatrack and went back to the van.

"We still clear?"

"No motion from any of the windows," Farhad said.

"Good. Let's get him out. Put the coat on him to make him look like Aslam and then we'll carry him inside. Make it look like we're bringing him home from a long night drinking."

Once inside, they laid Wasim gently on the couch.

"Now, what?" Farhad asked.

"The only thing we can do. Wait for Aslam to come home."

"That could be hours."

"You got somewhere else to be?"

Farhad shook his head.

"You hungry?"

"Starving."

While Thrasher went upstairs to keep an eye out for the doctor, Farhad closed all the blinds and raided the doctor's fridge. He cooked up a traditional dish, called Baghali polo, which contained rice, saffron, fava beans, green dill, and some leftover lamb. Thrasher had never had it but found it surprisingly good.

The next several hours became a grueling waiting game that ran its fingernails down Thrasher's impatient nerves. He kept checking in with Dub and Jenkins, but there was nothing to report.

Whether he liked or not, Farhad had been designated as Wasim's nurse. He wrapped a large, thick blanket around him, and tried to keep him hydrated. As he cleaned up another round of spilled water, Thrasher came running down the steps.

"He's here. Take Wasim into the next room."

Thrasher screwed the silencer into the barrel of his gun and waited. Moments later, he heard the key turn in the front door. Once he heard it close, Thrasher came out from around the corner.

"Hello, Doc."

He pointed his gun at him.

Aslam stopped, frozen stiff.

"Come on, you can't be that surprised. Take a seat."

As Aslam sat on the couch, Thrasher whistled for Farhad.

With Wasim slumped over his shoulder, Farhad saw the doctor's eyes bulge from behind his oval glasses. His eyes darted back and forth between him and Wasim. It was hard to tell who he was more surprised to see.

"You . . ."

The doctor lunged for Farhad but stopped in his tracks when Thrasher stepped forward and put the steel barrel of the gun against his forehead.

"Eh-eh. Sit down."

Aslam glared at Farhad.

"How dare you bring that scum to my house!"

"Take it easy, Doc. We need your help. That's all."

"No."

"That wasn't a request."

As Farhad placed Wasim next to Aslam on the couch, Thrasher tucked his gun into his waistband and got down to business.

"What's he doing here?"

The doctor pointed at Wasim.

"*He* is our problem, Doc. You administered the drugs that put him in this vegetative state. We need you to give him something else that will bring him out of it."

The doctor laughed.

"Is something funny?" Thrasher said.

"It's not like I'm a pharmacy that can give him over the counter drugs to help with a cold. Mahmoud's chemical mixes were self-made. He was always tweaking the formula. I was only there to observe the patients and report on their status. I have no idea what he gave them or even how to go about doing it!"

Thrasher's face flushed with anger. He didn't have time for any nonsense. He grabbed the doctor by the collar and pulled him to his feet.

"I don't care about what you don't know. I care about what you *do* know. You're a doctor. Find a way to fix him."

Thrasher tossed Aslam toward Wasim. Aslam pulled out his pen light and looked at Wasim's pupils.

"Hand me the sphygmomanometer from my bag."

"The what?"

"The blood pressure cuff."

The doctor pumped up the canvas sleeve and looked at his watch.

"The good news is, he's stable."

"And the bad news?"

"I don't know how long he will be unconscious or if he'll even come out of this. Like I said, Mahmoud made his drugs in-house, and whatever he gave him was strong."

"What can you do for him?"

"He needs a special mix of serotonin blocking agents and amphetamines to help counter everything Mahmoud put in his system. That may be his only chance."

"Can you do that here?"

"Are you deaf? I'm not a chemist. I'm a doctor. Anything I give him will fall short. He needs fluids and complete rest to recover plus a *special mix* of the pharmaceuticals. Only Mahmoud can do that."

"Well, we don't have time for him to rest and I killed Mahmoud's sorry ass, so what's plan B?"

"He's dead?"

"Pulled out that bastard's throat myself."

Aslam sat next to Wasim and put his hand on the soldier's shoulder, relieved at the news of Yazdani's death. He was a doctor who wanted to help his patients, not watch over them as they served as someone else's personal Frankenstein.

Aslam's cell phone suddenly rang. Thrasher's jaw dropped when he saw the name on the caller ID.

SUPREME LEADER

Thrasher jammed his gun against Aslam's head.

"Are you kidding me?"

"I am the Supreme Leader's personal doctor."

Thrasher looked at Farhad.

"Don't look at me. I had no idea."

"Put it on the speaker, Doc. And don't attempt to grow any brain cells, got it?"

Aslam nodded and answered the phone.

"Yes, Supreme Leader? What can I do for you?"

"My servant can't find the extra vials you left. Where did you put them?"

Aslam glanced at Thrasher, whose eyebrows shot up.

"I put an extra vial in your nightstand with three more syringes and I have another order coming. It should arrive tomorrow."

"Do I need to remind you what happened the last time I ran low?"

"No, Supreme Leader."

"Good. I'm going back to Tehran tomorrow. Don't be late."

"Yes, Supreme Leader."

Shir-Del hung up and Thrasher released his gun from Aslam's temple.

"You want to tell me what that was about? Is he sick?"

"I can't. He'll kill me if anyone finds out."

Thrasher threw the doctor down on the floor, planted his knee on Aslam's throat and jammed the barrel of his silencer into the doctor's right eye.

"I don't give a shit about your oath as a doctor or your oath to him. Start talking. What are you treating him for?"

"I can't . . ."

Thrasher twisted the gun, putting more pressure on the eyeball with each turn of his wrist. Aslam started to cry out in pain. Thrasher grabbed the dishtowel Farhad had been using and placed it over the doctor's mouth, muffling the sounds of his screaming.

"Doc, you've got two eyes. When this one pops, I'm going to the next one. The choice is yours."

The doctors legs began to kick, but Farhad jumped in to hold them down. When he couldn't take any more pain, Aslam nodded, and Thrasher got up. After giving Aslam a moment to recover, Thrasher let him sit on the couch.

"Well?"

Aslam sighed.

"The Supreme Leader suffers from Chromosome Six Deletion Syndrome."

"Huh?"

"People are generally born with twenty-three pairs of chromosomes. He only has twenty-two. The specific one he is missing is chromosome six. It's incredibly rare. Chromosome Six Deletion Syndrome causes a person to not feel pain, hunger, or the need to sleep like the rest of us. I've seen him go three to four days without sleeping or eating. One time, he fell down a flight of stairs and fractured his hip, but got right back up. Another time, he broke his arm and didn't notice for three days."

Farhad and Thrasher had no idea what to say.

"He's only susceptible to pain when it is brought on by his own stress. One of the biproducts of this condition is that he suffers from a reduced blood cell count and is known to break out in rashes. The symptoms are often brought on by emotions running high, often leading to violent outbursts, which is why he needs a daily shot of Carbamaze-pine. He can administer it himself, but I have to refill it for him, and he insists that I give him the shot when a new batch comes in. While most people with his diagnosis have some form of mental retardation or learning disability, Shir-Del was never affected like that. I can't explain it, but his intelligence seems to be higher because of it. He's much more dangerous than you think. The concept of fear is foreign to him."

"He doesn't understand fear? How?"

"I don't know how. His brain simply doesn't process it. He was once crossing the street in Tehran with members of the Guardian Council when a car came racing around the corner. The others ran, but he walked at his normal pace while the car headed right for him and he never worried about getting hit. The car's passenger side mirror clipped him on the elbow, but he acted as if nothing happened."

"The leader of a terrorist country has no sense of fear. This is great! How much of that stuff does he have left?"

"I gave him enough for a week, but it depends on how he behaves. He's been extra stressed lately so he's been giving himself extra doses, despite my objections."

"What did he mean when he asked you if you remembered what happened last time?"

247

"I was late getting him his medication. He was stressed and his body was starting to feel the effects of not having it in his system. After I gave him the shot, he repeatedly kicked me. My ribs are bruised badly."

Thrasher could tell there was more. The man was holding back, but he'd been tortured enough. It was time to take another approach. Thrasher tucked his gun back into his waistband.

"Tell me about your daughter."

"What?"

"What was she like?"

The doctor paused. He was confused at the request, but a smile formed as memories came back to him.

"She had a lovely voice. I remember listening to her sing in the shower."

"What else?"

"She wanted to be a beautician. I'll never forget the first time she found her mother's make-up kit. She ended up looking like a clown because she must have used every product in there. 'How do I look, Daddy?' she said. I wanted to be mad at her, but I couldn't. She asked me for a special make-up kit for her birthday. I had come from buying it when I got the call that she died in a car crash. *He* robbed me of so many moments with her when he sold her that alcohol!"

Aslam pointed at Farhad.

Farhad began to speak, but Thrasher cut him off.

"Take it easy, Doc. I'm not trying to upset you. But think about this. Did you know that Mahmoud's first experimental subject was his wife?"

Thrasher proceeded to tell Aslam the same story about Mehry that Donya had told him. When he was finished, Aslam looked astonished.

"You're lying."

"Doc, look at him."

Thrasher pointed at Wasim.

"He's all the evidence I need. The Supreme Leader commissioned Mahmoud to perform those experiments. If they were willing to find ways to increase someone's intelligence, and they had succeeded, what was going to be next? You've seen the research. You can't tell me that they wouldn't have eventually experimented on women. Maybe to find a way to make their breasts bigger or suppress their thoughts to make them more slave-like. That's the kind of future the Supreme Leader wants for Iran. Is that what you would have wanted for your daughter?"

"I wanted my daughter to live."

"Would it really have been living if they were engineered to live the way someone else wanted?"

"No. Of course not."

"Alright then. There's something else you know about the Supreme Leader, isn't there? I can see that you want to tell me something."

Aslam nodded, but Thrasher noticed something else. The doctor's phone was face down on the edge of the blanket wrapped around Wasim, but he could tell the screen was lit up. The sound was off, but he must have had the vibration on. He didn't hear the text message come in because the blanket absorbed the sound.

"Farhad, take Wasim into the next room. Now!"

As Farhad hustled Wasim out of the room, Thrasher swiped the doctor's phone and looked at the message from two minutes ago. It was from someone named Yousef.

Heard a noise out here. Are you okay?

"Who the hell is this?"

Aslam grinned.

"I told you. I'm the Supreme Leader's personal doctor. He's not going to let anything happen to me. Yousef is part of the security team."

Thrasher nailed Aslam in the back of the head with the butt of his gun and pushed him to the ground. He grabbed the phone and texted the man back.

Fine, but need your help. Can you come in?

Thrasher turned Aslam over so he could look at his face. In trying to get more information out of the doctor, he had made the mistake of trying to appeal to the paternal side of him instead of seeing him as an enemy. The tactic backfired. Aslam had felt the phone vibrate, and used it as an opportunity to stall and wait for reinforcements to arrive.

After peeking through the blinds, Thrasher saw a lean man in an IRGC uniform approaching the house. He dragged the doctor across the room, and stomped on his bruised ribs to get his attention. Aslam curled up in the fetal position.

"Keep your fucking mouth shut, asshole."

Seconds later, Yousef entered the residence, and saw the doctor on the floor but he couldn't see Thrasher hiding next to the couch. He closed the door and rushed to the doctor.

"Watch out," Aslam coughed.

It was too late. Thrasher popped out from his position, and shot Yousef in the head. He jerked backward as his skull exploded. Aslam remained on the floor, shocked at what he'd just witnessed. Thrasher flipped the doctor on his stomach, pressed his knee on his back, sure to put pressure on the injured ribs, and placed the barrel of his gun against Aslam's neck with such force that it left a circular impression on the skin.

An image suddenly popped into his head.

That's gotta be the connection.

"Slick move, Doc, but not slick enough. I'm done playing nice with you. I saw those experiments that Mahmoud was doing in that basement, and I saw the swastika tattoo on his neck. You know more than you're

250

telling me. Now, you either start talking or I'm going to take you upstairs and make you watch as I burn every single item in your daughter's bedroom."

"No, that's all I have left of her!"

The doctor struggled to speak because of the pressure Thrasher was putting on his ribs.

"Then, talk!"

"The plans I overheard him discussing the other day are frightening."

Chapter Forty-Five

BAHRIA TOWN, PAKISTAN

Despite doctor's orders, Jenkins released herself from the hospital and had Dub drive her immediately to the ops center. She'd been out of the loop for too long and a lot was happening. She couldn't afford to stay in a hospital bed where she couldn't get anything done. The problem was, the doctor was right. Her body hadn't fully healed, especially her cranium. When she stepped outside the hospital, the sun was so bright she had to ride in the car with a towel draped over her head to curb a splitting headache. At the house, even though she was working alone in a room with the curtains drawn and a single light from a desk lamp, it felt as if she were being stabbed in the eye with an ice pick. Though she rested her eyes for a few minutes at a time, she had no choice but to battle on, and review the reports from the embassy bombing.

She distinctly remembered that Hyat had asked her about his nephew, Hasan Wasim, and knew it was no coincidence that Wasim ended up being India's poster child for the bombings at the global service centers. His disappearance near the Iranian border didn't sit well with her either. The facts didn't add up.

There's something missing.

Jenkins was staring at her handwritten flow chart when Griffin entered the room.

"Just came to check on you. How are you feeling?"

"Terrible. Do you have the report on Wahab Malik?"

"Yeah, I sent it to your inbox. It's all up to date and has the phone info your buddy Farhad gave Thrasher."

"Thanks. What about the autopsy report on Hyat?"

"You don't have it? I gave it to Dub a few days after the bombing."

Jenkins squinted. She'd had problems before with Dub being forth-coming with information. She thought it had to do with him feeling jealous over her being picked for the position he wanted, but she had addressed the issue with him. Since then, Dub was transparent with the flow of information. But, she didn't have the file and there was no record of it on the CIA server.

"No, he didn't. I'll have to ask him about it later. Send me another copy, will you?"

"Sure thing."

After her inbox pinged, Jenkins's phone vibrated, and the sound of it rattling against the table sent a surge of pain through her head. It subsided somewhat when she saw who was calling.

"Hey, girlie. How you holding up?" said Delang.

Jenkins smiled. His term of endearment for her helped relieve the chronic throbbing.

"I'm a little banged up, but I'll live. How about you? Dub told me about what you've got going on."

"You don't know the half of it. Beth, Senator Walsh was behind the attack on me, and she was coming after Kirk Kurruthers next."

Walsh.

"How certain are you about this?"

"Heard it straight from the hitman's lips, and I'm certain he wasn't lying."

Jenkins paused. Sparks flew in her mind as she connected the rele-vant dots.

"You still there?"

"Yeah, I'm here. Can you do me a favor and sit on this for a few days?"

"It'll mean having to babysit the hitter, but for you, I'll do it. Why? What are you thinking?"

"I don't know yet. I need to check on a few things first. I'll call you back."

Jenkins hung up and texted Griffin to come back into the room.

"What's up?"

"Did the crime scene team recover the safe from my office?"

"Yeah, it's downstairs. Why?"

"Is my iPad intact?"

"I'll check with the guys but that safe couldn't be opened with a bulldozer. I'm sure it's fine."

"Would you mind going down there and grabbing it for me? I want to take a look at my file on Tom's capture."

"Sure. Be right back."

Before the door even closed, Jenkins scanned Hyat's autopsy report on the new laptop she'd been given. Most of it was standard stuff: cause of death, stomach contents, status of the organs at the time of death, etc. However, despite his clothes being severely burned, there was evidence of a partial GPS tracker hidden under the back of the man's shirt collar. All GPS trackers are different but this one had been a sticker with a small chip built into the adhesive. If ISI was keeping track of him then she wouldn't be surprised. What alarmed her was that the tracker was known to be used by CIA personnel.

Jenkins closed the file and reopened the report on Wahab Malik. She was looking for the report on the embassy bomber's phone. She'd read it earlier, but Griffin made her want to recheck something, which she found immediately. Though damaged, the CIA tech team was able to confirm that the phone contained an app synched to a GPS tracker.

Malik was tracking Hyat's movements.

Jenkins sat back to collect her thoughts and tried to remember the conversation she had with Hyat before the RPG hit. Nothing particular about it jumped out at her. But then she remembered that she'd flipped the switch to kill any electronic signal in and out of the room before she entered. This would have momentarily killed the beacon to the GPS app, so why launch the rocket at that time?

Her eyes popped open when she made the connection. Malik knew where Hyat was going, and when the signal to the GPS tracker went off, he knew that Hyat had reached his destination. Hyat wasn't the target. She was.

Jenkins closed the file and logged into the CIA's secure administration server. She had a hunch, which she hoped was wrong, but she needed to look at Dub's agency file.

Chapter Forty-Six

PISHIN, IRAN

Thrasher couldn't believe his ears when Aslam told him what he'd overheard outside the Supreme Leader's library. Shir-Del was a devious genius and his plan fit perfectly into all the events that transpired.

Thrasher put the pieces together like LEGO blocks. Iran needed the money to break away from economic sanctions President Cannon had put in place. The pipeline it shared with India and Pakistan was the perfect catalyst to trigger a war that would send money flowing their way. It was impressive how the presidents of India and Pakistan were stupid enough to fall for such a parlor trick, but given how much animosity Sharma and Raja held for one another, it proved how badly emotions can get in the way of decision making. Thrasher knew this from experience.

Once the money seal was broken, Shir-Del decided that Iran needed friends in the international community who weren't afraid to show their support. In order to do that, he took a page out of America's playbook by convincing Libya, Syria, Yemen, and Lebanon to put sanctions in place against Pakistan.

The only way to do that was to hold Wasim hostage because he was the key to proving Pakistan's innocence. Raja's balls had been put in a vice, and his hand was being forced. Thrasher didn't know that for sure and he figured that Raja was probably getting something else out of the deal, but he was willing to bet on his hunch. He also knew that the Supreme Leader had no intention of surrendering Wasim in good condition. It was a brilliant plan.

Thrasher wasn't sure how the embassy bombing fit into the equation. He considered it a distraction while other pieces were put into place. There was no bona fide evidence that the Iranian government had anything to do with it, but after he got Wasim across the border, he was sure as hell going to dedicate his time to proving it.

After hearing what the doctor said, Thrasher called Jenkins. Unbeknownst to him, the President of Iran had called a press conference in three days where he would announce a "new step in diplomacy that would unite the Middle East forever." Conservative media outlets and conspiracy theorists were inciting a frenzy by claiming that this step would launch an Islamic Caliphate that could destroy the world. Thrasher didn't have the time, energy, or desire to partake in the panicked hoopla, but he knew that their concerns about having the world blown to shreds were valid.

According to Jenkins, President Cannon was doing his best to keep Israel's blood pressure down, but it was turning into a full-time job. Thankfully, the Israeli government had their own reservations. It was one thing to order a pre-emptive strike against Iran. Going to war with the entire Middle East was something entirely different. They had defeated multiple Arab countries during the Six Day War, but that was fifty years ago. Despite the increased strength of the current Israeli military, there was greater strength in numbers on the opposing side and the fanaticism was worse than ever. Resistance throughout the West Bank was at an all-time high, and there was no telling who else would join the fight. Israel's existence was being threatened like never before.

Cannon assured the Israeli president that he was gathering evidence to prove Iran's guilt. Once in hand, he promised that he would release it for the world to see. He hoped it would put a serious dent in the Ayatollah regime, and place them on a path to be rid of their evil forever.

The dream was nice, but it put Thrasher's mission front and center. It was imperative that he got Wasim across the border so that he could get the medical treatment he needed and snap out of his current state. That was the only way he could testify about how he was set up and that Iran, not Pakistan, was responsible for the bombings at India's global service centers.

Whether he liked it or not, Thrasher knew that his country, and perhaps the future of the world, was depending on him. Most people would consider it a shitty position to be in, and maybe that was true, but being part of a mission like this is what he signed up for when he joined the agency. Someone had to get the job done. He took great pride being that someone, but not for the glory or accolades. He simply did not want countries like Iran making the world unstable on its personal whim. The only path to stability was to have peace and the only way to pull that off was to have people like him in place to fight for it.

Meanwhile, Wasim's condition made him difficult to move. Fortunately, the doctor had an IV drip and enough saline solution in his home to hook Wasim up for the day-long drive from the doctor's house outside of Qom to Pishin, near the Iran-Pakistan border. Getting across the border wasn't going to be easy, but Thrasher had an idea. He would need Farhad's help, which meant he would have to keep him and Aslam away from each other. For one, he needed the doctor to put his full attention on tending to his patient. Second, he didn't need another dead body or risk Wasim being further injured by any type of assault the doctor had in mind for Farhad while they were driving.

Farhad borrowed a car from one of his PMOI buddies, and loaded it up with energy drinks to keep him and Thrasher awake for the long drive. Donya, concerned that she might lose Farhad on the mission, joined the convoy in a third car. Thrasher wasn't thrilled about her being involved, and made it clear that he couldn't protect her, but he admired Donya for standing up for one of her people.

Thrasher called Dub to see if he could get one million Euros wired to different banks in Iran. When Thrasher told him what it was for, Dub said he was nuts.

"We gotta roll the dice," Thrasher said.

Donya's finance couriers picked up the first four batches of money from two different banks in Qom and delivered them to Farhad. Although Thrasher disliked the idea of Farhad picking up the other three batches from banks in Isfahan and Kerman en route to Pishin, there were no other options.

Ten miles outside of Pishin, Thrasher pulled the convoy over to check on Wasim and to go over the plan one last time. The boost from the energy drinks and his adrenaline were wearing off, but he pushed on. Like every other mission, there was no second place.

Wasim was showing some signs of improvement. He was still unconscious but showed signs of life by moaning from time to time.

"Everyone know their assignments?" Thrasher asked.

"Yes, I've got what you need. Here," said Donya.

She tossed him two grenades. Thrasher panicked a second before he caught them.

"Relax, I didn't pull the pins."

She laughed and turned to Farhad.

"I'll meet you on the other side."

"I know what I have to do," Farhad said.

Aslam was quiet and stared at Farhad.

"Doc?" Thrasher said.

"Get me across the border," he said, "and I'll do what I can for Wasim."

"Here," Donya said, "put these on."

259

She tossed two clean IRGC uniforms to Thrasher and Aslam. Farhad was still wearing the one he had on at the air base.

The doctor nodded. He got the message.

Thrasher's phone rang. It was Dub.

"You about ready?"

"Yeah, we should make it to the border station in about twenty minutes."

"Okay, we'll meet you there."

While Thrasher was on the phone, Farhad couldn't help but notice Dr. Aslam continuing to give him a contemptuous glare.

Chapter Forty-Seven

THE IRANIAN BORDER

When Thrasher received word from Donya that she'd reached the Pakistan side of the border, he and Farhad switched cars, and headed to the border station. Farhad drove the van with Aslam and Wasim. Thrasher drove the money car and would try and get them all across the border. The doctor insisted that he ride in the back so he could continue to monitor Wasim, but Thrasher shut that down. There was no way he was going to let Aslam sit behind Farhad and try to avenge his daughter's death, not when the mission's success was at stake. Before they left, Thrasher went nose to nose with the doctor and grabbed him by the balls.

"Don't even think about trying anything. The soldiers at the border may end up taking me down but not before I take you with me. Got it?"

Wincing in pain, Aslam nodded.

Thrasher whispered to Farhad.

"Be sure to keep one hand on your gun."

"Way ahead of you," Farhad said.

He patted the sidearm on his belt.

Thrasher hated the idea of putting Farhad and Aslam in the van together, but there was no other choice. He couldn't be in two places at once, and he wasn't trusting anyone but himself with the cash. He regretted not asking Donya to bring another one of the PMOI members, but he couldn't dwell on those thoughts. It was go-time.

When they got in line at the border, Thrasher thought it made the U.S.-Mexico border look like the line to Space Mountain in Disney World. There were six lanes, all at least fifty cars deep, and the constant honking was bringing out a new level of road rage in Thrasher that even he didn't think was possible. He cranked up the radio and hoped the music would drown out the maddening racket, but the percussion from the Arabian chords were equally annoying.

He saw that the civilian platform used for transients to walk across the border was just as jammed. But there was only one bulky line and all the people were crammed in like sheep. He switched off the radio and tried to deal with the noise. He was dog tired, sweating from the heat, and felt as if he literally had the weight of the world on his shoulders. At the same time, he needed to keep an eye on Farhad in the van.

Then, he received a text from Dub.

SANDSTORM COMING IN FROM THE WEST.

Perfect.

Thrasher thought about aborting the mission, but he and Farhad were stuck in the middle of traffic. They needed to act fast, but the elements were out of his control. It wasn't like they could just turn around and go the other way. They would have to wait for the border guards to officially close the border.

Dub also relayed new intel about the incident at Hashemabad Air Base, that it had created paranoia within the Iranian government. This wasn't unexpected, but no one anticipated General Lajani leaning on the Border Guard Command and ordering IRGC soldiers to join border agents to assist in inspecting cars. Thrasher was so alarmed he called Dub immediately.

"Are you serious? You couldn't have told me this earlier?!"

"I just got the intel a few minutes ago. I debated telling you, but I thought you needed to know. I don't know what to tell you. I'm sorry."

Thrasher hit the dashboard so hard he cracked the plastic frame.

"Where are you?"

"Two miles out and awaiting your signal."

Thrasher hung up, too pissed off at Dub to speak to him any further.

They had been in line for an hour when he texted Dub that they were approaching the gates. Thankfully, it seemed like the imminent sandstorm caused activity at the border to speed up. Thrasher was in an adjacent line, half a dozen cars behind Farhad when the van neared the front of the line. He watched nervously as the guard interacted with Farhad. His stomach dropped when the guard pulled his gun.

***

There was an awkward silence in the van. Farhad kept one hand on the wheel and the other on his gun. He knew that Aslam despised him, so he tried to break the ice while he waited for the guard to make his next move.

"I hope you know that I'm sorry about what happened," Farhad said.

"Yes, I'm sure it keeps you up at night."

"Dr. Aslam, you have to understand, we're all trying to make a living under the Ayatollah. I had no idea your daughter . . ."

"Berina! Her name was Berina! I can't believe you don't even remember her name!"

Farhad paused. He wanted to deescalate the tension between him and the doctor, but he quickly realized that bringing her up was an obvious mistake.

"Okay, okay. Berina. I'm sorry. I know her name. Believe it or not, it's still hard for me to say it."

"Why would I bother believing you? You didn't even have the courage to show up at the funeral and face me."

The doctor spit in Farhad's face. As he wiped his cheek, the guard knocked on the window. Farhad rolled it down and froze when he saw a large gap in the man's front teeth and the name on his tag.

263

"Is it just the three of you?" said Sgt. Bameri.

"Yes," Farhad replied.

Barmeri looked at Wasim, laying in the backseat, hooked up to an IV bag.

"What wrong with him?"

"He needs medical attention," Farhad said. "We need to get him to a hospital across the border. This is his doctor."

Bameri leaned into the window and saw a familiar face.

"Dr. Aslam?"

Farhad froze. It had been a slip of the tongue. Aslam hadn't been with him when he, Thrasher, and Payman talked their way past Bameri at the air base gate. He didn't realize that he and the guard were acquainted.

"Wait a second. I know you. You're the same guy I talked to a few days ago. And that guy was in the back of the truck!"

Bameri grabbed the handle of his gun. He waved another man over.

"General, we've got a situation here!"

Farhad and Aslam stiffened. The man that approached from the passenger side leaned down to look inside the car. Though the driver's face was vaguely familiar, he was well acquainted with the doctor and the passenger in the back seat.

"Doctor?" Lajani said. "What's going on?"

"Arrest him!" said Aslani. "He's working with the Americans. They're trying to sneak this man across the border!"

Bameri pulled his gun and put the barrel to the side of Farhad's head.

"Get out of the car, now!" Lajani ordered.

Farhad slowly exited. Lajani grabbed his radio and was about to call for additional assistance when an explosion rocked the lane next to them and knocked everyone off their feet. Lajani slammed into the side of an adjacent cargo truck and hit the back of his head before he collapsed to the pavement, unconscious.

When Bameri came to, he looked up and saw bills of money floating in the sky. Pandemonium ensued as everyone in line exited their cars and rushed toward the scene, snatching whatever cash they could.

Some IRGC agents hurried over to control the scene while others joined in on the calamity of free money.

Bameri held Farhad at gunpoint.

"Stay where you are!"

Farhad's eyes darted back and forth. He didn't know what to do. He had to help Thrasher get Wasim across the border but he couldn't move and reaching for his own gun would be a sure recipe for getting shot. As he debated his next move, he noticed Bameri's face freeze in a shocked expression. He slowly lowered his weapon as blood began leaking from his mouth before he dropped to the ground.

***

When Thrasher saw the border agent pull his gun, he wasted no time pulling the pin on the grenades that Donya had given him and tossed them in the back seat as he hauled ass to take cover. After they exploded, Thrasher smiled as he saw everyone trampling over each other, clamoring to grab the cash, which had exploded out of the trunk and up into the air. He imagined that in their minds it had probably been sent from Allah himself.

Then, Thrasher saw one of the guards holding Farhad at gunpoint. He didn't want to shoot and alert the other soldiers. He also needed the chaos to continue as the crowd scrambled for the money. He couldn't afford to scare them. With his options limited, Thrasher pulled his boot knife and snuck up behind the border agent. He was less than ten feet away when the soldier stood up.

Thrasher heard him tell Farhad not to move. The soldier had no idea Thrasher was behind him as he jabbed the blade between the man's ribs. After yanking out the blade, he shoved the body to the ground.

"Come on, Farhad," Thrasher said. "We don't have much time. Help me get Wasim out of the car."

Thrasher unhooked the IV and they pulled him out. Once they were able to get Wasim to his feet, Thrasher looked over to the walkway. Most of the crowd that had been standing there had run over to take their chances at getting the cash, but some were still there watching the chaos. Only two border agents still guarding the gate. The scenario was as good as it was going to get, so Thrasher lifted Wasim into his arms as if he were carrying a bride across a threshold.

"Hurry, let's get him to the gate!" Thrasher said.

When they looked up, they noticed that Dr. Aslam had picked up Bameri's gun and was pointing it at them. He fired a shot and Farhad went down.

Chapter Forty-Eight

Farhad dropped to the ground and rolled over. Blood was starting to pool around him.

"That was for my daughter," Dr. Aslam said.

Thrasher glared at the doctor. He tried to slyly reach for his gun in his waistband, which already had the silencer attached, but the doctor noticed.

"You're not going anywhere. I'm going to march you to the Supreme Leader myself. He'll reward me with whatever I want."

Before the doctor uttered another word, a helicopter landed just across the border. The huge gust of wind from its whirling blades hurled sand and dirt in everyone's face. As the doctor held up his arm to block the debris, Thrasher drew his gun and shot Aslam in the head. Because of the sounds from the chopper, the doctor never heard the sound of the shot that dropped him.

Thrasher checked on Farhad. The bleeding was worse than expected.

"Hold it!" Lajani shouted.

He was holding the side of his head and the gun in his other hand was shaking, but he knew that he had to stop Wasim from getting away.

Seeing that Lajani was clearly disoriented, Thrasher ripped off two more rounds that hit him right in the chest, knocking him down once again. He kneeled down by Farhad.

"Can you walk?"

Farhad shook his head and reached for his partner.

"Don't leave me," he said.

Thrasher shrugged him off and threw Wasim over his shoulder. He shuffled away as fast as he could, lowering his head as much as possible to avoid the sand kicked up from the helicopter.

Is this the sandstorm Dub was talking about?

Thrasher kept moving toward the pedestrian gate. When the pedestrians waiting saw that he was wearing an IRGC uniform and carrying an injured man, they gave way so that he could make it to the front of the line. The guards there were shouting and signaling to the helicopter pilot to shut it down. Thrasher saw that it was Dub. Thankfully, he'd been smart enough to put the tags of the Pakistani military on the side of the bird, so the Iranians had no idea it was an American. For now, that was the only thing keeping the IRGC goons from taking a shot at him.

"I've got an injured man here. I need to get him across!"

Thrasher yelled in Farsi over the sound of the helicopter. The guards took one look at him and knew something wasn't right.

"Where's your medical clearance?"

Thrasher wasted no time shooting one of the guards. He gave him one in the gut followed by another to the head. The guard's partner was too inexperienced and slow on the draw. Thrasher shot him between the eyes before he could raise his assault rifle.

Thrasher hustled through the gate, but he still had to pass through a two-hundred-yard walkway, encased by a fence with barbed wire. It was a neutral zone used in case the border agents on either side changed their mind about who they let across. He ran with Wasim on his shoulder as fast as the man's weight would allow. Suddenly, a bullet from the watchtower plugged the ground in front of his feet. Thrasher stopped in his tracks.

"Don't move!"

Thrasher threw down his gun. There was no way he was going to get a shot off before the guard did. As he turned around, another shot rang out. The guard tumbled over the edge of the tower and plummeted to the ground. Thrasher didn't stop to see the mess. He saw Griffin at the other end of an SR-25 sniper rifle.

"Move it, will ya?!" she yelled.

When Thrasher finally reached the chopper, he tossed Wasim in the back.

"Do everything you can for him. I gotta go back."

"*What?*"

Thrasher didn't answer Dub. He sprinted back to his gun, plowed past the people shoving their way through the gate with cash in hand, past the Pakistani border agents, who'd been ordered to let him by and stood stupefied as they watched him run back into Iran.

"Out of my way!"

Thrasher yelled in Farsi.

Farhad was barely conscious with blood surrounding him.

"Come on, Farhad. I need you to move your feet."

Dub and the others were back in the air by then. Farhad was too weak to move, so Thrasher grabbed him as best as he could and rushed to the chain link fence, where he spotted Donya's car. She'd gone through the border station from the Iran side and then turned around on the Pakistani side to come back into her homeland.

Since the fence was topped with barbed wire, Thrasher's only option was to push Farhad over the top of the adjacent cement wall divider. There was no gentle way to do it. He warned Farhad to brace himself for the fall. All he could do was hope that the words registered and that Farhad didn't crack his skull when he hit the other side. He used every ounce of energy he had to lift Farhad over his head and push him over the top.

With the chopper gone, the burst of wind and sand died down. All of the cash had finished falling from the sky. Some people were still searching the ground for any cash that might have been missed, but the scene of disorder was starting to calm itself. Some of the Iranian border agents were laughing as they counted their money. However, one of them noticed what Thrasher was doing. Just as he slipped Farhad over the divider, a bullet narrowly missed his head. Thrasher returned fire and hit the agent in the torso before jumping the wall.

He landed on two agents who were inspecting Farhad. He pulled his knife and mercilessly stabbed them in the neck. Then, he carried Farhad to Donya's car.

"What happened to him?"

"He's hit. I'll explain later. Let's get the hell out of here!"

Chapter Forty-Nine

TEHRAN, IRAN

Three days later, Avesta paced the floor of the Razi International Conference Center. He was in high spirits and practically bouncing off the walls with excitement. It was going to be a great day for Iran and the Muslim world. The leaders of Syria, Yemen, Libya, Lebanon, and Pakistan had flown in for the coalition signing ceremony and were waiting for him. They would finally be united in their common interest against Israel, on their way to burying the putrid country, once and for all.

Avesta had also promised President Raja that he would deliver the Pakistani soldier after the ceremony, but the Revolutionary Guard had lost him. A few days ago, General Lajani had received word about a break-in at the testing facility at Hashemabad Air Base. Wasim had been taken, and Captain Yazdani has been brutally murdered. There was no sign of which country was responsible, but the Supreme Leader was livid. He not only wanted to push the ceremony up; he was inclined to put Lajani's head on a stick. While his future was in limbo, Avesta convinced him to leave the ceremony schedule alone, afraid that moving it up would raise too many questions in the international community. Lajani conducted his own search and hadn't been heard from since, although there were reports of a tussle at the southeast border with Pakistan.

Despite repeated calls and texts to Lajani, the ceremony was set to begin in five minutes and there was no word from him. Wasim was still in the wind. Oddly, Raja had made no inquiries about his soldier. Looking down the hall, Avesta saw that he was currently on his cell phone, no doubt arranging things at home for when Wasim was returned. After the ceremony, Avesta would have to use his political savvy to keep him at bay.

Avesta's assistant, Navid Dorri, entered.

"Everyone's ready for you, Mr. President."

Avesta nodded. His concerns about Wasim would have to wait. It was time for the Supreme Leader's vision to be realized. Iran would step up and take what was rightfully theirs. He walked to the waiting area, took his place at the head of the line, and led the other leaders into the auditorium.

Cameras flashed and the capacity crowd applauded as the leaders entered. The stage was set with a table on each side of the podium. Leather chairs and name plates were assigned to each of them, and they would sign the documents as they came around. Overhead a giant, high-definition projection screen displayed the ceremony, which was being broadcast to the Muslim world via Al-Jazeera from the state-owned broadcasting channel that had a trailer set up outside.

Once the applause died down, the leaders took their respective seats. As Avesta took the podium, his face appeared front and center on the big screen.

***

At the House of Leadership across town, Shir-Del sat alone in his private study. He checked his watch. Avesta would be taking the stage at any moment to help him realize his dream of Iran becoming the true leader of the Middle East. He checked his phone again, but still no message from Lajani. He noticed a new, dark blotch of skin on the back of his hand. He'd taken a shot earlier but was running low on his medicine. He had texted Aslam about getting the extra shipment but he wasn't answering. His rage was building and he slammed his fist on the arm of the chair, but he soon calmed down when he saw Avesta appear on screen.

"My dear Muslim brothers and sisters. For too long we have debated and fought against one another, regarding the leader of our wonderful faith. We are not here today to put that debate to rest or fight it any further. Instead, we are here to unite ourselves against our common enemy. The Satanic country of Israel has waged their private war against us for decades in the name of what they claim is their own security. We declare that they have no such security because we do not recognize the legitimacy of their existence. They have enslaved our Palestinian brothers and sisters on the West Bank, fought mercilessly against us, and aligned themselves with the Great Satan, the United States. Today we say, no more."

The crowd erupted in applause. Avesta waved and then motioned for them to be silent.

"Each of us is here today to strengthen our position in the region as we merge our individual national securities into one. It will be called the Persian-Arab Coalition. From this day forward, any attack by Israel against one of us will be deemed as an attack on all of us. And thanks to our Pakistani partner in this endeavor, the option of a nuclear response is now squarely on the table."

The auditorium exploded in cheers and applause as did people watching in homes across the Muslim world. Shir-Del couldn't help but smile. The applause died down as Avesta sat and aides from each of the countries passed around the documents for each leader to sign. The cameras zoomed in on each of their signatures above the legal name of their respective country and displayed it on the big screen.

It took ten minutes for the alliance to be formally completed. Once the paperwork was handed off to the aides, each of the leaders stood center stage and raised their hands together for the world to see. Shir-Del's defining moment had been realized.

As the leaders took their seats to field questions from the media, the giant screen above them went blank. Rainbow-colored bars indicated that the signal had been lost. When the image returned, what was displayed was not the face of anyone on stage.

"Hello, Mr. President."

The voice startled Avesta. He didn't know where it was coming from. When he turned around to look at the big screen, he was stunned to see the face of President Roger Cannon.

"Mr. President, you are not invited to this meeting. What is the meaning of this?"

"Well, Mr. President, I've always had a nose for a good party, so I thought I'd crash it with some news of my own. First of all, I'd like to congratulate you and the leaders of Yemen, Syria, Libya, Lebanon, and Pakistan on your coalition. It is a bold statement, indeed. But it got me thinking."

Shir-Del stood up, shocked at what he was witnessing.

Oh no.

"After 9/11, many citizens of the free world wondered what country we should attack in order to exact revenge. Alas, our president at the time had to tell them that no such country exists. Until now. Thanks to the document that you and your fellow leaders on stage just signed, the coalition you spearheaded now provides legal precedent in the international community for a terrorist organization."

Avesta was shocked. He looked to his fellow leaders. Each of them had a similar look. But he knew that the penny wasn't finished dropping. He had caught on to one of the words Cannon used.

"We?" he said.

"Oh yes. I'm sorry. Where are my manners?"

The camera on the president zoomed out. Standing next to him in the East Room of the White House were the presidents of Israel, Egypt, India, Jordan, and the United Arab Emirates.

"Each of us," Cannon continued, "have signed our own pact, stating that any attack by any of your countries on one of us is an attack on all of us. And I don't think I have to remind you that our nuclear arsenal is substantially bigger."

Enraged, Avesta looked over to Raja, who gave him an approving smile. It was all the reassurance he needed to take the conference to the next level. If America wanted a showdown, he was going to give them one.

"Mr. President, we're not scared of you. We are here today, united in our cause. Thanks to our friend in Pakistan, we'll be glad to wage war with you."

"Yeah, about that. President Raja and I have had many discussions over the last few days, including one just before your conference. We have someone he's been looking for and he's got a lot to say."

Cannon motioned to the person standing off-screen. In walked a haggard but alert Hasan Wasim.

"I believe you and the rest of the world are familiar with Lieutenant Wasim as the bomber of the global service centers in India. What the rest of the world doesn't know, and what he will testify to at the United Nations, is that Iranian agents blackmailed him into pulling the C-4 out of the base in Pakistan by threatening the lives of his family. They then held him at gunpoint to plant the bombs in the corporate offices. Due to some quick thinking on his part, though, he was able to disarm some of the bombs under the noses of your Iranian agents in order to limit the damage. Is that right Lieutenant Wasim?"

"That's correct, Mr. President."

"Oh, I'm sure the world will be pleased to know that the Pakistani ISI successfully rescued his family from a warehouse outside Karachi an hour ago. Isn't that correct, President Raja?"

"Yes, President Cannon, they did."

Shir-Del grabbed the phone, and urgently dialed the trailer for the state-run news station outside the conference center.

"Hello?"

"This is the Supreme Leader. I order you to cut the news feed to the conference immediately!"

"I'm sorry, your call cannot be completed. Please try again later."

The voice on the phone hung up. Shir-Del stared at his phone. After cussing incessantly, he made another call.

"And there's one other thing," President Cannon said. "We've also discovered some serious human rights violations at one of Iran's military bases that Lieutenant Wasim will also testify to. In the meantime, here's a preview."

Avesta began to sweat. He motioned for Dorri, who ran over.

"Go to the news trailer and tell them to cut the feed!"

"Yes, sir."

The screen played a thirty-second clip of video footage Thrasher recorded in the basement of Yazdani's former observation lab.

"President Cannon, I'd like to speak," President Sharma said.

"By all means," Cannon said.

"President Avesta, you have dishonored and killed Indians and Pakistanis in the name of advancing Iran's global interests. While I can't speak for President Raja, India formally withdraws from our oil deal with you, and will join the United States in the sanctions against Iran."

"As will Pakistan," said Raja.

***

Outside in the news trailer, Thrasher held the producers and technical directors at gun point. The camera men who were supposed to be working inside were tied up behind him. The men working the cameras inside were some of Donya's PMOI members.

"You hooked in?"

"Yup, got it," she said.

Donya had successfully hacked the feed to the event inside. In the lower half of her screen was the video feed from the White House. She stopped the broadcast from the big screen with a couple of taps on the keyboard, and inserted the feed from America. Minutes later, the hardline phone rang inside the trailer.

"Hello?" Farhad said.

He was sporting a new arm sling.

"I'm sorry, your call cannot be completed. Please try again later."

He hung up the phone and smiled.

"I've always wanted to do that."

Thrasher cracked a smile.

Suddenly, Avesta's aide burst through the trailer door. Thrasher turned and pointed one of his guns at him. Dorri froze. Thrasher didn't want to create a mess or start a fight that would jeopardize the video feed. Farhad saved him a step by kicking Dorri in the balls. Thrasher reached into his back pocket and threw him some zip ties.

"Tie him up," he said. "If I had to guess, we don't have long."

Back inside, President Cannon continued.

"I guess that about concludes our business, Mr. President," he said. "Sorry to ruin . . ."

The world didn't get to hear the rest of Cannon's statement. As Thrasher expected, Shir-Del called the power company and had them cut electricity to the building.

"Let's get outta here, fast."

Inside, it didn't matter that the power was out. The damage had been done. Avesta sat in the dark room, shocked, with only the camera flashes and shouts from the media filling the room. The other leaders quietly filed out of the rear door. All except Raja. Before leaving, he dropped a note in front of Avesta.

Pakistan officially resigns from the Persian-Arab Coalition.

Chapter Fifty

BAHRIA TOWN, PAKISTAN

Jenkins woke Dub up at three a.m. with an alarming phone call.

"Thrasher's in trouble. You need to get in here. Now."

Dub popped in his contact lenses, and was still hopping into the legs of his pants as he ran out the door. The normal forty-five-minute drive from his apartment outside Islamabad took him less than twenty. Jenkins was standing in the corner of the third-floor office, reading a file, when he entered.

"Hey, what happened to him?"

"Take a seat and read this."

She handed him her iPad.

Dub sat across from her and started reading an autopsy report on Izad Hyat, the same file he had tried to hide from her. He was about to explain when the clicking sound of a gun being cocked grabbed his attention. She was pointing a Walther PPK at him.

"You set me up, Dub."

Dub slowly raised his hands.

"Whoa, no, I didn't."

"Yes, you did. Tom called Izad Hyat's wife. She told him that he was scheduled to meet with you on the day of the bombing. Then, he unexpectedly came to see me. The autopsy report in front of you says that a GPS tracer was found on him. It was damaged by the blast, but the techs were able to identify it as one the CIA uses regularly. You planted it on him, didn't you?"

Dub nodded.

"Why?"

"I owed someone a favor."

"Let me guess. Vivian Walsh."

Dub cocked his head and gave her a curious look.

"How'd you know that?"

"When the agency was about to medically discharge you, your father called in a favor to save your career. All it took was a little digging to find out that person was her. Knowing your history with Hyat, I put two and two together. When did she contact you?"

Dub sighed and let his hands fall onto his lap.

"Keep your hands where I can see them, Dub."

Dub reluctantly raised them.

"A few weeks ago. She said that I owed her. All I needed to do was place the tracer on Hyat and walk away."

"And you believed her? You know what kind of person she is!"

"She was friends with my dad, and she laid the guilt trip on me pretty thick. I swear to you, I had no idea it was going to put you in danger, and I sure as hell didn't know it was going to mean getting the embassy bombed. I thought it was another one of her games where she needed dirt on Hyat."

Griffin knocked. She nodded at Jenkins, gave Dub a disdainful look, and left.

"Looks like the last phone number that called the bomber also called you a few days ago. Was that her?"

Dub nodded.

"She wanted to know about you. I hung up on her and haven't spoken to her since."

Jenkins lowered her gun.

"What am I gonna do with you? How could you be so stupid?"

Dub shook his head.

"I know. The only thing I can say is that family pressure is a bitch. She had a good relationship with my father, and believe it or not, she was once a good person. All I can tell you is, she knew exactly what buttons to push. But I *swear* to you, I had no idea what she was up to. When the dust settled, I was planning on looking into how she knew Wahab Malik. My guess is that she paid off the right people in the Pakistani ISI. She probably covered her tracks pretty well, but I was going to give it a shot."

Jenkins chewed her lip as she tried to decide Dub's fate. Overall, she knew he was a good man and a good agent. He'd been caught in a situation he didn't fully understand, and certainly wasn't the first to be trapped in a web spun by Walsh. He was stupid, not evil. But this wasn't an incident that could be swept under the rug.

"You know that I have to report this to the Director."

Dub nodded.

"I know."

"I can't guarantee that he won't fire you or have you brought up on charges, but he and I both believe in redemption. That is, if you're willing to try and make things right."

"Of course, I will. Just tell me what you need me to do."

Chapter Fifty-One

PHILADELPHIA, PENNSYLVANIA

Vivian Walsh was riding in a limo on her way back from a meeting downtown. The pouring rain made it easy to get lost in her thoughts. On the surface, she was about to make a ton of money. Her company that produced prepaid cell phones was about to be bought out. As a senior board member, she stood to personally gain more than sixty million dollars. But at the moment, money was the farthest thing from her mind. President Cannon had delivered a spectacular blow to the Iranians when they weren't looking, and embarrassed them on global public television. It was thrilling to watch. She was even a little jealous.

The Iranians were the root cause of ruining her Congressional career and setting them up for the bombing was her attempt at payback. But when the Islamic Republic brokered peace between India and Pakistan, the world thought that the deranged nation had miraculously turned the corner under the rule of a new Supreme Leader. Doing so cleared the board of the embassy bombing headlines that she'd worked to put into place. Thanks to President Cannon's efforts, though, the eyes of the world were now glued on Iran.

Prior to her board meeting, she'd spent a good deal of her day using her contacts in the media to get them to double down on their attacks on Iran, and linking the embassy bombing back to them. But she got few nibbles from journalists who owed her favors. The embassy bombing was weeks ago. Without a huge smoking gun, it was yesterday's news. Apparently, a call from the phone number of a Revolutionary Guards-man to the bomber wasn't good enough. Walsh was convinced that she could find a way to get it done, but she needed time to think.

When she walked into her home, she unbuttoned the jacket of her pink Alexander McQueen suit, poured her seventh Maker's Mark of the day, and took a seat in her living room. She was drinking more than usual. The buzz helped dull the pain of knowing that all of her power had been stripped away by a bunch of degenerate Iranians and meddling CIA agents. An unfortunate biproduct of her increased alcohol consumption was her tendency to drink and dial. It had become such a common occurrence that her ex-husband had filed a restraining order. Her blackouts were frequent enough that the judge on the case was on the verge of recommending rehab. Not that she was worried. One phone call would be all it would take to squash the restraining order. She knew that the judge in question had a liking for young strippers and had paid for more than one to have breast enhancements.

After a few more gulps, Walsh lit a cigarette and turned on the TV to see if there were any developments in the Iran story. But as soon as she did, the TV clicked off. She groaned, figuring that the rainstorm had knocked out the reception.

"You're not going to hear anything you haven't heard over the last few days."

Walsh spun around and saw Dub, calmly standing in her living room.

"What the hell are you doing here?"

"You set me up, Vivian."

Walsh grinned.

"You let yourself be set up. All I had to do was sprinkle a few words about how your dad and I always had each other's back, and you didn't hesitate. Some spy you are."

"I never would've helped you attack an embassy, and you know it. Christ, you almost killed my boss!"

"The only thing I did wrong was send the wrong person to get the job done. For her and Delang. Neither one of them has paid their debt in full yet."

Delang came out from around the corner.

"Oh really?" he said.

Walsh stopped mid-sip of her bourbon as Delang sat in the chair next to her.

"You need to be more careful about who you call, Senator."

"Excuse me?"

"Your plan to use a Tehran number from one of your company's burner phones was clever, but you hit a patch of bad luck. When your company assigned you the same number that had previously been used by someone in the Revolutionary Guard, it should've been good for your little plan. But one of our sources on the ground used to receive calls from that number and we know for a fact that the person who used to call from that number is now dead. He was killed outside the embassy after I made it in."

Walsh took a slug of her bourbon.

Shit. That wasn't in any of the reporting.

"And, I don't know if you were in one of your drunken stupors or if you were trying to frame Dub, but when you used that same number to call him a few days ago, the number pinged off a cell tower a mile from here. And guess what I found in the hidden compartment of your nightstand?"

Delang held up the cell phone.

"That puts you back in the spotlight."

Fuck.

"I can't believe you tried to set up the Iranians for something they actually *didn't* do," said Delang. "With your help, we could have gotten them on any number of things. Doing so may have even improved your image."

"They set me up."

"Welcome to the club."

"What do you want, Delang?"

"I want all of these self-labeled debts cleared. We're not going to be the poster children for your career going down in flames."

Walsh licked the bourbon from her lips.

"You don't know me well at all, do you?" she said.

Delang turned to Dub and nodded. Dub screwed in a silencer and shot her below the kneecap. Walsh screamed in pain.

"And I guess you don't know us either. The only reason that I don't kill you right here and now is that we might need you down the road. Then, *your* debt will be paid in full."

Dub and Delang slipped out the back, leaving Walsh writhing in agony.

Chapter Fifty-Two

ASHEVILLE, NORTH CAROLINA

Everyone in the Kurruthers' home was in good spirits. Wheaton flew in from Los Angeles and Delang drove over from the Highlands so they could all put their heads together to finish the screenplay. Simin was especially excited to be involved in the Hollywood process and gave her insights into the inner workings of the Iranian black market. She was in social media heaven and couldn't resist making multiple posts on Instagram. Since Jenkins had to make a special trip to Langley to talk with the Director about Dub, she decided to attend. It gave Wheaton a chance to pick her brain on the incident in Beirut and how she dealt with the time when she thought Delang was dead.

The discussions were therapeutic and jovial. Too much had been left unsaid since Delang returned to the States. It dawned on everyone that they'd never had the opportunity to put all their cards on the table. For the most part, Wheaton remained silent and hammered away at his laptop, making notes. The gang consumed multiple bottles of wine, which led to popcorn fights and plenty of laughs as Kirk and Delang relived their Iranian adventures. As they described their ordeal, it was hard for all of them to believe that they had actually survived.

The party shifted gears when Kirk asked Simin to video something for her. When she turned the corner, she saw Kirk down on one knee with a diamond ring in his hand. She nearly dropped the phone but managed to keep recording and get the whole proposal on video. Jenkins took the phone so they could embrace. Simin, of course, posted the video online for everyone to see. Within an hour, she'd gotten thousands of hits.

A short while later, Jenkins pulled Delang aside on the second-floor patio.

"You okay?" he said.

"Yeah, it's been a while since I laughed so much. Those two make the cutest couple. It makes me sick."

"Tell me about it. So, what's the problem? I can tell there's something on your mind."

Jenkins pursed her lips. Delang knew her as well as she knew him.

"It's just a hunch, but there's something I think you should know."

"Okay."

"Thrasher told me about all the experiments the Iranians performed on the physics students. After Wasim's blood work came through, I had one of the agency doctors compare his tests with the one we got from you in the hospital in Ashgabat."

"And?"

"Although your test showed smaller doses, both of you had elevated levels of serotonin. Your description of one of the Revolutionary Guard soldiers matches the one that Thrasher killed. I would say it's likely that he experimented on you."

"I can't say I'm surprised, and it shouldn't surprise you either. Why the long face?"

"It always bothered me why Izad Hyat was the one that Walsh targeted for her plan at the embassy."

Delang sighed. He finally understood.

"And when I testified to Congress behind closed doors, I named Izad as one of the possible sources I gave up under torture."

Jenkins nodded.

"I can't say for sure that you gave his name up to the Iranians because of the experimentation, but all Walsh had to do was get a copy of the report."

287

Delang lowered his head.

"So, it was my fault he got killed."

"No, I wouldn't say that. But I thought you would want to know why she chose him."

"Thanks for telling me, but I'm not sure how I live with this now. If I got him killed, who else did I put in danger?"

"I'm still looking into that, Tom, but I think it was an isolated incident. Walsh at her best. Or worst. Depends how you want to look at it."

"No. This is on me."

The patio door slid open.

"Hey, am I interrupting something?" Wheaton asked.

"No, we were just reminiscing a bit," Delang said. "What's up?"

"We've probably got another hour or two of work. You ready to come back in?"

"Be right there."

As soon as Wheaton went inside, Delang turned back to Jenkins.

"Does the Director know about this?"

"I haven't told him yet."

"Make sure that you do."

"Are you sure about that? It could hurt you in the end."

"Nothing can hurt me more than the emotional pain of giving up one of my friends."

Delang joined the others. Jenkins stayed on the patio, looking at the hazy sky of the Blue Ridge Mountains, and debated her decision.

Chapter Fifty-Three

NEW DEHLI, INDIA

Thanks to Donya, Dhoni's body made it back to India so it could be properly laid to rest. In the Hindu culture, the body of the deceased is normally held at the family home for twenty-four hours before it is cremated. Unfortunately, in Dhoni's case, this wasn't possible because the body was already starting to decompose by the time it got back to India, but his family was grateful, and proceeded with the cremation.

Although he knew it was dangerous and that Jenkins would not approve, Thrasher had Farhad sneak him out of the country so he could visit Dhoni's grave. He knew it was going to be a pain getting back into Iran, but that was tomorrow's problem.

The funeral was small. Thrasher didn't want to be seen so he stayed in the background while the purohit, a family priest in India, performed his services. At the national cemetery, the Indian government honored him as they should have, as a soldier, complete with a three-gun salute that startled his grief-stricken wife. When the ceremony was over, the family led the procession to the Yamuna River. Thrasher had no idea why this spot had been selected to spread Dhoni's ashes, only that it was a place of importance to his family.

For the next hour, family members sang Hindu hymns and paid their respects. It was one of the few times Thrasher could remember being able to keep his emotions in check. He remembered attending a funeral for one of his team members who died in Beirut. That day in Arlington National Cemetery wasn't all that different than this one, but that didn't make it easier. It hurt losing someone you knew, especially seeing the pain in the eyes of their loved ones. In both cases, Thrasher couldn't bring himself to confess to them that it was his fault that they were gone. It was an anguish he would have to learn to accept. When his time came, he hoped that people would attend his funeral, although given his mistakes, he wasn't sure he deserved it.

When the ceremonies concluded, Thrasher took a short walk around a nearby bird sanctuary to collect his thoughts. As he watched them fly around in their cages, he remembered the patient in the Iranian lab, yelling at him that the birds would kill them all. Thrasher had discarded his words as the hallucination of a man who had been drugged beyond belief against his will. But when he spoke to the nuclear proliferation team at the agency, what the man said actually made some sense.

One of the particles in nuclear physics is a Lambda. It's symbol, Λ, looks like a bird that is flying. There was no way to know what the man was working on or how far he had gotten in his equations, but it was enough to make the agency team nervous. While this put the CIA watchdog in charge of keeping an eye on Iran's nuclear developments on high alert, Thrasher found solace in knowing that stopping them had forced Iran's nuclear aspirations to take a giant step backward. This wouldn't have been possible without Dhoni's help.

When his family had left, Thrasher stopped to pay his respects. He didn't know what to say to Dhoni because of their turbulent relationship, but one thing unquestionably needed to be said.

"I just want to tell you thank you for saving my life."

"What was that?"

Startled, Thrasher turned around quickly and reached for the gun inside his jacket. He settled down when he saw that it was an old Indian woman with greying hair who looked to be in her sixties. Hindi women typically wear white saris to a funeral, symbolizing purity and respect for the dead, but this woman was wearing blue, which symbolizes courage.

"Did you say that my son saved your life?"

Thrasher nodded. He desperately wanted to avoid a conversation like this, but it was too late. He was shocked when the woman walked up and hugged him. Sharing emotions with others did not come naturally for Thrasher. Not knowing what else to do, he hugged her back.

"How did you know him?"

"We, uh, worked together."

"Were you two friends?"

Thrasher paused.

"He was probably a better friend to me than I was to him, but he called me, forgive my language, an asshole, as he died in my arms. So, I couldn't really say for sure."

The old woman grinned.

"If he called you that then your relationship sounds about right. Kedar was never great about making friends. I guess that's why he went into the business he was in. In that world, relationships are so grey, and often temporary. I know my son. If he called you that, then he considered you to be close to him."

Thrasher smiled and looked at the water where Dhoni's ashes had been poured.

"Well, ma'am, then I guess it is my privilege to tell you that he was my friend."

She kissed Thrasher on the cheek.

"Thank you for coming. I know he'll be watching out for you. Please try and visit him again soon."

"I'll try."

Dhoni's mother smiled and walked away. As soon as she was gone, Thrasher picked a tulip from a flowerbed under a tree and tossed it into the water. Maybe he wasn't as different or alone in the world as he thought.

Epilogue

BANDAR ABBAS, IRAN

When news of Farhad hanging up on the Supreme Leader spread around the PMOI, he became an instant celebrity. They wanted to honor him right away, but he was still weak from his injury. With the help of black-market pain killers, he slept more than usual. When he was awake, he was often groggy and not himself. The party would have to wait.

A week later, Farhad's arm was still in a sling but his shoulder was healing and he weaned himself off the painkillers. Even though he was limited, he needed to get back to work. When the American president interrupted the coalition conference, the broadcast went viral. Iranians who had previously only dared to criticize the Supreme Leader in private suddenly became more vocal. Protests were occurring in the streets of Tehran during the day and parties were being held at night. The Guidance Patrol was busy trying to squash them wherever they could, but they couldn't be everywhere.

For the first time in his life, Farhad began to understand what true freedom felt like.

The best part about the parties was that everyone had an appetite for alcohol, which kept Farhad in business. The bad part was that alcohol supplies were not unlimited and the PMOI had to double their efforts to smuggle it into the country.

Given all the social discontent, the IRGC was being more vigilant than ever about locking down the borders and keeping illegal goods from entering. Fortunately, Farhad still had sources that were easy to bribe, and others who could get non-alcoholic beer, which he could later ferment. Unfortunately, when he finally felt well enough, he had to get the booze for his own party. Normally, this would have annoyed him, but he decided that he'd been recovering long enough.

On a sweltering, sunny day along the coast, he watched his source unload beer and wine off the boat that had come from Hormuz Island. He kept his distance and didn't say a word. His source only nodded, acknowledging that he had the stash. By the looks of it, the load didn't appear to be as large as he would have hoped, but he wasn't about to complain. His source covered the booze under a quilt and pushed it on a dolly over to a van. Once everything was loaded up, he drove down the road and Farhad followed him to the village of Bostanu. His source exited the vehicle and walked to one of the snack vendors to get a falafel.

Per his normal routine, Farhad slumped low in his seat and gauged his surroundings. Bostanu was one of his normal pick-up points, and he knew it well. The streets were a tad busier than normal, but he thought that played to his advantage. At the right time, he could slip out of his car and into his source's van to drive off with the hooch. His source would take his car, which had his payment in the glove box, and he would catch up with him on a later run.

He was on the lookout for Revolutionary Guard soldiers mingling about in disguise. He knew from his previous experience with Aslani that he was a marked man, and he felt certain that the rumors about him hanging up on the Supreme Leader had reached their ranks. Donya had tried to convince him not to go, but his source would only work with him. Farhad hoped that the hat and glasses he was wearing, along with his sling, would keep him safe.

When he thought the time was right, he strolled casually toward the van, and kept his head down, hoping to sell an image of being in pain, which wasn't much of a stretch. As he opened the van door, a hand covered his mouth, and pulled him through the door of a building behind him. A sack was thrown over his head, followed by a punch to the gut. His kidnapper squeezed him by his injured shoulder, and threw him in the back of a waiting car.

Farhad was panic stricken in the backseat. He'd hoped that this day would never come but was always worried it would. His heavy breathing was noticeable as the bag rose and fell with each breath. He wished Aslani was still alive. If that were the case, maybe all he would get was another lashing. This time felt different.

After what seemed like a thirty-minute ride, he was pulled out of the car, had his sling ripped away, and seated in a chair with his hands zip tied behind him. All he could do was wait. Moments later, he heard footsteps approaching. When the bag was snatched off his head, it took a moment for his eyes to adjust to the light.

"Hello, Farhad," said the uniformed man.

Farhad nearly soiled himself. It was General Lajani.

"You're not an easy person to find," he said, "but you didn't think I was going to just forget the incident at the border station, did you?"

"You got shot," said Farhad. "How are you still alive?"

Lajani lifted his shirt to show two tennis ball sized, purple bruises in the middle of his chest.

"Bullet proof vests are a wonderful thing. Too bad they are too expensive for us to issue to all my soldiers."

Farhad nodded.

"So, I guess this is it for me. If I can have one last request, I'd rather you finish me right here than take me to Evin Prison."

"That depends on your answers to my questions. Who was the man with you at the border that saved you? CIA?"

Farhad didn't answer.

Lajani bent over and looked Farhad dead in the eyes.

"I take it by your silence that the answer is yes."

Farhad didn't answer but was surprised when Lajani clipped his restraints and tossed his sling back to him.

"What's going on? What do you want?"

"I want to take down the Ayatollah, and you and the CIA are going to help me."

THE END

"The essential difference between emotion and reason is that emotion leads to action while reason leads to conclusions."

—Dale Carnegie

Author's Note

While I am aware that some authors in a variety of genres have chosen to include the COVID-19 pandemic in their storylines, I have chosen to avoid it. I believe that fiction should be an escape from reality.

Acknowledgements

Like musicians, authors have a lifetime to plan their first novel. Amending it and perfecting it is the easy part because one has all the time in the world to work on it. Getting it published is the hard part because that's when deadlines come into play.

Truthfully, writing my first novel was a joy but writing this second one was scary, as I had to face my own doubts as to whether or not I could do it again. I would like to thank the following people who helped me during this process.

To **my wife, a.k.a. "Fireball"** for her unwavering support. I could not have done it without you.

To **my parents**, for believing in my talents and being my silent investors behind the scenes.

To **Josh Lanier, Alan Scott, and Martha Scott**, my number one team of beta readers, who gave me much-needed feedback and kept me pointed in the right direction. You guys are the best!

To the real **Kathy Patel and her husband Ketan**, who are true friends to me and my wife. Good friends are hard to find. Thank you for being ours!

To the real **Chad Ward**, who I was not able to include in the first novel. I hope you enjoyed your character. See you on the bourbon trail!

To **Jason Gregory**, the real "J-Dub" who originated the "I'm good if you're good" line. We always keep one another going and you're the best friend a guy like me could ever ask for!

To **my agent Nancy Rosenfeld**, who took a chance on me when so many others said no. Thank you!

To **David Tabatsky**, who is one hell of a tough editor but always does a fantastic job of sharpening my novels. I have learned so much from you. Thank you!

To **Kurt and Erica Mueller**, and the rest of the hard-working team at Speaking Volumes for tolerating my continuous questions regarding the publishing process, and for allowing my dream of being a published author to come true. Thank you!

To **all of my readers, fans, and supporters**, I want you to know how much I appreciate you. I love hearing from you. Every time you recommend one of my books to someone you know or leave me a great review, I am humbled beyond words, and you fill my heart with nothing but happiness. You're the best! Thank you!

Upcoming New Release

THE AYATOLLAH TAKEDOWN
SURVIVING THE LION'S DEN SERIES
BOOK 3
BY
MATT SCOTT

Unbeknownst to the Supreme Leader, chief commander of the Revolutionary Guard, Ramin Lajani, is conspiring with the People's Mujahadeen of Iran as well as CIA operatives Ben Thrasher and Beth Jenkins to overthrow him. But Lajani has enemies of his own. General Mohammed Nassiri of the Basij has been suspicious of him for years. Will Nassiri discover Lajani's motives before it's too late or will the Supreme Leader make one last stand?

For more information
visit: **www.SpeakingVolumes.us**

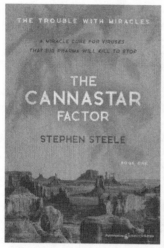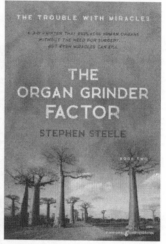

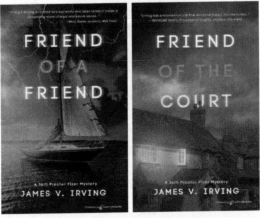